Praise for *Beyond the Ripples* . . .

D0034391

"Memoirist Dede Montgomery has the uncanny ability to create the quality of presence inside story. This time, it's through her fiction. Whether at the Columbia River shoreline with a man struggling to gather up a bottle with a note inside or in a restaurant with a waitress witnessing a meeting that will change lives, we are there, moved by these characters, cheering them on and celebrating how interconnected we humans are. *Beyond the Ripples* will capture your heart." — Jane Kirkpatrick, Award-winning author of *Everything She Didn't Say*

"In *Beyond the Ripples*, Dede Montgomery takes us on a moving, heartfelt journey through the lives of a cast of characters fatefully joined by a note in a bottle set adrift in the Willamette River. The characters—the young girl who launched the bottle, a kind octogenarian who finds it, his successful daughter who feels inexplicably unfulfilled, a salesclerk struggling to rise above an abusive partner and a controlling mother, and a burned-out teacher searching for meaning—all live and breathe with human authenticity. This beautiful book is a story of love, friendship, and growth, and a meditation on the abiding need we all have for human connection." — Warren C. Easley, author of *Moving Targets,* Book 6 in the *Cal Claxton Oregon Mysteries*

"An old fisherman, a letter, an unlikely friendship and the big rivers of Oregon—the Willamette and Columbia, inspired this fictionalized multi-story, threaded from the stories of a bygone era and rippling with the power of synchronicity that occurs whenever someone finds a message in a bottle. An enduring, reflective, and soulful read for a winter's night." — Jenny Forrester, author of *Narrow River, Wide Sky: A Memoir*

Other books by Dede Montgomery

The Music Man

Beyond the
Ripples

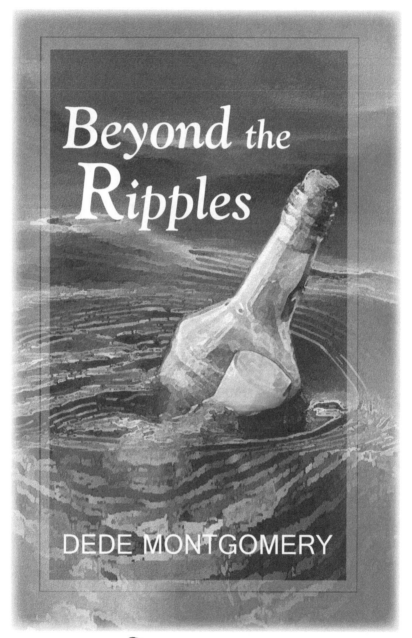

Beyond the
Ripples

DEDE MONTGOMERY

Bink Books
Bedazzled Ink Publishing Company • Fairfield, California

paperback 978-1-945805-96-7

Cover Design
by

Bink Books
a division of
Bedazzled Ink Publishing, LLC
Fairfield, California
http://www.bedazzledink.com

For Mom. The best friend any daughter could hope for.

In every moment the Universe is whispering to you.
~Denise Linn

Chapter 1

The bottle
June 2013

THE BOTTLE WAS partially hidden, stuck in a stag of some fallen cottonwood branches. Winter's rain and winds had been cruel to the trees and shrubs growing along the banks of the Columbia River. This particular cottonwood crept closer to the rippled current, until, one day, it slid sideways, pulling some of its roots out of the soil, severing its lowest branches. Through winter and spring, the trunk rested in the water's edge, submerged remaining branches collecting floating river debris.

Ernest had been keeping his eye on the bottle for months, first as he tossed his cast out into the wind-whipped ripples of the river channel as the current crashed on its bank early in the winter. When he first noticed it, rough waters carried broken fir branches and severed paper mill remnants in a muddier than normal torrent enhanced by winter rains. It exuded the smell of fish and he told himself he should pull the bottle out. Clean up the river view. But the extra effort and possibility of getting wet commanded him to wait; to let someone else get to it. Perhaps an exploring kayaker or boater, or someone whose curiosity might get the better of them. Or better yet, melted snow pushing even higher spring waters might nudge it forward, furthering its journey to wherever it was supposed to go, he figured. Yet, the next week and then the next, the bottle remained.

Ernest had started wondering if others might have noticed it: a handful of locals occasionally frequented this spot of his, although he was lucky enough to usually be the only visitor during his early morning excursions. In this spot, he would rest and ponder, and in times now gone, even pretend a fish might bite. Then it began to happen that he'd near the bank and neglect to bait up his line. Picking up the rhythm of the river instead; looking out, thinking, remembering. A bit of rocky beach with edges overrun with grasses and shrubbery of Oregon grape crawled down to the water. He would often strain to look across to the expanse of Washington state on the other side of the river, peering beyond Puget Island as it separated the Columbia into two channels, always glad, although he couldn't put into words why exactly, that he was born and bred an Oregonian. Even if others grumbled about missing the good old days, and all the "no good" folks taking over the state. But not Ernest. He knew there had always been good and bad people around. He still preferred to think the lot of them now to be mostly good. And those that weren't had some attached baggage steering them in that direction.

On this morning as he brewed his morning tea, seeping the black bag extra-long to elicit its caffeine jolt as he sat at his bare kitchen table, the image of the bottle interrupted his thoughts of the day. The bottle overtook other typical first morning notions: imagining what his daughter might be doing or worrying about his dwindling savings. Instead, for whatever odd reason, he was suddenly terrified maybe someone else had claimed it. This silly bottle, he thought, peering into his tannin colored tea, wondering why this small thing wouldn't escape him? Good thing he had never mentioned it to his daughter, Amelia— it would only cause her more worry. He questioned if he could summon energy on this day to take it on, as lately, it was harder and harder to get going each new morning. Perhaps the buzz of the tea would give him just enough lift to leave the warmth of his small, dingy, yet warm, house. A house, he kept telling himself, needing a new coat of paint along with a roof, and although his sense of smell wasn't what it used to be, he knew mold and mildew seeped along inside corners of his home's walls and windowsills.

Finally, he drained the tea, but left half of the toast on the chipped plate. Ernest grabbed his jacket, the one with the IBEW logo under the collar, and his favorite ball cap, so faded he couldn't remember what its original color had been. He made his way down the lane, not bothering to lock his door as he left. He never locked, although he would never admit it to Amelia. His knees hurt more than usual, the arthritis acting up especially with the chill sting clinging to the June morning. It had been a stormy, rainy, cold June which those natives living along the

Columbia River knew to be pretty typical. His heartbeat picked up, and he wondered for a second if this might be the morning that would take him? Maybe he would be visited by one of those early morning heart attacks that seemed to claim so many of his friends. *Why is it always early morning?* He forced himself to slow his steps, and then finally, to stop for half a minute. He heard a rustling in the brush and turned his head in time to spot a blue heron disturbed into flight. Ernest tried to remember his daughter's advice—to breathe from deep within the diaphragm, although he never seemed to understand how, even when she forced him to practice with her.

Finally, he moved his feet again. He felt his shoulders cave into the hunched posture of the old as he walked, his feet shuffling loudly on the gravel road as he failed to lift them fully off the ground. After a few minutes of walking, he neared the river and chuckled at the irony. As if anyone else would be out on this cold and foggy morning! Most of the old crowd, at least the ones he knew, were having a harder time getting around, if they hadn't already left this earth. The serious fishermen, up with the dawn, selected spots more likely to entice the Columbia's gourmet offerings.

On this morning, he saw fewer than the usual number of birds and figured there would certainly be no fish. A good reason not to bring his pole again, as if he still needed to defend his recent laziness. It never used to happen, but lately more often than not he arrived without it. He knew, even if he tried to pretend otherwise, it was the spot that drew him, and the way his memories spilled out alongside the river as it splashed against its bank. Releasing from his brain like air rushing from a pinhole in an inflated balloon. Although these days, he admitted to himself, a glimpse of the bottle in the snag was what compelled him to visit. These past few seasons he had believed one day fate would blitz a stormy assault, tossing the bottle back into the current and beyond. But no, as he spotted it on yet another morning, nothing had launched it back on its journey. Now, with summer arriving and the river receding lower in the bank, he knew enough about the seasonal life of the river to believe the bottle could be stuck for much longer than he had ever anticipated.

Nearing the river edge and the snag, he figured he'd likely have to wade into the muddy muck if he hoped to grab the bottle. He could barely make out the green glass from where he stood, so covered it was with river scum, wondering how he had even noticed it in the first place. Ernest realized his worries about someone else chasing after it were quite silly: after all, it was just a piece of litter embedded into the crotch of an old cottonwood. Sharon's voice propelled him further: "Go for it, Ernie!" His feet stopped moving abruptly as he forced himself to slow his breathing. He couldn't decide if this newer feeling in his chest was true pain, or simply his clock winding down. He wondered how long it might take someone to find him if this turned out to be his final resting place? He'd been thinking about life's end more often, knowing it would happen sometime; hoping it would at least be quick.

Recently he found himself thinking about Sharon all day long, her needling laugh accompanying him most mornings as he trekked along the road toward the river. Some mornings he'd notice himself missing her desperately; and yet it hadn't been so long ago when it was more common for him to have nighttime arrive only to realize he hadn't thought about her all day. But on this damp morning, for some reason, it wasn't only Sharon who was captive in his memories. Ernest rested against the same smooth, cold boulder he leaned against so many mornings before. The quiet rush of the current rang in his ears, and his eyes were mesmerized by the river ripples, as his breathing slowed. Something prodded his brain to get back to the task at hand, but the memories hooked his focus.

Thinking back in time was different here, next to the river as it flowed on toward the mouth of the Columbia where it propelled its waters into the Pacific. Back home, lots of days he'd sit in his chair, alone in his living room, and drift off, not to sleep but slipping softly into moments that happened decades before. And on these days, especially lately, he teased through memories, as if watching frames from an old movie in slow motion, knitting together what he remembered about his dad, Chuck, and father-in-law, Jackson. The meeting of those two men had once seemed unlikely to Ernest, as did the friendship created between Ernest and Jackson. A bond made after his own dad had died. And yet, after years mulling it over, it was only recently Ernest understood. Maybe it wasn't so unlikely. Because, as Ernest believed, more now than ever, there are spaces in our lives when our individual spirits intuitively know who to reach out and touch. It is only sometimes much later when we understand what it is we offered each other.

IT HAD BEEN at the beginning of World War II as Portland shipyards stretched for man power, luring newcomers to Oregon. And some may have been identified as different than those who were native, but all of them, in truth, were newcomers in the timeline of history. And in all of Ernest's own brothers and sisters of the trades he had known over the years—welcomed in the union hall as if their own home—few had wired together the nooks and crannies of Liberty Ships like Chuck and Jackson.

So, in the end, it wasn't odd when Chuck and Jackson came to depend on each other while sharing shifts. For Ernest knew as well as the next IBEW Brother—if you can't count on a fellow electrician, one might as well anticipate the day you don't make it home. Those two, Chuck and Jackson, were true buddies. Ernest heard from others later how the two knew their trade better than anyone. Jackson, decades after those war years, explained how their friendship reflected shared personal traits: commitment and fastidiousness.

"Do it right the first time or don't bother," Jackson told Ernest once, or something like it.

Jackson or Chuck would give the other sad head shakes when an inexperienced sparky ignored this work ethic. Later, when Jackson retired early, his knees and fingers worn out, and Chuck grabbed private jobs on his own, they'd still see each other at the union hall. Ernest too experienced the power of union hall visits. His father and Jackson might grab a cup of coffee, and back in the earlier days, Chuck, a cigarette. When Ernest learned it was Jackson his dad called first after his diagnosis, keeping it from his own family for much longer, it had taken Ernest a long time to forgive. To forgive his dad for not letting his own son or wife know earlier, to give them the news a few of their brothers had already received, multiplying as years passed. A diagnosis Jackson fully escaped, for reasons attributed to luck, genes, and perhaps things none of us are ever privy to know. All these things Ernest never learned much about. Until later.

LEANING AWKWARDLY AGAINST the rock, Ernest felt the sharpness of the stone dig into his thigh, and he shifted his body. An intruder poked at him, interrupting his focus on what he came to the river to do. Leaving him no choice but to prepare himself for the memories that would next flood him. For it was as he first grieved over his dad's death all those years ago, his previous loss of Dixie was amplified. He had been just a kid then, overwhelmed in his personal battles: falling in love so early, at sixteen. In love with Dixie, the pretty, flashy one: different than him, the quiet guy who hid in classroom corners and the shadows of flamboyant jocks and circles of rich kids. Quiet, but solid.

Back in those days, Ernest went to church every Sunday and spent free time helping his dad, learning early how to rewire their house. He had already decided on his trade, but was told he still needed to graduate from high school. But that Dixie, she simply shined. Ernest had never been one to whistle, but if he had, just her memory would have caused him to release a quiet air-filled attempt. And unlike the other girls who traveled in her flock, Dixie would look at Ernest each morning and speak to him or ask him how he was. She'd hesitate as if she actually expected him to answer. He swore silently at the blush he knew to be slowly moving from his neck to his cheeks, leaving him tongue-tied. Ernest could feel the eyes of his classmates on him, or at least he imagined so.

Then there was the day Dixie asked him to the Sadie Hawkins Dance. She had stopped him in the hall after school while he helped Mrs. Southward empty an overflowing classroom trash can. As he returned to the quiet, abandoned hall, there she was, in her flowing skirt and white blouse, with collars that always lay down perfectly.

"Hi, Ernest," she said.

Ernest stopped. He was a statue without a single muscle moving, until, finally, his mouth twitched, and he set down the trash can and reached his arm out to the wall to balance himself. "Hi," he replied. He still remembered how he had searched his brain to say something that wouldn't make him sound like an idiot. Instead he remained tongue-tied.

"That's nice of you to help Mrs. Southward. Some days I think she might just pass out on the spot," Dixie said. She had looked as if she might laugh, but then added more seriously, "She always looks so tired!"

"Yes," Ernest said, his brain still searching. He was distracted as he wondered how long it took her each morning to tie her sweater so neatly around her neck: it looked such a perfect, soft arrangement of cashmere as it rested there.

"Well, I was wondering," she started. "Do you have a date for the Sadie Hawkins Dance?" She looked at him, searchingly.

Ernest almost took a step backward, but tried hard to focus on being still. He self-consciously pulled at the collar of his button-down shirt, giving himself air.

"You know, it's the one that girls can ask boys?" Dixie said, stumbling a bit as if she worried he might think her too forward. Instead, she continued on boldly, "It's next Friday night."

Ernest so badly wanted to have a good line. *What would Dick say?* His friend Dick always knew what to say to girls. Instead, he blurted, "Dixie. I don't know how to dance." He looked down at the ground, attempting to shield his fully reddened face. "And no, I don't have a date."

Dixie grinned. Her smile radiated through her whole body, and she delightedly almost danced a jig. He watched her saddle-shoed feet move quickly back and forth twice. Her white socks caught his eye, and he could hardly take his eyes off her ankles, until he heard her say, "Oh good! Then you will go with me?"

Ernest no longer recollected what he had said after that. But he remembered knowing right then that this girl was determined to get what she wanted in life. And she blew into him like a burst of early spring air, picking him up and carrying him along in her gust.

Ernest noticed for a moment the coldness of the rock sinking through his pants, interrupting his thoughts. He touched the faded denim of his pants, feeling their dampness. But the distraction couldn't stop his brain from moving along its path. It was so easy to remember, even now, how from that moment on, Dixie was his life. And for a long time back then, he had kept wondering: what was the catch?

The few friends he had shook their heads and cautioned him. "Just watch out," one would say; or another, "You just wait." They all believed Dixie was after something; some way to embarrass or simply dump him. As Ernest began to uncover what he found to be the true essence of Dixie, he knew his friends were wrong. Plain wrong. And soon, he came to realize how he loved her. Pulling his courage together, he took a chance and brought her home to meet his parents. Dixie was more cautious about sharing hers: the sole barrier Ernest uncovered that caused his courageous Dixie to lose her nerve. Until, that is, when the moment arrived when Dixie knew she had to stand up to them. For it was immediately after their high school graduation Ernest and Dixie married, against the protests of her parents who had strived to get her to understand how they knew best. She was young, they'd say, adding she'd get bored with him. Dixie was honest enough to share some of these conversations with Ernest, assuring him how the problem lay with her parents, rather than any weakness in him.

Dixie never did tell Ernest, however, a few things her parents had said. "Dixie, dear. He'll never appreciate those things that are important to you. The things you love," they might say. They would remind her about her devotion to piano lessons and catechism. In the end, Dixie's parents may have spoken some truth, as Ernest did struggle to avoid embarrassing her around friends and family as they talked of things he knew nothing about.

But now, Ernest thought, looking back so long ago only some of the memories were still crystal clear, in the end, it simply didn't matter. None of it. Dixie and Ernest had two years together in marriage that were mostly good. Sure, they had an argument here or there, but he had loved her. Truly, truly loved her. And he always felt she loved him. But none of that love prevented an accident from destroying everything late one night when she was out with friends. The curvy road. The dark sky with misty Portland rain pelting the ground, creating stormy, mud laden gushes of water along the road. She had been out with her childhood friends, some still unwed. To be girls again. A phone call came later from the hospital three hours after he expected her to be home. This many years later, he can recall the feeling he had that night. A sensation still capable of numbing his body if he allows himself to think back, on lonely nights as he sits in his worn upholstered chair, its seams now unraveling, in his hushed living room near his telephone. That one late night, Ernest's fatigued body and spirit became alert as an undefined fright seeped into his blood, shocking him awake.

Before the call as he awaited her return, he began to imagine what he had believed to be the worst: maybe she had tired of him and had found a man who could give her everything her parents thought he couldn't. This man wouldn't be like Ernest, a hard-working electrician who pulled a paycheck and assured her she would never need to work. Most of the girls back in those days didn't if they could avoid it, it seemed to him. Not like now, Ernest knew, thinking of Amelia. No, Dixie had not chosen to go to college and instead dabbled in art classes at the local museum, something he knew bothered her parents. And Ernest told her, time after time, he could put her through college. But on this night, no. He was so fully convinced she had left him for an anonymous refined man who would offer a perfect line for every conversation, that when the phone rang to tell him otherwise, it took him a full thirty seconds to register the message, as it slowly dawned on him that, no, he had not imagined the worst. And while he needed to leave immediately, to identify her body, all he could do was sit for ten minutes solid, stunned. He knew he needed to notify her parents but couldn't imagine how he could tell them.

But he did it and the worst night of his life progressed into an awful misty morning. He still remembered how when he got home he made himself a cup of coffee to start the day. A day proceeding without a night's sleep. In the act of putting coffee in the percolator he realized the last time he had made coffee was on Dixie's last birthday in April. And it was only then, the dreary morning after, that he had cried. Finally. Ernest called in to work intending to call in sick, something he had only done once before as a flu bug ravaged his body, to learn his boss had already been notified. It was years later when he wondered who made the call for him. Instead of heading to work, he sat back in the armchair and looked out the front window at the dripping rain.

Later, at the Catholic funeral, he sat with Dixie's family in the front row and struggled to kneel and sit and pray at the right times. Since he hadn't converted, he didn't join the family in the taking of communion. He knew that her whole family viewed him with disgust, blaming him for all the things they felt he hadn't done for their Dixie. Ernest had been frightened at the service to seek eye contact with either of Dixie's parents. His head pounded through the ceremony, after too many nights consisting of only a few hours of sleep. As soon as he returned to work after her death, he had surprised his co-workers by asking for overtime, finding work to be his only solace: the thing he could do without thinking. Without feeling. But then, at the service, he saw the crowd rise, one final time, and he spotted it. Her casket. His most beautiful wife's casket was to be carried down the aisle by her father, still young enough to help heft the load, accompanied by her brothers and uncles. He worried he didn't know if he should be helping to shoulder it or not. He did know that the casket would not be open, and he was thankful after seeing her crumpled body in the hospital morgue. No loved ones could have handled that grief, he had told himself.

As if in a trance, he followed the procession to the hearse, and on to the cemetery, deaf to words, sounds, noises. Someone held out an umbrella to him, but he shook his head. He knew he needed rain to seep through his body, down between his raincoat and the neck of his collared shirt and tie, and into his lower pant legs and socks. For after all, Dixie had astounded him with her adoration of rain. They would go on walks and after the first few times of holding open an umbrella for her, he left it at home, knowing she would laugh at him and dash away from the domed nylon's protection. Often, to Ernest's horror, she might splash through puddles in her shoes. He would force himself to smile at her joy. But during this final goodbye to his love, the rain seeped through the open collar of his jacket, chilling him in the late winter cold. He felt it in the toes of his socks, and its wetness migrating into his sleeves. It was the rain that allowed him to spill his tears, and not worry if anyone was watching.

Finally, back at the church where sandwiches made of white bread were arranged on pretty platters and two young women ladled a pink sparkling drink from crystal punch bowls, he had to escape. The sandwiches would only cling to the back of his throat, and the pink, stickiness of the punch would make him vomit. But first, he knew he must see Dixie's parents. He felt hopeless—he didn't know what to say. And worse, to face what he knew to be their hatred. As he went to get his jacket, out of the corner of his eye, he saw Dixie's mother, Patty, nudge her husband. They both slowly moved toward him, and it rooted him in place, leaving him unable to pull his left arm through the coat sleeve. His coat dangled behind him as if he were a toddler.

Patty reached down to gather the top of his jacket, and held it open for him as she guided his arm. She paused, and then awkwardly gave him a hug. Thomas reached out his hand and Ernest shook it, after which Thomas placed his other hand on top. Ernest slowly focused his vision to look Thomas in the eye, and then, back at Patty. Through her tear-stained mascara she tried to give a small smile.

"Ernest. We know how our daughter loved you," Thomas began. Ernest looked back at him. "And you have been good to her." He started to cry and cleared his throat. "We just want you to know that," he said as his voice cracked.

Ernest tried but couldn't get a single sound out. He began to weep.

"We will give you a call. Soon," Patty said. And with that they stepped away and Ernest hurried back into the rain, toward his truck and into the safety of the raindrops.

WHEN ERNEST WAS eight or nine he complained to his dad. "It's not fair," Ernest had said when his dad wouldn't let him play baseball with the boys from school. Ernest didn't now recall the reason his dad had given, but he did remember his dad saying, "Life isn't fair. Remember that." And then he added, "Ernie, get over it."

A few years after Dixie died, this phrase from his dad was one of the things from childhood that came back to him. Ernest knew Chuck had been having difficulty catching his breath for a number of years. His dad would minimize his worries, telling Ernest it was a cold or a cough, or just "sparky breathing" like other electricians. It was only these few years later, after he'd had a minor heart attack, that Ernest and his mother wondered if Chuck truly did have a breathing problem. But then they'd remind themselves how he was still working hard to provide for his family. He was never a complainer, and seemed to practice what he told Ernie all those years ago; that life wasn't fair and to just get over it. He loved his wife, and was there for his son.

After Dixie died, Chuck did not repeat the phrase, and was present for his son in his silent and gruff manner. Occasionally, he might give Ernest a partially stiff, half hug, although his dad always looked uncomfortable in this father-son touching. For their unique bond was more about what they shared together rather than chatter or touch.

When Ernest turned twelve, Chuck gave him his first screwdriver, and each subsequent year he added another tool to slowly build Ernest's electrician's tool kit. These many decades later, Ernest couldn't remember the first time he was allowed to help his dad with a task of the trade. For that was, in fact, what his dad did: he shared his knowledge and love of his trade, even occasionally taking Ernie with him to the union hall meetings.

It wasn't until Chuck's funeral where suddenly his dad's whole life lay open in front of him, for the first time and almost without warning, did Ernest understand the impact his dad had made on those around him. Those guys he had worked with all those years ago in the shipyards. The guys who mostly had moved on to other jobs, but still gathered at the union hall for coffee and meetings, surrounded by signs shouting "We are all one for safety" and "Once a union man always a union man." For now, unlike the Catholic funeral for Dixie just a few years before, these old friends of his dad's united together as both Ernest and his mother were caught in slow motion. In a local community center, Ernest watched grown men look down at their worn work boots and shed tears for their union brother.

Ernest sat next to Helen at that service back then. Although his dad had not been one to be demonstrative, he put his arm around his mother's heaving shoulders. Helen avoided eye contact, knowing such a glance would set loose tears she struggled to contain deep inside. Or, incite the anger she was feeling: an upsetting and confusing emotion. She couldn't admit to anyone how, yes, she was angry Chuck had left her. How he never admitted to her how much he struggled to breathe. She wondered how tired he must have been, and how it was he kept working, day after day, minding his own business without complaint, until forced to admit the advancement of his lung cancer. Too young, her Chuck seemed, to die. To her.

Two of the union wives arose following the service and came over to stand next to Helen. They whispered something Ernest couldn't make out, gently gathering Helen's arms to help her rise. One of them, an older woman still with jet-black hair, looked at Ernest and said, "We'll be over near the coffee in the corner." She pointed with her head in a direction.

Ernest nodded. "Thanks," he whispered.

He got up and tried to anticipate what it was he was supposed to do next, the only son of this man who was much more loved than Ernest could have imagined. The room's walls were bare and though the lighting was dim, he could see how the crowd had cleared out, mourners getting on with the remainder of a Saturday afternoon with chores to finish and places to get to. It was only then, he now reminisced, when a man moved toward him.

"You must be Ernest," the man said simply. He put out his hand and in shaking it Ernest could feel the calloused grip of a fellow tradesman. This hand ran many shades deeper than his own. "My name is Jackson. I don't know if your dad ever mentioned me." He looked at Ernest for recognition. The whites of his eyes were almost bloodshot. "Your dad and I worked together a long time ago back in the shipyards."

Ernest had struggled at first to remember, although not for long. *Of course!* Jackson was the guy his dad mentioned as he told Ernest about some of the ships they had built back then, and about how surprised he had been at the shoddiness of some of the completed work.

"Um yes." Ernest struggled to get out of his mouth. "Of course." He was quiet, until suddenly, words bubbled out. "Were you the one that almost got hit that time the crane cable snapped? I still remember Dad being so thankful you weren't crushed. That it was so close. Yeah?" He pictured a crane high above, its cable snapping and the crashing of a shattered, dropped load.

"Oh yes," Jackson smiled for the first time, and issued a quick snort. "That was me. The first of a few lives." He laughed. More seriously he added, "Your dad was a great guy. But you must know that?" He was quiet and then shook his head. "Oh, but I had never seen him so angry as he was that time they misjudged that load."

"Yeah," Ernest replied, not quite sure what to say next. He had begun wondering how much about his dad he didn't know.

"It's the shits," Jackson said. "Of course, I wouldn't have said that around Chuck. I never heard him swear. Not once, in all those years."

Ernest was distracted in acknowledging the oddity of neither he nor his dad using foul language among so many others who did, and he shuffled his feet, hating the tight dress shoes he had bought years back to please Dixie. He was late to realize on this sad occasion how he should have known the other guys would wear their work boots. He felt stupid not to have known that.

"It's just not fair," Jackson continued. "When the big guy takes the good ones. Hell, I could point out a good five guys still left in this crowd that I would have given up first, if it were my choice. Of course, that'd make your dad uncomfortable too, to hear me say that. Though he always gave me some leeway, reckoned I'd had to put up with a lot more than him."

"Oh," Ernest muttered, again. Feeling stupid he didn't know how to respond to this side of his dad. *Had he known him so little?*

"Well," Jackson hesitated. "The wife and I would like to invite you over to dinner one of these days. You might not believe it, but I've got a few pictures of your dad and me, from the early days. Some kind of promotional thing. Hell, I have no idea why the two of us were chosen. Maybe a Mutt and Jeff kind of pair." Jackson looked at him for a response.

"Um, yeah. I'd like that," Ernest spit out finally. "Yes."

"Okay. Good. Living at your dad's place, right? I mean, um, since your wife and all." Now Jackson looked uncomfortable. "I'm so sorry about that, by the way."

"Yeah. Thanks. Yeah, we're there. For now, at least," Ernest said. "I guess Mom and I have some talking to do. I just don't know."

"Oh, of course," Jackson said quickly. "Of course. Perhaps next weekend? My wife, she's the best cook, maybe this side of the Mississippi. Truly." He patted his rounded stomach and gave an embarrassed smile. He looked around the room. "She couldn't be here today or I'd introduce you. I'll check in with the boss and then give you a call. But maybe Saturday?"

A date set so many years ago, Ernest thought, shivering in response to cool morning air. He had no idea, back on that mournful day, how much one conversation would set in motion.

ERNEST HEARD A distant horn. Or was it a siren? His hearing wasn't what it was once, yet he refused to pay for hearing aids. Nonsense, he had told his daughter. He heard everything he cared to hear.

But now, the sound, whatever it was, broke him out of his reverie, and he knew he finally must take care of what it was that brought him to the river edge on this damp morning. He stretched up, ever so slowly, so that he was standing, rubbing his aching back and hips. He slowly plodded toward the water, stopping briefly to awaken the tingling foot that had fallen asleep. He shook it, being careful not to lose his balance, and then took slow shuffling steps down the bank. As he edged toward the snag, the cold water slowly seeped into his right work boot. *Shoot.* He would have been smart to have worn something different today, even the pair of old sneakers he didn't care about.

But now, it was too late to turn back. He grabbed the alder branches jutting out from the bank, stabilizing himself as he gingerly boosted his other boot up onto the decomposing debris abutting the snag. He hadn't realized how difficult this would be, and how much it would challenge his now imperfect balance. He thought he could just about finish the task without much more water damage to his leather boots, although he wondered why he should worry much about them. They'd served him well all these years and a little mud and water could hardly do much to them now: they may not find many more days of wear.

He heard a rustle in the tree near him as another surprised heron was rousted to activity. Startled, Ernest grabbed the slippery branches with his second hand as he peered into the sky to the harsh "kaark" as the bird took to flight, momentarily shocking him into forgetting, again, what he was doing. But then, a moment later as he recovered his stability, he let go with his right hand, and reached out just long enough to grab the neck of the bottle. The vessel was almost smothered in the dried muck of leaves and sticks, trapped during the wilder currents of the winter and spring: halting its river journey. Holding the bottle mid-air by its neck, he willed himself to slow his breathing and steady his heartbeat. Then—he couldn't help it. He smiled. *Finally, he had it!*

Ernest looked toward where the road ended at the river's edge. Had anyone seen him uncover the seeming treasure? Nothing. Only the stillness of the morning accompanied by sounds of the river. Still holding the branch with his left hand and grasping the bottle in his right, he maneuvered himself around to face the shore, dousing his left boot this time with seeping mud. He didn't care now. He had finally rescued it, and he let out an audible chortle. He wondered what

Amelia might think about this act he took on this morning: certainly, she would scold him. But, thankfully, he figured, she'd never know as his heart slowed to its regular beat. He didn't believe it was his ending, not this day. Though he knew that good feeling stuff they said that sometimes got released in your body might be masking the real state of his heart. He didn't care, he told himself. He felt confident he still had some time left.

He carried the bottle back to the perch on the dirty rock, twenty feet up from the shoreline. The river water sloshing in his boot left his wool sock soggy, and the rough skin of his heel chafed against the leather. But finally, the difficult task finished, Ernest knew he could look beyond the mud and film covering the outside of the bottle. He scraped at it with his finger. *What in the world?* He peered at it, more curious now than ever as he spied a cork in the top, partially covered by tin foil. The bottle was coated with so much scum he couldn't see anything inside, but for the first time he wondered how it had floated along the river without water seeping in and sinking it. He shook it, but didn't hear or feel any liquid swishing inside.

Ernest partially crouched so he could lean back against the rock and look toward the road and path, suddenly suspicious a neighbor or visitor might see him. If they didn't know him, they might imagine him to be a passing vagrant hitting the bottle early in the morning. The chill of coldness from his feet spread throughout his body. He stood up, his legs stiffening, and knew he should begin the slow steps home, tucking the bottle carefully under his left arm to give his frigid hands relief. He rubbed his right hip with his aching right hand, reminding himself it was just a short walk home. He took a few steps but curiosity overwhelmed him, and he stopped for a minute, took the bottle by its neck, and peered inside. He saw a cylindrical shape, and his heart quickened once again. He put the bottle back under his arm and willed his cold feet to make their way back home.

LATER THAT NIGHT, well after he'd returned home, warmed by trudging along the road but having changed out of his wet pants, boots, and socks, he finally sat in his chair in the living room. He had earlier made a simple dinner, feeling lucky to have leftovers from his meal at the café the day before. The evening's darkness edged itself through the dirtied windows of his front room, not penetrating the edges where moisture condensed. Ernest turned on the lamp next to his chair and looked into the shadows it created across the room, thinking more than seeing. He no longer could hear the ticking of his clock, the only interruption to the silence around him.

Earlier in the day his excited spirit overcame his body's exhaustion to deliver him, finally, home. He was so drained he didn't stop to remove his muddy boots until after entering his house and plopping his body wearily on the kitchen chair, at first struggling to determine what to do next. He set the dirty bottle on its side on the table, creating smudges of mud on its wooden surface, and steadied it with his hand. In his wet wool socks, he dragged across the kitchen floor to extract a pair of needle-nosed pliers from a drawer. Having a plan improved his energy, as he returned to sit again in the chair. His hand trembled and he wasn't certain he would be able to still it enough to use the pliers to grab the edges of the coiled paper barely visible inside. But slowly, rotating his aching arthritic wrist, throbbing pain developed after years of overuse, he painstakingly removed a spiral of paper from the bottle. Ernest released a relieved sigh of exhaled breath.

But now, as the sun faded through its sunset, the note rested on the coffee table near him, its edges crumpled, and the ink slightly smudged from its travel and his already repeated reading. Earlier that day, over and over he had read the little girl's message, this twelve-year-old Annie who he had never before met or heard of.

Ernest struggled at first to make out the handwriting. After reading it the first time, he felt the urge to tell somebody about it, but soon after held on to it as if a special secret. *A note in a bottle.* A little thing. So easily missed. And yet, how often in anyone's life, did they find something like this, he asked himself? He had to think about what it meant, and just what he should do. And as he poked at his brain, its tendency toward routine caused him to think of Sharon, his second and last wife. For it was at this time of night, most nights for all those years they had together, he remembered her most: the time of night when they would sit together after their long work shifts. And on this occasion, he imagined her belting out her melodic laugh, teasing him with, "What you thinking, Ernest? Some special directions from God?"

On this evening, the imagined conversation made him laugh! In their life together, he had been the one to bring reality to her dreams. It was then that he knew. If from God or a little girl or something else beyond his understanding, this bottle and its contents were, in fact, a special message. A message that deserved his reply.

Chapter 2

Times long gone

THAT SATURDAY NIGHT, the long-ago week after his dad's memorial service, Ernest made it across town to Jackson's family's home. He remembered he couldn't at first understand then why his heart pounded so. Soon enough, he figured out there was so little he knew about parts of his dad's life. And he wanted to make a good impression, for his dad's sake, he had told himself. Ernest had knocked lightly on the door, looking around the neighborhood. *Working class, just like his.* By this time in his life, and after having spent time in Dixie's old neighborhood, he could tell the difference. He knocked again on the door, grabbing the bottle of wine he held more tightly, then switching hands so he could wipe his sweaty palms on his pants. Daring—his own parents didn't drink and he had no idea what Jackson and his wife might think was polite. He had only once bought wine, for Dixie's parents, and Dixie, of course, had been there to make the selection. This time Ernest asked a clerk in the store to choose, as his face blazed with embarrassment.

"A good red wine is best for dinner," the clerk had said as she led him to the cash register.

A woman had then appeared at the door, and greeted him by reaching out her hand. He nervously moved the wine to his left hand. She firmly grabbed his right hand and held onto it just a few seconds longer.

"Come on in," she said. "You sure are the spitting image of your dad." And she smiled at him, reaching out to touch him on the arm.

As shy as he felt, Ernest blurted out, "You knew him too?"

"Oh, I met him only once. A long time ago," she said. "Let me take your coat."

As he walked into the small entryway and handed his coat to her, he heard a familiar voice.

"Ernest. So glad you could come!"

Ernest looked toward another room, a small, but cozy living room, to where Jackson sat in a recliner, slippers on his feet, propped up on a stool.

"Come on in and sit down, and we'll follow the missus's orders." Jackson gave his wife a quick smile, as he stood with a grimace. A bit softer he added, "You don't want to get in the way of that woman around mealtime. Trust me. Good to see you." He clasped Ernest on the shoulder. He left his hand a bit longer than Ernest expected. It felt warm and comforting.

"Pay no attention to him, Ernest," Jackson's wife said. "We all have learned to ignore a lot of what he says. You'll catch on soon." She looked at Jackson with a wicked smile.

Ernest didn't mean to stare, but he couldn't take his eyes off the slippers on Jackson's feet, thinking how his own dad never owned a pair.

As if reading his mind, Jackson said, "No staring at my house shoes. An old man is entitled to comfort finally for all these wasted joints."

Ernest felt a bit like the first time he tried to ride a two-wheeler: a strenuous effort requiring full concentration with this first exposure to such marital jovial sparring. A type of communication absent between his own parents.

"Would you like something to drink? We have Coke, water? Or wine, I see?"

Now Ernest met a new test that must, he was sure, have only one correct answer. "Um, no thank you, Ma'am. I'm fine just now," unwilling to chance it.

"Call me Janet, please." She turned toward her husband. "Jackson?" she asked, with just a bit of impatience in her tone.

"A coke would be great. Thank you dear." He laughed, but this time, restrained.

Ernest moved his body nervously on the couch and tried to calm the shaking in his right leg. *Why did he feel so nervous?*

"Ernest," Jackson said, with a serious expression on his face. "I have a bit of an apology to make. I didn't realize when we invited you, that our daughter would be staying with us this weekend. I really wouldn't

Beyond the Ripples 31

have done this had I known. You know, I want to focus on those old stories tonight."

Ernest didn't know what to say, so he stayed silent.

"It's just that our Sharon . . ." Jackson stopped, gave a quiet partial laugh, and shook his head back and forth. "She's a bit exhausting, I guess you could say. Of course, we love her, don't get me wrong. You just have to . . . well . . . I guess, be a bit prepared."

Ernest was confused. "It's okay. I'm fine." He wondered how horrible this daughter could be?

"Well, don't ever tell my wife I said this." Jackson theatrically looked toward the kitchen. He cupped his hand around his mouth, leaned toward Ernest, and asked, "Have you ever been in a tornado?"

"Um. No sir," Ernest answered.

"Well, you might want to plan for that tonight. You know, it's a dizzy, get me out of here soon, too much coming at you at once, kind of feeling. Because that's a bit how it is around our dear Sharon." And then, yet again, Jackson laughed his deep, joyful laugh.

Ernest found himself wondering how in the world a man who laughed following most every sentence, and a man seemingly as even keeled and serious as his father, could ever be pals.

About five minutes later, a young woman burst through the front door. And really, Ernest thought, although he had never been in a tornado, he had enough imagination to believe this just might be the kind of wild energy packed into such a turbulent stream of air. And if there was a human equivalent: perhaps this Sharon was just that.

"What a day!" Sharon exclaimed, almost yelling, as she burst in and slammed the door. "Mom, did you see that article on the front page of the Examiner? Oh my God. I tell you. I'm going to kill them!" As she pulled her coat off she suddenly noticed Ernest sitting on the couch and immediately flung an accusatory glare at her father. She wore jeans that ended at her calves and a pair of tennis shoes. Her black hair streamed down in a multitude of tiny braids.

"Sharon," Jackson began calmly. "We have a guest for dinner. A guest who, I bet, didn't prepare himself for two days to be able to survive an evening of wildness."

Sharon turned to look at Ernest, and then back to Jackson. "Dad, that's not fair! As if you are the picture of calmness. Ha." She turned and strode over to Ernest. "I apologize for my dad. I'm Sharon." She held out her hand.

Ernest silently shook her hand. He sat in such shock that he didn't even stand up, in this household so different than his own. This young woman, he realized, terrified him. Although Dixie no doubt had her own kind of energy, it was very different than this Sharon. Disciplined, perhaps. And Dixie's parents were rather quiet and careful to follow whatever they imagined to be the politeness they believed society dictated. Or at least it seemed that way around Ernest. But this girl! *Wow. She knows who she is.* And suddenly he felt as if he was just thirteen years old and prayed that he wouldn't be expected to communicate with her.

"Ernest, I don't know about you, but I really do need something to drink. Are you interested?"

Ernest suddenly had an urge to throw up. How could such a question and decision be so intimidating? He yearned to be back home with his mother as she silently stared out the window, and then perhaps later they might turn on the television to find an escape. He needed to be someplace where very little was expected from him.

"Ernest!"

He was jolted back to Sharon. He finally stilled his brain and looked at her.

She gave him a big smile and laughed. "Where are you?"

Again, he didn't know what to say as he stared at her smiling face, and finally offered boldly, "I'm right here on the couch."

Sharon laughed. She looked over at Jackson. "Oh, so you invited in a joker. Okay, last chance. I'm grabbing something—of course my parents never have much but can I get you something as well?"

"Sure," Ernest settled on. Relieved to come up with a useful word. "Thank you," he added, pleased to find two more.

After she had left the room, Jackson followed her with his eyes, and then with a mysterious look on his face offered, "See? Don't tell me I didn't warn you. She doesn't live with us anymore but is nearby and seems to stop by plenty. We figure her roomies toss her out from time to time." He smiled broadly.

Sharon returned with two wine glasses filled with a clear liquid. Ernest's hands grew clammy as he wondered if the red wine he brought had been a poor choice, or if she hadn't spotted his gift, but was too intimidated to ask. He wiped his sweaty palms on his pants, hoping she wouldn't notice, and reached out to take the glass.

Before he had much time to worry, Sharon shepherded him up. "Come on. Mama's ready. And let me tell you, if Mama's meal is ready, you damn well better get yourself to the table."

Stunned, and without any idea of what else he could do, Ernest followed her to the table.

And that was that. Really it was. As unbelievable as it might seem now. Over the many years, Ernest had often wondered how it could be that the only two girls he ever loved came from such different worlds than he. And yet, he could never imagine loving anyone else like that. And while a few of his friends later in life wanted to know which woman was his true love, they never seemed to believe him when he answered, simply, "Both. I loved them both so much."

When he had been with Dixie, all he ever heard from his high school buddies was how they couldn't believe she would have settled on a guy like him. Those few years later, the men he worked with couldn't imagine he would marry a woman like Sharon. But he didn't care. It wasn't as if after that first night at Jackson and Janet's home it was some fairy tale, like the stories his own Amelia would read when she was little. But that first evening was a night filled with stories about Chuck, and laughter, and perhaps, he realized much later, life. Something Ernest hadn't felt for so long. Sharon exuded a different form of life energy than Dixie's. And he understood, all these years later, how Sharon knew who she was, even if at times she took wild stabs at new opportunities.

Ernest, back in their early years, didn't know himself. He just kept trying to do those things he knew were the right things to do. But slowly, with help from Sharon and Jackson and Janet, he learned about humor and to be able to comfortably show and accept affection. And unlike Dixie's parents, Jackson and Janet folded him in to their lives, helping him understand how the kindness they shared wasn't only due to Jackson's bond with Chuck, but because they truly cared about Ernest. And it was Jackson, just prior to his death several years later, who shared the fears he held for the new couple—but rarely expressed at the time—against the backdrop of Portland's race relations.

After five repeat four-some dinners, one night, Sharon caught him alone in the dining room. Jackson had gotten up and offered to help Janet in the kitchen which seemed a bit odd to Ernest. As kind and considerate as Jackson was to his wife, he still made it clear where he thought a woman's place was when it came to domestic chores. But on this night, he arose, looked across at Sharon, and stated that "the missus" needed help. Ernest stared across the table at Sharon, realizing how the two, for the first time, were alone together. Ernest had progressed to where he wasn't nervous around her, at least when Jackson and Janet were there, and he had begun to enjoy her funny outbursts and her teasing of her parents. More recently, he noticed Sharon taking an interest in his stories, often offering a smile directed to him.

"Well?" Sharon asked. No smile this time.

"Um. I'm sorry? Was I supposed to do something?" Ernest asked.

"Well, if I have to say. I kind of thought maybe you'd suggest that we do something together. Sometime?"

Ernest was stunned. *How could a girl, well a woman really, be asking him this?* How could such a beautiful woman, so beautiful especially when she smiled, have any interest in a guy like him?

"Well, we are together," he sputtered, unable to think of anything else to say.

"You goof. I mean just us. Don't you maybe just want to go somewhere without them?" she asked, jerking her head toward the kitchen.

Ernest stared at her. And then he released a smile. Not as wide and bold as Sharon's, but a smile, nonetheless. "Yes. That would be good."

And that was it. For the rest of their years together—through both easy and tough times—Sharon would remind him, often in front of their Amelia, how if it wasn't for her, their little girl would never have entered this world. Her humor was one of the things he loved most about her, always reminding him of his father-in-law. Ernest didn't know how anyone could both think *and* get words out so quickly, almost simultaneously. Even all those years later with Sharon still at his side, he might find himself tongue-tied if he wasn't careful. But by then, he was astute and confident enough, to detect traces of a small smile slowly progressing on Sharon's face, reminding him, how much she loved him. And almost as often, Sharon would take a deep breath, let it out, rest her head on his shoulder and mutter, "Oh, how I love you."

ERNEST TOOK THE breath and let it out slowly. He grabbed at both arms of his chair and closed his eyes. Alone. In this little house where he had lived alone for ten years. When he lost his Sharon, he knew he couldn't stay in that home of theirs—a house foreign after she passed. Cold and unfamiliar. He had walked through its starkly quiet kitchen and stood in the doorway to this room where he had built an area against one wall for her sewing machine. Gone was the hum of the machine. Its absence for him amplified Sharon's unrequited hope for small grandbabies to sew for. It was that room, more than any other, even their bedroom, that he couldn't bear being in any longer. The same gray house they lived in together after they married and where his parents raised him, Helen living with him even after they married. His mother had never forgotten her anger and sadness over Chuck's abrupt passing. Helen had struggled at her son's decision to marry someone she felt to be so different than her son, telling him she was worried how the community would treat them. Her concern lessened later, the moment she held her granddaughter, tiny Amelia, and she never spoke of it again. Helen passed away early in their marriage but not until after teaching Sharon to sew, strengthening their friendship while working together at her old Singer in the corner of the family kitchen.

When Sharon died, years after Amelia had grown up and moved out, the memories captive within his house were beyond what Ernest could face each day. He chose this new spot along the Columbia River to live out his final years.

Chapter 3

An invitation
June 2014

IT FELT LIKE the longest day ever by the time Gloria got home that night. She could barely keep her eyes open, and her feet dragged noisily on the porch steps. It took her a minute to realize the key wouldn't fit in the lock because she was using her car key, only to remember she generally failed to lock her door anyway. As she turned the unlocked door handle, she spied a brown paper package on the doorstep. Abstractedly, Gloria wondered how long it had been there—tucked behind the gardening pots she neglected to plant the previous spring. She struggled to hold both her grocery bag and purse, while simultaneously opening the door, and by the time she stumbled into the house, she had forgotten about the package on the doorstep.

She saw it again the next morning as she was leaving. This time she stopped and picked it up, trying to remember what she might have ordered. When her mind came up blank, she groaned as she squinted without her glasses to find a return address or any clue to trigger her memory. All that was written on the package that she could decipher was her address, scrawled in black ink adjacent to the postmark and postage stamps. She reached in her pocket for her reading glasses, came up empty, so instead she stooped over to pick up the package. *It was so crudely wrapped!* She hated to admit how lately, little things, such as a poorly wrapped package, so easily perturbed her. *Wasn't she once easier going?* Yet, there had always been, in her mind, a right way to do everything, further evidence to support Sarah's claim about her mother's anal retentiveness. Fixated now, Gloria asserted to herself that proper wrapping was necessary to get parcels delivered on time through the inefficient postal service.

Finally, Gloria brought the package into her house, irritated at one more thing to slow down a day she already felt late for. Even if nobody was expecting her. *When did it happen that she became cranky all the time and everything was so difficult?* The package reminded her how lately, amid the stress of daily living, she had lost her curiosity. Most times she didn't notice it, but times like this made her sad. She lowered the package to the wood floor and clumsily kicked it to slide under the coat rack, momentarily losing her balance and catching herself on the nearby table. She'd deal with it later she told herself as she instead crept to her soft plaid rocking chair.

"Ah," she groaned, as she let herself drop down into it. *Just for a minute.* She needed a few minutes relief already from a day that had only just begun.

Years ago, she may have gleefully imagined what treasure hid within this unannounced package. Now, it was just one more thing in her way, at this time when life was unlikely to hand out any interesting surprises. *God.* Embarrassing to confess when she was not even seventy-five years old: her own grandmother at ninety had more spunk than she. *Seventy the new fifty baloney!* She laughed disdainfully. Her cramped toes ached, smothered as they were in her lace up shoes, and she felt compelled to pull them both off. *The darn shoes!* Why couldn't someone make a pair to accommodate arthritic toes? She closed her eyes and sighed. Reluctantly, she opened them to peer at her large-dialed Timex watch, a scratch blurring its face. *How had she lost track of time so quickly?* She reached down to the floor and stuffed her sore feet back into her shoes.

Chapter 4

Trepidation
September 2015

WHEN SARAH RECEIVED the emergency phone call, all she could think about was an incident with her mother a month before. She had stopped by Gloria's house in the middle of the day, responding to an odd phone conversation she had with her that morning. Her mother had sounded so needy. Of all things Gloria had been over the years, *needy* was never one of them. Sarah had forced herself to stop by Gloria's house as soon as she could that day on a "good will visit." She tried hard to rouse up some type of genuine, which she hoped to be daughterly, love. Instead she was annoyed to be compelled to respond to what was sure to be another bothersome exchange.

As Sarah pulled her car up to the house, she was surprised at the visibly untended yard, the lawn overgrown, and flower beds filled with weeds. Large dandelions popped out between clumps of scraggly grass. She tried to be positive by reminding herself that at least her own landlord kept up his part of the bargain by providing landscaping services. It was only then she realized Gloria's car wasn't in the driveway. This good deed wasted, she complained to herself. *Fuck it.*

Sarah opened her trunk in spite of it and grabbed the small plastic bag of groceries she had purchased at Safeway on a spur of the moment. The few last times she had seen Gloria, she couldn't help but notice how much thinner she seemed, her pastel polyester pants hanging off her body, creating uneven fabric pleats rather than stretching tightly over curves. She lacked bulges above her waistband or below her chin, like other old women Sarah saw at the mall. Carrying the grocery bag up to the front porch, she pulled the extra house key from the zippered part of her purse. Before fitting it into the front door lock, though, she found the knob turned freely.

"Good God, Gloria," Sarah muttered as she pushed open the door and entered the house, wondering if her mother ever locked up anymore. "What a fucking disaster!"

It had been almost a month since Sarah had visited, but she didn't remember it being this messy. *I can't do this!* She routinely insisted to herself she shouldn't feel responsible for her mother, reminding herself of legitimate excuses. She held a demanding, sometimes demeaning, job that was grossly unlike the one she once dreamed about and often worried about her grown daughter. *Just how much more could she take?*

Sarah often felt she was the only person to discern the real traits that lay behind her mother's facade of strength and independence. Although Gloria might occasionally rile those around her, she had exhibited a determined pluck that Sarah knew others admired her for. A pluck that grated against Sarah and contradicted a truth that she held from events so long ago.

But now on this visit, Sarah admitted something was amiss. Parts of Gloria's presence teetered from what she once had been. Although never immaculate in her housekeeping, it had always been at least "organized disorder," piles and boxes here and there, yet always in the appropriate part of the house. But now, Sarah noticed, looking around, the place was a pigsty. So much of this extra stuff had once been part of her mother's strategic plan to help others: her offerings of friendship. But now, Sarah wasn't so sure if any of the crap lying around was intentionally planted.

After setting the groceries in the kitchen: sliced turkey and cheddar cheese in the fridge, bananas in the fruit basket, and a loaf of white bread on the counter, Sarah dashed into the bathroom with a sudden urgency to pee. Across from the toilet in the corner next to the toilet brush sat a box of groceries, a milk carton peeking out from the top. She felt the carton, it was warm to the touch.

"What the fuck?" Sarah demanded, out loud. She pulled down her pants and underwear to sit on the toilet seat, feeling relief with the flow of urine, hearing it splash into the water below.

Her phone vibrated, and she pulled it out of her zippered jacket pocket, looking at the caller's number flashing.

"Yes?" she answered, a frustrated response to this intrusion. "Yes, I'll be back as soon as I can. Even I can take a lunch break, can't I?" She slammed off her cell and jammed it back in the pocket. "Damn!"

She would regret talking to Betty sharply and knew her feelings were juvenile and selfish. She dabbed at her eyes, wishing she could force her tears to retreat back inside. She sat on the toilet seat and covered her hands to her face, believing each time she cried she was an even greater failure. She sunk her head onto her folded arms, resting them on top of her naked thighs.

"I can't do this. I cannot do this any fucking more." Sarah tried to slow her panting and sorrow-filled heaving chest, until it all dissipated into a series of soft hiccups. It's always one more thing, and never ends, she thought as she pulled toilet paper off the roll.

She wiped herself, and then grabbed another swatch to wipe her eyes and nose and tossed both into the toilet before flushing. She got up, ran cold water from the faucet over her hands, and splashed it on her face, carefully to avoid further smudging her mascara. She strode back into the kitchen and through the living room, grabbed her purse, and slammed the front door, making sure to lock it.

"Fuck this," she said as she returned to her car.

Although she had been relieved when she reached Gloria later that day and her mother had sounded more like her old self, Sarah couldn't forget about what she had seen. When she told her mother about how frustrated she had been during her noontime visit, Gloria had apologized.

"I'm sorry, hon," her mother had said. "Sorry to worry you. I was just not quite myself, maybe a touch of a bug. And then I realized I had to get to the church and I didn't think you would worry so."

Gloria paused, and Sarah imagined her mother taking a breath to control her voice, to prove to Sarah that she was, in fact, fine.

"I would have called you back if I thought you'd actually come check up on me," Gloria said resentfully.

Sarah felt only a small bit of her frustration disappear, and she tried to put the entire incident out of her mind, including the groceries she spied in the bathroom, even though she continued to wonder if her mother would ever notice the old carton of milk. She had turned her phone off, stretched her arms up above her head, and groaned at the relief she felt in her tight shoulder muscles.

EVEN AFTER THE passing of time since that upsetting day, Sarah knew deep inside her how something equally or even more disturbing would happen. And when it did, it was *déjà* vu like—as if she had dreamt it, and the low-lying worry embedded within her arose as if to say, "Told you so." She had been driving to visit Alison when she received the call. She reacted instinctively, emotionless, hurrying without thinking to the hospital emergency room ten miles away— later not remembering where she parked her car—to where she faced Gloria lying in the metal-railed hospital bed, with purplish bruising on her forehead and above one eye. Her eyes were closed and her head was raised awkwardly on a pillow. Gloria must have heard Sarah's footsteps as she struggled to open her eyes. Sarah saw her mother cringe, her mouth melting into her worry look, as she identified her one daughter.

Only then panicked by her mother's appearance, Sarah blurted, "Gloria, what did you do?" She bit the inside of her cheek, wishing she had made herself sound more worried and less irritated.

Gloria forced a weak smile. "It's nothing. I tripped. Really, it's not a big deal. I was just a little tired." She looked away from Sarah and slowly closed her eyes.

Sarah then spotted Gloria's friend Flo, the one her mother volunteered with at church, sitting in the corner of the room, a glossy gardening magazine unopened on her lap. She looked at Flo, who caught Sarah's eye and almost imperceptibly shook her head, as if commanding her into silence.

Flo's worry lined her face as she spoke up. "The doctor said they want to keep her a bit longer while they evaluate the CAT scan. And her wrist is broken, so they will need to cast it."

Sarah turned to look back at Gloria, but her mother's eyes were still closed. Now Flo stood up. She was at least ten years younger than Gloria and had been a close friend for more than a decade. Sarah tried to remember if she had first met her at their church, although Sarah had only been to one or two events there, or whether they had made an earlier connection. Now Flo went to Gloria and took her left hand, the one not splinted.

"No, Gloria, keep your eyes open for now. It's okay. It'll all be okay." She tried to sound calm, but to Sarah it sounded fake and alarming, rather than reassuring.

A young male nurse entered the room. "Time to check your vitals," he said perkily, smiling at the three women. Sarah noticed his biceps pushing up through his short-sleeved maroon scrubs, and she wondered how many patients he had to move every day.

"Wow, Gloria, lucky you," Flo said and winked toward Gloria, but lacked any real humor. Gloria didn't respond. Then Flo looked at Sarah. "Sarah, can you come down the hall? There's a print I want to show you."

Sarah gave her an odd look, tempted to snap back at how she had no interest in art now or ever. Instead, she reluctantly followed Flo out of the room as the nurse with the badge identifying him as "Peter" began to check Gloria's oxygen saturation.

Once they were safely out of the room and down the hallway, Flo grabbed Sarah's wrist, stopping her. "You have to do something. Your mother cannot live by herself anymore. It's not safe."

Sarah stared at Flo. Horrified. Yes, she knew there were small nonsensical events happening here or there. But to have her mother's close friend speak with this fear that bordered hostility unnerved her. "What are you talking about? She just fell. Right?" She wracked her brain to remember if Flo had brought up concerns before.

"Sarah, I'm sorry, but you have no idea. Don't you remember the thing I told you about months ago? I left you a voicemail," Flo sounded exasperated. "Have you not wondered about where she was when she fell? Or what she was doing?" She was almost yelling as she struggled to control her voice, the veins in her neck bulging. She hesitated and took a breath. "I'm sorry. I am just so worried. And I have tried to talk to her, but she pretends things are fine. She dismisses anything I say."

"Well. What was it? I mean, tell me what happened," Sarah said, as the pulsing of her heartbeat pounded in her chest and sweat formed in her armpits.

"She was in her pajamas. In the broad daylight. Without a coat or anything. Her neighbor, that old man Winston, found her on her rear end outside his back window."

Sarah simply stared at her, her eyes opening wider as the startling news shocked her into silence. "What?" was all she could get out.

"Yes. Thank goodness, he is such a kind man. And not really a talker, either. Just like the gentleman he is, he just walked her back to her house. Probably pretending as if it was no big deal. But, Sarah, it was the middle of the day." Flo looked again at Sarah.

Sarah only stared back, her mouth slightly open.

"He called me," Flo added, "thank the Lord, and just made up an excuse like she was having a bad day."

Sarah shook her head. She looked for a chair and held her stomach, afraid she was about to puke. Flo sat next to her on the adjacent plastic chair lining the wall. Chairs for people awaiting news: hoping for the best, expecting the worst.

"But this was today, right?" Sarah asked. "It's Wednesday and she always volunteers at church on Wednesday. This doesn't make any sense."

Flo nodded. "Yes, I know. And what was even odder was that right after Winston called me, I immediately called her, and she said she was fine. I said, 'What do you mean you are fine?' Heaven's sake. He should have called 911. I drove over so fast it was lucky I didn't get a ticket." Sarah had never seen Flo so upset, she gripped the chair so hard with both hands that her knuckles were white. "When I got there, she had tracked her muddy shoes through the house and had blood dripping down her face."

"No. No. Please tell me this didn't happen." Sarah sank even lower in the hard chair, slouching downward, so that her head rested ever so slightly against the top of the chair back. She stared up at the white ceiling and then, briefly, closed her eyes. The antiseptic odors of the hospital permeated them.

"And now . . . you can see," Flo continued. "She can't even use her wrist. I asked her what she had done and she just looked at me with this faraway look in her eyes, and said, 'Nothing.' I don't want to pester her, but I'm not sure if she can even really remember."

Sarah looked desperately for a trash can, her guts warning her she was going to lose it. She also knew the two of them had already been away from Gloria's room much longer than they should. Certainly, handsome Peter would be done with his pricking and prodding. She took a deep breath to try to steady the nausea caused by the churning of morning yogurt and coffee.

"Hell. Okay, we've got to go back in," Sarah said.

As Flo and Sarah re-entered the room, Gloria was lying in the bed with her eyes closed, although Sarah sensed she wasn't asleep, but figured if Peter had left her like that, perhaps there was no real fear about concussion. Or else he had too many other patients awaiting him and call lights blinking, that dragged her case to the bottom of his worry list.

"Mom," Sarah tried. Gloria's fragility forced Sarah to refer to her as she did so long ago, rather than the more impersonal "Gloria" of recent years. "What's going on?"

Gloria's eyes remained closed.

"I need to be going, Gloria," Flo said.

Gloria slowly opened her eyes, and looked at her friend.

"I'll call you tomorrow, okay? Chin up, friend. It's all going to be okay." She smiled first at Gloria, and then gifted Sarah a sadder mutation of the smile. Flo picked up her rain jacket and purse abandoned earlier on the spare chair, ignoring the magazine, and silently walked out the door.

Sarah and Gloria were alone, immersed in the repetitive sounds of a hospital: electronic beeps and liquids swooshing, voices emanating from patient rooms, and punctuated by door slams. The offspring of technology's tracking of bodily functions, all trying to keep patients alive.

"Mom," Sarah tried again. "I think we need to talk."

Gloria opened her eyes, and sadly met her daughter's. "Honey. I'm old. I'm just really old. I can't keep doing this."

"Gloria, I mean, Mom . . . what do you mean?" Sarah said, raising her voice. Unable to keep herself from calling her what she was used to. "You're not that old. Hell, you still scare the check-out clerks at Safeway." She wanted to smile, but her lips were stuck in place, tight against her teeth, the forced smile feeling as if it would split her lips.

Gloria shook her head. "No, really. Things really aren't good. But don't worry. You have your life. It's not for you to take care of." She looked away, out the window to where the afternoon sun was masked behind dark clouds. It had poured the previous night, and a storm was threatening again.

"Gloria. This is crazy. I don't know what is going on." Sarah was trying not to sound exasperated, but couldn't stop herself. She tried to discount the times recently when she had felt Gloria wasn't handling things as well as she once had. She had tried to remind herself it was all normal aging. That it had been nothing to worry about. And as much as she argued now, the deep foreboding sensation built within her; dark worries that haunted brains even in the middle of ordinary thoughts. It was at this moment, Sarah admitted to herself there was more evidence than simply the disorderly appearance of her house, or complaints about others. "Please. I promise to try to understand. What do you mean?" The temporarily subsided nausea rose up again, making her want to burst out of the hospital into the fresh rain laden air and scream obscenities at the world around her.

Gloria was quiet. Finally, she met Sarah's eye. "I'm getting mixed up sometimes." She paused. "Once in a while I'll leave to go somewhere in the car, and then before I know it I won't know at first where I am." She stopped as if to gauge Sarah's reaction. "Or why I am there. Like last week I was just driving, and I found myself at a donut shop in Beaverton. I don't even like donuts. And I had absolutely no idea why I was there, or even how I got there." She looked at Sarah who could only stare back at her.

Gloria continued, as if unleashing deep secrets she'd been holding inside. "Today I was so embarrassed. With my neighbor, Winston. I don't know why I was outside. I had breakfast but then I told myself it was time to get to church. And then I remember thinking about why I couldn't go today, but I can't remember why that was. When Winston found me in his yard and walked me back home I just about died. Winston of all people. What he must think of me, prowling around. And I can't even remember what I said to him. Anyway . . . I don't know. I just don't know." As if exhausted, she lay her head back deep into the pillow and closed her eyes.

Chapter 5

Transitions
January 2016

"SARAH! WHAT'S THE sale price for the black cardigans on rounder four? Sarah?"

Sarah looked up from staring fixedly at the inventory list on the computer, and spun around.

Marilyn looked at her impatiently. "Hello? Anybody home?"

Sarah sent Marilyn a look of embarrassed surprise and shook her head to hide her resentment for this co-worker catching her like this. "Sorry. I didn't sleep very well last night. They are 19.99."

Sarah stood up and walked away from the computer, knowing she had been simply peering blankly at the screen. She focused on refolding an ugly purple flowered tee shirt on sale on a shelf closest to the counter. Then she looked at her watch. *Thank God.* This day felt like the longest shift ever. Being back on the floor again was killing her, and she hoped it would be only temporary, although she worried, given how slow retail business seemed to be. She knew the popularity of online shopping wasn't simply a blip like everyone had said at first.

Sarah carefully looked back at Marilyn, relieved to find she had already moved on to something else. It wasn't that Sarah didn't like her: Marilyn was one of her less annoying co-workers. She just didn't feel like she had the energy to deal with her, or anyone else, on this day. She knew she should appreciate this job and its benefits, although it did make her feel she was settling on something she had never intended to be her life work, and lately she had less energy to deal with anything extra. She looked at her watch again, not remembering the time when she had checked only a few minutes before. *One more hour.* She returned to the computer to update the inventory, total the daily sales, and straighten up the mess of curled yellow paper receipts and returns littering the sales counter. Maybe if business stayed slow she could get the end of shift busywork done and sneak out earlier than normal.

Just then two teenage girls came in. Damn, she thought, as she stared at the girls' identically French-braided hair, her attention now heightened to watch for early indications –were they the type to try on dozens of items without intention to buy, moving piles around into synthetic chaos requiring straightening after they eventually got bored and wandered away? Those kinds of shoppers, although annoying, weren't as bad as the type who flat out stole, requiring her to follow them around the store as if she was their mother.

Sarah had been around long enough to pick out the ones who dared each other to score some cheap piece of clothing and stuffed it up the billowing shirt they were wearing, or quickly into an oversized handbag. She made sure these prowlers knew she was an unfriendly viewer who wanted them to hustle on out of at least her department, if not the store.

This time, though, she noticed these girls lacked the belligerent confidence of the slightly older would-be shoplifter and decided she didn't need to follow their every move. Instead she returned her attention to the sales receipts she was organizing. Within a few minutes her cell vibrated but she forced herself to ignore it, not even looking to confirm the caller. If it was Gloria, she thought to herself, she would have to wait. She could call her back, although the familiar urgent worry scratched below her consciousness. Different than a year or two ago when she knew the call to be an innocuous reminder that could wait another week, now it would poke at her until she returned the call.

Finally, eight o'clock. It felt as though clock-out time would never arrive. She walked through the store, glad she didn't have to do the final closing, tightly grabbing the straps on her purse to create the beginnings of tiny indentations into her neck as she pulled them close to her body, believing she'd never entirely recover from that one night. She strained to remember if she had parked her late model Honda in her usual place: a few times she stumbled in after-shift stupors to an empty space where she was certain she had parked her car. But this time, she was relieved to spot it in her usual location. So far, no surprises. Thank God, given how vulnerable she felt. She hit the remote, the lights flashed, she climbed in, and quietly groaned as she bent down to sit on the cold vinyl seat, pushing aside the crumpled napkin lodged into the seat crease. The door beeped as she locked the doors, and she simply sat, waiting for the overhead light to dim.

The chilly air seeped through the denim of her jeans, and her toes felt cold and clammy inside her flats. She closed her eyes and wondered if she could fall asleep as she started to shiver. What would a co-worker think if they saw her here in the morning, sleeping? Most of the team might kindly ignore it, but she knew at least a couple who would feel compelled to start a rumor, especially on the heels of her more recent poor work performance.

They'd start a story about her being on the streets, or about Tony doing something weird. She felt sad, after all these years working at the same store, she didn't have anyone to whom she could speak honestly and confidentially. Or pal around with, invite for lunch, or just hang out. She knew she was older than many of the sales crew, but she never had a pal even before, when she was young. *Was she really such a bad person?* She knew she was feeling sorry for herself, sitting in the cold, as she searched her brain to remember the last good friend she had, the one she could share her deepest thoughts with. Probably Maggie, she figured; fun Maggie. Until all the bad began.

She stretched and shook her head, trying to pull herself together. She started the car, hoping the heater would warm her up soon. The radio shouted out a talk show, and she channel surfed to find a song she might recognize. The warm air melted the goosebumps on her legs and arms, and she released the emergency brake. She heard Tony's voice criticizing her for setting the brake even though the parking lot was level as she put the car into drive and pulled out of the lot toward the freeway entrance. All she really wanted to do was go home, take a hot bath, and go to bed. Thank God, she didn't have to work the next day.

But instead of heading to her empty apartment, she pulled into the visitor spot at River Crossing. After going through the front door, up a set of stairs, and down a long, too bright hall, she first knocked on the door, hesitated, and turned the handle, confident it wouldn't be locked. She opened the door.

"Gloria?" she asked. The apartment was quiet. "Don't worry, it's just me."

"I'm in here," Gloria said.

Sarah went into the small bedroom where her mother was sitting on a wicker chair looking out the window. She didn't turn her head to look as Sarah entered the room, but kept staring out at a parking lot, where street lights cast their glow off the few cars, and one van parked there.

Sarah sat on the bed as she tried to gather her thoughts; to try to predict which tact might be most useful. "Hi."

Gloria turned suddenly toward her, her face naked without its usual makeup dressing.

"Just thought I'd stop by for a minute on my way home from work," Sarah added.

Gloria turned back to the window and stared into the darkness on this winter evening. Sarah tried to decipher if she was still angry with her or simply sad.

"Was dinner okay tonight? Can I get you anything?" Sarah asked.

Gloria remained silent. Sarah noticed she was wearing the same matching light blue sweat suit she had on the last time Sarah visited. She wondered if Gloria had figured out how to do the laundry at this place.

"We could have a cup of tea?" Sarah added.

Gloria turned her head toward Sarah and looked her in the eyes. "No, I'm fine. You should go home. I'm sure you've had a long day."

Sarah could tell Gloria was attempting to smile, but it was fake. Forced. Not the broad smile always accompanying her loud cackle that had annoyed her all their years together. Her inner voice begged. *Bring back my real mother.* Even though she knew how much she battled against that mother, seemingly now, of the past.

"I will in a few minutes. It just seemed maybe we could talk." She looked around the room. "Hey. It really looks homey in here." She tried to sound cheery and positive even as she stumbled to get words out.

Gloria looked outside again. It was not like her. She had always been one to fill the air with words and statements. Commands and assertions that had annoyed Sarah so many hours of her life. But now, excess talking seemed to be a thing of the past.

"Really. It's going to be okay." Sarah tried to keep her voice gentle, but knew she was failing. "Really. Here let me get you a cup of tea." She went into the kitchenette and put water in the electric tea kettle. As she pulled two cups out of the one cupboard, she wondered how Gloria, previously an apparent commander of her universe, could go from a full kitchen to this dollhouse-sized space. Sarah, though, was beginning to think she herself might be honestly relieved to live in a space like this. To be devoid of expectation from others for doing anything more than the minimum. Then, if Alison dropped by, she'd have a real excuse for not being able to attempt to create the elaborate meal to prove to her daughter how much she really did love her, even though she wasn't sure, even then, that Alison believed her. Sarah knew Alison would never believe how she, Sarah, had been available for her all along, or as supportive as Gloria.

Sarah re-opened the cupboard, found two boxes of tea, and chose chamomile, even though she hated it: but reminded herself the tea was supposed to be relaxing. She knew she needed to find a way to get sleep, especially on the nights Tony wasn't around. The water rumbled to a boil, and she poured it over one of the teabags. Before she poured the steaming water into the second cup, she put the kettle back on the counter and returned the cup to the cupboard. She heard shuffling footsteps and looked up to see Gloria had made her way into the small living room to sit in her rocking chair next to the window. As Sarah looked past Gloria toward the window, she was relieved to be reminded of the view from the apartment, even if it was dark now. At least by being on the second floor she could look into the horizon of the valley rather than an asphalt parking lot. Not that Sarah would bring that up now, though.

Sarah pulled the hot tea bag out and shook it into the cup so not to drip all over the counter before tossing it in the trash. She was glad she hadn't brewed a cup for herself –the steam's scent reminded her of rotten daisies. She'd have to pick up some better choices for Gloria. She carried the hot china cup and set it on the scratched wooden table next to Gloria, who smiled a more authentic smile than before, though still weak by Gloria standards.

"Thanks, dear. You should get on your way. Do you work tomorrow?"

"No, Mom. You know it's Sunday." Thank God, she never had to work Sundays, she thought, unfairly irritated. Her mother should know she didn't work that day, ever.

"Do you have any plans tomorrow?" Sarah asked.

"Oh, I'm sure I'll figure something out," Gloria said simply.

Sarah paused for a moment, and debated. "But you're not driving. Right?" She tried not to sound like a bitch.

"Sarah, just leave that. I'm not an idiot." Gloria took a sip of the tea and closed her eyes.

"I know," Sarah said, trying to keep her voice even. "I just worry about you. You know. I mean, I just don't want anything to happen to you. How about I call you in the morning when we aren't both so tired, okay? Maybe I can see you later in the day and we can get some groceries." She remembered Gloria didn't have a big need for groceries now with meals provided as part of the package. As bad as they may be. "Or maybe we can get a bite to eat," she offered, reluctantly.

It had taken months to get Gloria into a place, with Sarah ultimately accepting how her mother would never be happy with any selection. Luckily, Gloria's lease was ending, and the rent was going up again, although this place was off the charts compared to what she had been paying in rent. A cost Gloria could never have afforded without a lifetime of thriftiness. Her brother had argued with her about making the decision "unilaterally," as he called it. He felt sure Gloria was fine living on her own, and that living independently was a much better use of *her* money. That's when they had their first real argument in recent years with Sarah shouting at him that all he cared about was having something left over for him when Gloria died. Ted had hung up on her, and they hadn't spoken again for several weeks—never discussing it once they did talk again. And now, after months trying to convince Gloria that this living arrangement would be better, not just safer, Gloria still wasn't adjusting very well. Sarah knew she needed to visit her more often, but, so far, it always wiped her out, making her procrastinate each time.

"We'll see," Gloria said. "I might have other plans. And they involve someone else driving, not me. Anyway, don't worry. You worry too much. And don't hover. I can do this." But she didn't sound confident.

Sarah arose from the small sofa next to Gloria's chair and stifled a groan from the pain in her lower back and her aching feet. She was so tired: as if she could simply lie down on the carpet and fall asleep immediately. Anyplace. Gloria continued to sit.

Sarah had been slow to realize, at first, but now couldn't ignore how much her mother had changed in the last year or two. Gloria had always been so bouncy, the first to take care of anyone other than herself. Now, Gloria looked up at Sarah, wordless, then took another sip of her tea.

"I'll call you soon." Sarah fingered keys in her pocket and only then realized she had never taken her jacket off and the heat of the apartment felt smothering, her forehead sticky with sweat.

"Goodnight, Gloria," Sarah said as she headed out of the unit. Wishing for an immediate, cool jet of air, she stepped into a stale mixture of Lysol and potatoes. *Who would ever have thought?* She headed down the hallway, through the stairwell and back to her car.

SARAH CRAVED SLEEP—hours and hours of sleep—during these interminable last few months. She tried to shield her brain and heart from darts of worry during her busy waking hours. But there was so much to do. At night when her body should be sinking into exhausted sleep, unanswered questions pinged at her like a triggered smoke alarm. Although Gloria's landlord granted her several extra months at a reduced rate, something Sarah was certain Flo had arranged, she struggled as if wading in a mud-filled swamp to ready the house for the landlord.

She knew she couldn't depend on Ted for help, he was still angry with her for initiating the move. She repeatedly swore at him when she was alone, wishing she was brave enough to show up at his house and tell him in person. In front of his prissy wife and perfect children. Deep down she wondered if his issue with the move was his inability to accept the changes in their mother rather than the money he complained about, but she couldn't bring herself to have a heartfelt conversation with him.

There was no way she could meet the landlord's deadline. Against her better judgement, she dialed Alison's number the next morning to remind her. She hated to ask her for this help, knowing how unpredictable she could be. But if one thing was true about her daughter: she loved Gloria, in good and in bad.

"Morning. Are you still able to help out a bit today?" Sarah asked.

"Hi, Mom," Alison said, groggily. "Well of course, I said I would, didn't I?" She was suddenly edgy and razor sharp. "But how about a little later, okay? Can we do it like at one or something?"

Sarah tried to keep her voice under control: immediately concluding Alison to be hungover in her bed, after a night of too much something. "Whatever works." She knew she sounded frustrated. "There is so much to do. Just get there when you can, okay? And do you think Tom can come by too? There are still some heavy things to get to Goodwill. Or somewhere."

The phone line was silent.

"I'll try, Mom. He's just got so much going on. You know . . ." Alison said.

Sarah listened to Alison's indecisive breathing for what felt like too long.

"I'll try, Mom. Really. I'll try to get him to come for a while."

But Sarah knew that asking Alison's newest boyfriend Tom to help was the last thing Alison wanted to do.

"Thanks," Sarah said simply, forcing herself to sound positive. "That'd be great." She hesitated. "And maybe he can bring his truck?"

"Sure, Mom," Alison said abruptly, indicating to Sarah she merely wanted to get off the phone. "I'll text you a little later but I'll get there as soon as I can."

Sarah set her cell down next to her as she continued to lay in bed and shut her eyes. Her closed eyelids softened over her eye sockets, giving a glorious but false anticipation of relaxing into nothingness. Oh, if only she could sleep for a bit or have the luxury of spending the entire day in her sweats alone at her own place.

She sighed. *When did she sign up for this?* And why did she still feel so damn guilty about everything? Guilty about how she had felt about Gloria for most of her life. Guilty to be the one who had to initiate the move, against Gloria's will. Almost bullying her to do what felt to be the only option, ignoring an unspoken alternative to bring Gloria into her own apartment. The thing, she refused to admit, any *real* daughter would do in a heartbeat: no questions asked. *Nobody warned her this part of life would be so hard.* She tried to take those deep breaths somebody was talking about on the radio, although every time she tried she gave up in the middle of the first one. Leaving her with a cough, rather than a stilled mind.

A stray thought jarred her back to present time: she had forgotten to call Gloria's doctor back on Friday. *Damn!* She strained to remember if she was supposed to pick up a prescription. She told herself she could drop by the pharmacy and see if there was anything waiting. Just one more stop in this whirlwind of the shits of life.

Sarah opened her eyes and dragged herself out of bed, put on her robe, oversized with the tie missing, and walked barefoot to the window. Not that she had smoked since college, but if she did, now would be the time to take a long drag on a cigarette, releasing wisps of smoky exhalations into the chill of the morning while sitting outside on her tiny porch. *What a goofy thought.* Better yet would be if she had a close girlfriend she could call up, invite over to talk and laugh together.

Instead she flipped on the radio, just for noise. Two women bantered about the coming weather, rain again. She flipped to Gloria's favorite station, All Classic 99 hoping it might help her feel calm. Saturday morning opera shouted out at her.

"Jesus Christ!" she said, flipping back to the weather banter. Who would have guessed Oregon radio station commentators could find so much they felt had to be said, all the time, about nothing weather: dire storm warnings that half the time never materialized. She padded back into the kitchen to make a single cup of coffee, grabbed a solo strawberry yogurt carton out of the fridge, and ate it while waiting for the coffee to drip into her mug.

OUTFITTED IN A faded pair of jeans with frayed hems, a flannel shirt that had belonged to some previous boyfriend, and tennis shoes, Sarah pulled up the driveway to the house. It wasn't as though she was sentimentally attached to this place. Gloria had lived there only a couple of years. It's not like it was where she learned to ride a bike or played with dolls or any of that stuff. Or had a dad. No, that place, and its memories were captured but hidden in her brain in tiny gaps between pain and betrayal.

She wondered how Gloria had acquired so much crap in this short time? She questioned if, from here on out, Gloria wouldn't be Gloria? Or was it simply Sarah hadn't been paying attention to a shift that had already begun many months back?

After Sarah's dad left them, Gloria was a tiger. Too late, though, Sarah always reminded herself. Too late to recover from the missteps and miscommunications in their mother-daughter relationship. But now, Sarah felt uneasy. She had moments when she questioned so many of the things she had repeated to herself for so long. After all the years of reminding herself she didn't care, she suddenly wondered if she had been kidding herself.

Had she never given Gloria enough credit? How did her mother do it, really? She was relieved her own ex, Sean, inept as he was as a partner, stayed in her daughter's life, even though Sarah had been glad to be rid of him. Even if some days it was damn hard. Lonely. But Gloria did it for so long, and, if she was forced to be honest, a lot better than she, herself, was handling it.

Sarah pulled the key out of her purse, at first thinking she had forgotten it. A locked door was the best clue that Gloria no longer occupied the house. It would be quite the irony, if she was the one to lock herself out. At least there weren't any outdoor chores she would be responsible for with it being a rental. She tried to improve her mood by reminding herself she didn't even have to do much cleaning. Hell, for all Sarah was doing for her, Gloria could pay whatever cleaning deposit the landlord sent her way. Her mom wouldn't want her scrubbing her toilet in order to save a few bucks, that's for sure: though it'd embarrass her if she knew the house wasn't spanking clean when it was turned back to the landlord. She dismissed the thought, knowing the sheer amount of crap she had to get rid of might be more than she could pull off.

A putrid smell, a cross between rotted food and dirty diapers, shocked her nostrils the moment she opened the door and stepped inside. Before she could take stock of what needed to be done, she located the guilty paper sack of trash, its wetness seeping through the bottom of the bag to the floor from rotten fruit, the likely culprits perfuming the air. She carried the bag outside, holding the bottom so it wouldn't spill its contents onto the floor, while she tried to push old memories back deep inside her heart. When she returned, she left the door open to air out the unventilated space.

Forcing herself to move ahead in an organized fashion, she envisioned two piles: yeses and absolute nots. Yet, she realized, she would have to add a third pile for things requiring storage if she couldn't immediately figure out to which bucket an item belonged. Maybe she could get one of those Pod things, or whatever they were called, although she sure as hell couldn't have it in her parking space. Oh, she needed to rethink that. *That settles it.* Back to two piles with Goodwill for all that couldn't be used now.

Maybe she could simply take a picture of all the crap and post it on Craig's List where someone would miraculously claim it and offer to take it all away. Except, her luck, whoever came would mug her, tie her up or kill her, and dispose of her body somewhere deep in the depths of the Willamette, like that story she read once on Facebook.

At least, she had music to listen to as she pulled out her iPod and speaker. This won't be so bad, she lied to herself, although her brain craved another jolt of caffeine: she knew she was addicted. She was glad she needn't worry about Tony dropping in. He was one to run when the going got tough. Although Gloria had met him a few times, Sarah knew from the first meeting with him how much she didn't care for this boyfriend of hers. One could tell these things with Gloria, at least the old Gloria, as she simply tended to ignore making any comments at all and rattling on with whatever she'd rather discuss.

On her good days, Gloria still did fairly well. She had built her confidence up some following the months since she had been released from the hospital after the fall. For the first month, Sarah insisted to herself that Gloria was fine: how the incident had been an anomaly. Soon after, though, she couldn't ignore slip ups Gloria was unable to hide from her and she wondered what else might be happening that she didn't know about. After too many calls from Flo, Sarah knew it couldn't continue.

But on this day in the house, Sarah was surprised by how much Gloria had been able to do on her own to pack up the house. It made her momentarily embarrassed at how long she had procrastinated, yet repeated the consoling voice in her head: her little free time had been spent helping Gloria move and, though she felt as if she had failed, feel settled in her new home. Sarah couldn't refer to the new place as Gloria's new "home" without a loud protest from her mother. Several times Gloria had said, "Oh, I get it. My holding place till I die."

She wondered how she hadn't noticed the already packed cartons during those last days she had been with Gloria in the house. A number of full cartons lined the wall in both the kitchen and small dining room. Sarah was surprised—it hadn't seemed as though Gloria had been in the right head space to do all that. The front entry, however, was still a mess, with the overflowing toy chest Gloria had insisted stocking in case someone with little kids came over, even though her own grandkids had long grown out of them. In spite of her bossiness, Gloria always wanted visitors to feel comfortable

Reluctantly, Sarah opened the front hall closet. Gloria's favorite jackets were gone, but a few left-behind garments hung on the rod, and a pile of discarded items lay forgotten on the floor. She walked back to the speaker and blasted the volume, and then grabbed an empty box in the corner of the room, thankful there were some left still. She seized the remaining coats, gloves, and scarves by the handful and jammed them into the box. For the most part, she didn't have the patience to weed out things she or Gloria might like, although when she came across a pair of gloves she knew to be Gloria's favorites, she stuffed them in her purse. Another sign that Gloria wasn't at the top of her game. She moved back to the closet and picked up several old pairs of shoes, hidden back in the darkened far corner. She spotted the bright blue rubber rain shoes Alison liked, and set them out on the porch to make sure they weren't missed. Everything else fit into the box.

Sarah thought she had gotten everything, but when she looked again she saw another small box. It was covered with brown paper, and looked unopened. The name "Annie" was scrawled next to Gloria's address.

"That's weird."

She set it aside and gathered the final lone sock from the closet floor and stuck it in the Goodwill box. She shut the closet door with a grunt, and was glad when she tested the weight of the box to know she could carry it to the porch by herself.

Just then she heard the doorbell. She wondered how long someone had been trying to get her attention with her music blaring. She shut off the iPod, then walked to the open front door, where she looked into the eyes of an old man.

"Uh, hi there," he said, looking embarrassed. "I'm sorry to surprise you. I'm, um, Winston. Gloria's neighbor? I know you might not remember me, but we met last summer once." He was clean shaven, and although he had tucked his plaid collared shirt into his belted blue jeans, the front was rumpled as it made room for his belly.

"Oh yes, hi," Sarah said, trying to place where they had met. "I'm Sarah, Gloria's daughter."

"Yes, I know. I've gotten to know your mother pretty well over the past couple years," he said awkwardly. "In fact, I hope it's okay. But she gave me an extra key when I told her. Well, I just thought I could help a bit." He nodded toward the boxes in the living room. And then he held up the key to her.

Sarah was unable to hide her surprise. "Oh. No wonder. You didn't need to go out of your way. But. Well, thank you." She took the house key.

"Oh," Winston said. "It wasn't a problem at all. Your mother, uh, I mean, Gloria. She is very kind. Anything I can do to help?"

Sarah forced a smile at him. She wondered how much about Gloria this man knew, and she couldn't help but feel embarrassed for Gloria's sake. She could tell it was difficult for him to talk about Gloria.

"Uh, and I know you found her after her . . . um, you know. Her little incident." She looked at Winston for some acknowledgement, wishing she could learn more about that day.

Winston looked sad and uncomfortable, staring at his feet as he gathered his thoughts. "Yeah. Don't worry about it. It was just one of those things. It could have happened to anyone." He didn't look Sarah in the eye, but instead, over toward the packed boxes. "It looks like things are coming together."

"Well, I thank you," Sarah said, her skin stretching into an artificial smile. "You are very kind, and well, I hate to think about what might have happened if you hadn't helped her." She didn't particularly want to keep talking about it, even though she thought by knowing more details she might better understand Gloria.

Winston met her eyes again. He smiled. "Like I said, I care about your mom. She's been a good neighbor. She fed my cat a few times when I went out of town, and well, you could say, well, uh, we've enjoyed those old . . . Well, you know. At the mailbox kinds of talks." He looked out toward the mailbox.

"Well, maybe you can visit her?" Sarah asked, looking at Winston for encouragement. "She's not that far away now, although, well, she shouldn't be driving." She hesitated. She knew Gloria would hate to know she was talking about her like this. "I guess we'll see what the doctor says." She'd already prepared her argument if the doctor disagreed with her opinion.

"Yeah. We'll see. Maybe you can give me her phone number if you have it." He shuffled his feet and looked down at them again. "I didn't mean to get in your way. I know you have a lot to get done." He hesitated but looked at her again. "Is there anything else I can do to help?"

"No, no. Thank you so much. You have been so much help already." Sarah walked over to the table by Gloria's phone, only then realizing she still hadn't cancelled the service. Gloria was using only her cell phone in her new place. She grabbed a pen and scrawled Gloria's name and her cell number on a notepad, and then gave Winston the piece of paper, accidentally touching his sleeve. "Thank you." It made her sad to think about Gloria moving away from this kind man, and she wondered if he had any family.

She walked him to the door and remembered the small package. "Oh wait, I have a question."

Winston stopped on the porch and turned to look up at her expectantly. He put his hand on the porch rail to steady himself.

"Do you know anyone named Annie?"

His grey eyebrows rose toward his wrinkled forehead. He scratched his head. "Annie?"

Sarah stepped back into the house and pulled the box off the floor to show him the black scrawled lettering.

"Oh, that Annie." His eyes had a faraway look and he smiled. "Little Annie was one of a kind." He chuckled softly, and Sarah was certain his eyes lit up for a few fleeting seconds as he nodded. "Annie was the little girl who lived here before Gloria moved in. She and her family. She was a little firecracker." He chuckled. "A good little firecracker."

"What happened to her?" Sarah asked.

"Well, her family moved away. That was the last I ever heard of them." Sarah waited, hopeful Winston might say something else.

He scratched at his ear and brushed the air as if at an imaginary gnat. "She was a good kid from what I could tell. But her family." He looked at Sarah and then again at the porch. "Well. I hope everything turns out okay for her." He turned to the yard and grabbed ahold of the stair railing. He stopped, gripping the railing tighter, and looked back at Sarah. "Maybe just something that got lost in the mail. Probably not worth much, I would guess." He climbed down the stairs, stopped, and turned back to her. He reached into his top shirt pocket. "Oh, I almost forgot. Here is my phone number." He made an effort to climb back up the stairs, but Sarah trotted down the steps and took the paper.

"Please tell Gloria to call me. She might need someone to talk to once in a while. I will miss her," he added, softly.

Sarah watched as he walked with short choppy steps through the front yard and crossed the property over to his own. He bent down, as if to pick something up, and then moved on. She closed her eyes and let the morning stillness and winter smells of the river fill her. Then she went back in the house, leaving the door ajar, to pick up the package from the floor. She added it to her pile next to the door.

"No time for this now."

Late in the afternoon, Alison and Tom stopped by with his truck. None of them were in a chatty mood, with Alison and Tom working quickly to escape, proceeding onward to drop off the pile of unwanted clothes and household items.

HOURS LATER, SARAH made it back to her own apartment, where she filled her bathtub with steaming hot water and poured in a capful of lavender bath bubbles. She sat at the edge of the tub, breathing in the infusion of lavender and hoped the tension in her neck muscles would disappear. As the tub continued to fill, she headed into the kitchen and eyed a beer from the fridge. It was there for Tony, not her. She tried to tell herself how she deserved it tonight, even if it wasn't a brand she liked. Gloria had always spouted off about how wine is civil and cultured; and doesn't count as drinking. Even though she'd been known to piss a few people off after having a few. Although Oregon was known for its vineyards, it was hard to be serious about drinking it when the local brews were so good.

Thinking of her dad, she grabbed a can of Diet Coke instead, the non-caffeinated kind, opened it, and set it back on the edge of the tub. She took off her panties and bra, avoiding looking in the mirror, and eased herself into the hot, foamy water. She hoped she had locked her door, but worried for a minute that Tony might stop by anyway. She didn't have the energy to deal with him, pushing the thought out of her mind; forcing herself to save that worry for tomorrow. She knew she had to address the weirdness of how things had been for them lately.

"Ah." She sank down deeper in the tub and closed her eyes, enveloped in the sweet reassuring aroma. All day her busyness kept her from consciously worrying about Gloria and all that might come next. For the last few months she had been haunted by the doctor's words: it could just be mostly normal. Or not. It was hard to predict, Dr. King had said, how our brains, especially as we get older, react to stress. But Sarah latched onto the warning that, of course, it could be more. She thought back to her other Grandma, Lulu, who lived into her nineties but didn't seem to know who she was. Not that they ever had been very close. But still, this memory of Lulu when Sarah was in her early twenties, danced eerily in her brain as the first time she realized any one of us, no matter how smart or talented, could end up that way. *How could you not know who you were, or where you had come from?*

And with that thought, Sarah could not contain it any longer. Quiet sobs escaped, releasing tears of frustration that dripped into the bubbled bath. She felt so alone. Not that she and Gloria had ever been buddies: but now, she had to admit, Gloria had always seemed to have an answer for everything. Usually she had too many answers to questions Sarah hadn't even asked; and it had been largely that which drove her away in her teens. But more recently, as much as it bugged her, she admitted how Gloria's predictability had been oddly comforting and consistent, even if it pissed her off. After her own divorce and mostly single-handedly raising Alison, at least she knew Gloria was there for them. And in a weird way, although she didn't like to admit it, in all the hard years with Alison, Gloria seemed to be the one to know what to say to this granddaughter of hers. Sarah often found herself as the third wheel who reacted to her own daughter in a way that she herself detested.

Her bath water was getting cold, and her soda only half empty. She drained out a quarter of the tub, stoppered it and filled it with water from the hot tap. She was lucky the apartment building never seemed to run out of hot water: it was a luxurious temporary Band-Aid to life's crises. She knew it was one thing she couldn't imagine living without, although hot coffee ranked with it at the top. She slowly sank her head under the water, keeping only her eyes, nose, and mouth above. She listened to the weird echo emanating from inside the center of her tub, feeling momentarily removed from life's complications.

As she lifted her head and neck back up above the water, Winston's comments about Annie trickled back into her brain. Just who was this little girl and what might be in the package? Who covers packages with brown paper anymore? She told herself the whole thing really wasn't very odd—why did she kept thinking about it? After all, maybe it was just a birthday present that had gotten waylaid along the way. She chided herself that she had other more complicated and pressing issues to worry her minutes away instead of a stupid post office error. But still—why would the post office deliver something to an occupant who had moved away so long ago? Or, just how long ago did her mother haphazardly throw it into the corner of her closet?

The water was cool to the touch. Her upper legs were beginning to dimple and she shivered. She drained the soda can, and set the empty on the floor next to the tub. She gently caressed her breasts, suddenly thinking it might be okay if Tony did stop by. She attached the nozzle to the faucet and rinsed her head and body with yet again, warmer water, but decided she wasn't up to washing her hair this late at night. She needed to go to bed.

Even then, she couldn't shake the thought of the package. Damn, why had she left it in her car, now that she was warm and feeling relaxed? She put on her sweats, robe, and slippers—a pair that had a hole in the right toe and were so stretched out her feet slipped around inside if she didn't wear a thick pair of wool socks with them. She tried to put the package out of her mind, telling herself it wasn't going anywhere. But she couldn't stop obsessing, and gave in.

"Damn!" She grabbed her car keys from her purse and hustled outside into the dark.

A few minutes later, she sat at her kitchen counter, feeling perfectly alert as she held the package. She considered grabbing a beer, but forced herself to put it out of her mind. The label stared back at her and for the first time she noticed the postmark. Claskanie, Oregon. She had heard this name, although at the moment couldn't place it.

Feeling a little guilty not to be its rightful recipient, she ripped the paper with her fingers, thinking it was too much effort to get up and track down her scissors. She pulled away the crumbled newspaper and extracted the supposed treasure.

"Jesus Christ." She shook her head. "What's this?"

Chapter 6

Westport
February 2016

"HEY TED, IT'S Sarah," she said into her cell phone.

She had woken up early after only a few hours of sleep; instead tossing in her bed, unable to find a comfortable position for the remaining hours and minutes. At first it was her aching back that had her awake in the early morning hours, triggering the arousal of her brain. Her bladder urged her to stumble to the bathroom. She was tempted to have a beer to relax, but knew she would regret it, and forced the option from her mind. And then she found herself waking to a Sunday that might have been filled with endless possibilities, but instead gray fogginess crept between her blinds, hijacking her mood. She wondered if she had ever called her brother Ted before sipping her morning coffee. It must have startled him. Or just irritated him further.

"No, nothing's wrong. Yeah, Gloria's okay. At least she doesn't seem to be any worse. But I have a favor." Sarah shook her head, impatient, as she pretended to listen to him share something about the day.

"I just wondered if you're around the house today?" Again, she nodded vaguely as he dribbled on about some kids' sporting event, interrupting him louder than she intended. "I don't think you need to actually *do* anything for her." She tried unsuccessfully to calm her voice. "It's just . . . I have to go out of town. Just for a short bit, but I hoped you would be around in case. For once. You know, if she needs anything. If she remembers that it is Sunday, she might try to reach me."

Her anger rose, while he calmly talked on, ignoring her frustration, as if *he* wasn't listening to her as he driveled on lamely about Sunday plans. Ted, the ever precise and perfect appearing attorney. She knew this asshole brother never betrayed what was really going on in that heart of his.

"Well, it's just that I might not have cell service. Maybe you could call to check in with her." Sarah forced herself not to mention how she always was the one to remind him to call Gloria more frequently. She paused to calm her voice, silently urging herself on—it was not unreasonable for him to do this one act on this day.

"Yeah. Yeah," she answered again.

At first, she expected Ted to ask her where she was going, but soon recognizing how rarely he asked her much of anything. It was probably just as well. She would have made up something anyway. She knew he thought she was just a loser: he in his big firm, fancy house, two straight A kids, and all that. He didn't give a shit about anybody outside his perfect circle.

"Okay. I will call tonight when I get home and check in. And I'll let Gloria know before I leave." Sarah hesitated. She knew Ted expected her to thank him, but she remained silent until she heard the click signaling he had hung up the phone.

Sarah went into the bathroom, taking the phone with her. Sitting on the toilet she dialed. After six rings, she insisted to herself it was fine. Gloria didn't always like to answer the phone, and at least as far as Sarah knew, she still checked her voicemail. Although Flo had complained to Sarah that Gloria didn't always take her cell phone with her when she left her unit.

"Hi, Gloria. Just checking in, no need to call me back. Hey, I have to actually work a bit today so won't drop by." She hesitated for a few seconds. "But Ted will be calling. I think he'd love you to call him to check in. If you feel like, or, well, um, if you need anything." She hesitated again. "Okay, I'll call you tonight."

A FEW HOURS later, dressed and not nearly caffeinated enough, Sarah pulled out of her apartment parking lot, hauling a filled water bottle, an overripe apple, and her travel cup. As she stopped at the local gas station to fill up her tank, she wished she felt more excited: so rarely did she leave town these days. She had to use Google maps to figure out the route to take, even though her destination was not even two hours away: less than the amount of time it might take her to get to Gloria's place and back on a day of horrible traffic.

She felt like a loser—her destination foreign to her even though she'd lived in the area all her life. She took a deep breath and looked toward the freeway. What would it be like to get on the road, keep heading east, and continue charging her credit cards until they were denied? She'd only been to the east coast twice, and both trips had been so long ago. *How was it that so much time had passed in her life, and it had been filled with so little?* At least the early morning drizzle had stopped, and a bit of sun forced its subtle energy through the clouds.

After paying for her gas, the pumps empty except for her car, she entered the address she had found inside the package into her map app. Time estimated: 90 minutes. She stopped at the local coffee shop, now a Starbucks rather than the original Java for You. She had once committed herself to a cost-saving strategy—often failing—of buying the ridiculously priced coffee out only on her day off. She sat at a table to eat the scone she ordered and drink a cup of their strongest roast, black as usual. She looked around the shop. Who were all these people and what were they about? *We know so little about the people around us.* She spied a woman slightly younger than Gloria, seemingly contentedly sipping her cup of coffee and peering out the window. She had on a pair of black sweat pants, bulging at all the usual places, and a green Ducks sweatshirt, probably a gift from some grandkid. *Just what is it that gets each person through life?*

"No time for this," she told herself as she crumpled up the scone envelope with its remaining crumbs, and tossed it in the trash. She grabbed a fresh napkin and pushed herself out of the shop, back to her car.

Highway 30 weaved north along the Willamette River, taking her through areas foreign to her. She couldn't remember having ever headed out further northwest than Portland's St. John's Bridge, although she was sure she must have. She'd have to ask Gloria if they'd driven the route when she was a kid, her brain silencing her question as to whether Gloria would remember. It was easier to simply take Highway 26 to the coast, except for all the traffic slowdowns in burgeoning Hillsboro, home of Intel, and now, continued housing for more people: all wanting to live in Oregon. The freeway was usually packed these days at both ends of the commute with drivers. But today, at least where she was driving, did feel like a slow Sunday. She moved through the continuum of small towns, a few fast food restaurants, schools, and small grocery stores, without much of anything else. She tried to still the thoughts flooding her brain, and instead pay attention to all that surrounded her.

A small, inconspicuous sign welcomed her to Westport. The sight of a roadside diner reminded her brain that she had travelled this road before. She pulled over at the only significant intersection with its sole sign identifying a ferry crossing. She rubbed her eyes, surprised to imagine a ferry crossing the Columbia so far from any population center. Would it be a wild ride over this wide river, as compared to the ferries that still crossed the smaller Willamette River? Someone more courageous and curious than she would abandon her current route and find out. Instead, she was careful not to refresh her phone, in case she lost service. She peered at the map, noticing it routed her toward the ferry. She hadn't even thought about it before but was thankful the address wasn't simply a post office box number, or she would have been stuck. She was glad the side road was vacant: she could take her time without being bothered by a car nearing her bumper. The landscape was pretty, even if it emanated sogginess. And probably mold. She hoped she'd continue to keep a phone signal, carefully making a few mental notes of where to turn next just in case.

And abruptly, there it was. A mailbox identified the address, nodding to a short driveway on the right side of the road, ending at a small white house. The expanse of land felt lifeless, a place where time might stand still. She was suddenly devastated. She had imagined during the drive out, all that she might ask the sender of the package, only now realizing it to be a ridiculous thought.

She knocked at the door, and after waiting a few minutes in silence, she walked around the house. She returned to her car, sat in the front seat, and tried to phone Gloria, but couldn't find a signal and didn't want to worry her with a dropped call. She turned the key in her car and attempted to locate a radio station, but got mostly static. She turned the ignition off and simply sat.

If she were smarter and richer she'd have a better phone, and a more expensive car stereo. Minutes passed and the chilly air seeped through her. She walked back to the front door and knocked again. Nothing. She returned to the car to dig for a scrap of paper on the messy floor, littered with napkins, two empty plastic shopping bags, and a stained, empty coffee cup. She finally located one in her purse, and after scratching out a short note to the man named Ernest, returned to the house a final time to tuck it under the screen door. After sitting and waiting another few minutes—only after scraping mud from the bottom of her shoes—she unrolled her windows to amplify the silence of the countryside. She turned the key in the ignition one final time, closed her windows, and backed down the driveway. *What a wasted Sunday.*

Chapter 7

Stuck
October 2015

GRANT PICKED UP their favorite bottle of wine and splurged on Deadly Double Chocolate brownies from the newest bakery on Hawthorne on his way over. It'd been a long week, school teeming with kids needing far more than he could give. Although he'd like to be optimistic as he was once in his career, he had seen enough to know how the toughest cases needed more than almost anyone could ever give them. Those kids who already had worry marks prematurely etched into their biologically young foreheads. By now he could identify the kids who didn't sleep at night because their one parent was working a night shift, or their two parents argued, one violently threatening the other. Then there were the others—kids already graduated to the stage of not giving a shit: those believing nothing they did could make their life any worse than it would be anyway, so they didn't try anymore. These were the most challenging for Grant.

He shook his head as he walked on to the party, as if to rid his mind of the week's failures and instead, find a glimmer of interest in this annual dinner shindig. After all, it was Friday. He tried to count how many years he had attended this event? Three? Four? The two of them had experienced so many ups and downs during their three-year relationship, with disagreements often popping up recently. He wasn't sure where they stood, although it was clear Kelly thought they should be sharing the same roof by now.

He knocked on the door, the sound of his knuckles to the wood interrupting his private thoughts. A man with a brilliant blue short-sleeved button-down shirt opened the door. Grant blinked at him stunned.

"Hey. Come on in. Kelly is at the stove." He nodded smoothly toward the kitchen. "I'm Marty." He gave a mustached smile.

"Oh, hi. Grant," he said, putting out his hand.

Marty instead gave him a fist bump, his ring poking Grant's outstretched hand. He shut the door behind him and just as suddenly disappeared into the crowded apartment.

Grant was engulfed in noise: rhythmic percussion music mixed with loud exclamations typical of a weekend party. He dreaded attending this event where he knew only a few, and yearned to sneak back out the door to the comfort of his own apartment couch, put his feet up, and read the next chapter of a book. Friday nights weren't a good time for him to try to be more social than he actually was, already knowing the conflict his mood would create, as it did other Friday nights when he admitted his true desires to Kelly.

How did he ever think he could fall in love with an extrovert? Grant pasted his pathetic friendly look onto his face, wandered into the kitchen where he set his wine on the table carefully behind another five or six more expensive bottles, and crammed the container of brownies between the other dishes. A man in faded Levi's and a maroon Harley Davidson t-shirt with his back to him stirred a red sauce on the stove and held a bunch of basil in his other hand. It was hard for Grant not to suddenly crave food as the earthy aroma of garlic and tomatoes wafted from the pot to his nostrils.

"Hey, Kelly," Grant said, carefully bending toward the man stirring, speaking softly into his ear. He silently chided himself for not knowing whether to give him a more intimate greeting.

Kelly stopped stirring and looked at Grant, keeping his right hand on the spoon, and placed the basil on the counter, then rested his hand lightly next to it.

"Oh, hi. You made it," he said, without inflection. Then, as an afterthought, he touched Grant's shoulder with his left hand.

Kelly's delayed response and blasé expression told Grant that he was irritated he had failed to return his call earlier in the day; a day filled by demanding students. Grant never succeeded in getting Kelly to understand the impossibility some days of picking up his calls or returning a phone call anytime he pleased. And Fridays, for whatever reason, were always the worst.

"Hey, can you do me a favor?" Kelly asked, peering at the sauce he stirred. "Jack was supposed to show up with some mushrooms for this and I have no idea where he is. Can you call him? His number is in my phone. Over there." He pointed the spoon at the kitchen table, avoiding eye contact. He put the spoon back into the sauce and turned his head toward the kitchen door to welcome another arrival.

Dismissed and punished. Grant knew this treatment. Kelly understood how uncomfortable it was for him to phone people he didn't know, and sometimes, even people he did know. He debated completing the favor, hesitating before taking the few steps across the kitchen to the phone. He picked it up and looked through Kelly's contacts, stupidly realizing he didn't even know the guy's last name. As if in response, loud voices rushed into the kitchen, preceding a man and a woman, the man carrying a reusable shopping bag decorated with images of bright red, yellow, and green peppers.

"It's about time. Hey, Jack," Kelly called out.

Grant shoved the phone back on the counter, harder than he should, and looked at Kelly for acknowledgement. When it didn't come, Grant knew to escape the action in the kitchen, first grabbing a beer from the cooler in the corner before seeking refuge in the quiet of the living room.

Kelly's apartment was spacious: too much room for one, Grant had always thought, although he was never brave enough to comment on it for fear Kelly might nag him about moving in. He realized Kelly would be unlikely to notice if he took his can of beer and marched back out the front door. Except there'd be hell to pay for later. He knew. So instead, he slouched across the Berber dark gray carpet to the far side of the room—stopping briefly to stare out the huge picture window toward Portland's eastern skyline—before sinking into the cushions of a couch. He had always loved this soft and comfortable couch, even though he had been admonished for spilling food on it. Protective, Kelly was, of his expensive possessions.

Grant popped the tab off the beer, still finding it peculiar to drink a quality craft ale from an aluminum can. He took a slow, long drink, looked around the vacant room, and rested the can on his thigh. He lay his head back on the soft top of the couch and closed his eyes, wondering what Kelly might do if he found him out here asleep. Maybe this time he'd ask someone else to stay over.

Sometime later—unable to track whether it was one or twenty minutes—Grant felt the cushions shift and tried to force his eyes open, but his eyelids were too heavy to resist letting them flutter and close again.

"Oh sorry," a woman said. "I didn't mean to waken you. Maybe I can join you." She gave a soft laugh, as if teasing him. "I dread parties like these."

Grant considered feigning sleep. It wasn't such a stretch, as he felt he could sleep through almost anything at this moment, like most evenings by this time of night. *A real party animal.* No wonder Kelly acted as though he didn't care when Grant first said he wasn't sure he could make the party. He struggled to force his eyes open. When he succeeded, he looked into the eyes of a beautiful woman sitting on the opposite side of the couch. It was her hair, though, that caught his eye. Black, natural, so curly. He wanted to tell her he'd always wanted hair like that; realizing before he spoke how weird that would sound. Instead, he tried to focus on her last comment.

"Oh, really?" Grant asked. *God, he was so boring.*

"Yes." The woman slouched back into the couch. "Um. This is one comfortable couch." She rotated her shoulders backward several times, and sank her back and hips into the couch's soft comfort, a tiny mound of stomach showing through the tight top where it was tucked into the waistband of her skirt. Grant heard a clunk and looked at the floor at the woman's red flat, and she pulled her feet underneath her, both knees resting together, but held close to her body so not to invade his space. He guessed she must have dropped the other shoe earlier: he saw it laying nearby. She leaned against the arm of the couch, opposite him.

"It's a deal my husband and I made," she said. "Kind of a recent one, actually. I think it might be the ticket that keeps us together forever."

He smiled.

"No, really."

Grant simply looked at her.

"Each week, he chooses one night, and I choose mine." The woman looked down at her nails and rubbed one finger against the edge of another perfectly sculpted nail that shined without color. "That is, the weeks we're both in town. He travels a lot. The other thing that just might save us." She laughed.

"So, what do you do on your night?" he asked.

The woman gave him a look, and he didn't exactly know why, but Grant felt his cheeks warm.

"Oh no, nothing like that. I mean, not for my choice night." She smiled and then put her feet on the floor, as if she couldn't quite get comfortable while taking up only a small part of a couch that seemed to invite a full sprawl.

Grant wanted to tell her she could extend her feet over his lap, realizing, again, how weird that would be.

"Honestly? I'm aiming for the art museum, next. It's open late enough most nights."

Grant gazed at her, strangely envious.

"What about you?" the woman asked.

"Me?" He realized he no longer even knew what she was asking, so lost he was in his own world of solo, unspoken conversation.

"I mean, what would be your choice for tonight? If you could choose?"

"Oh, that. Actually, I really would just rather be home in bed." He felt his face flush again. *Shit. Such a dork.* "I mean, alone. To be honest about it. I'm tired. Sorry about that. I'm not much company."

A tall, striking man strode over to them. He sported a neatly trimmed dark goatee with tinges of gray, and held out a glass of wine to the woman. Grant neither knew or cared about fashion, but even he could tell this guy had style. He looked back and forth between them, assessing who was the more attractive of the two. A blue gemstone sparkled on what he assumed was the man's wedding band.

"Might you come over in a few minutes and meet a couple of people, Amelia?" The man smiled at the woman, looked over at Grant, nodded, and turned back to her.

Grant admired how confident and smooth he appeared and it made him even more self-conscious of his own nerdiness. He wanted to shrink out of the room and wondered how he might secretly be tutored by a man like this on the basics of being social.

"I'll be right there," Amelia said. "Just resting my feet. Thanks for the glass."

The man gave her a nod and a wink, and sauntered back into the dining room. Grant couldn't help but stare at his butt, and quickly looked back at the woman as he caught himself.

She took a slow drink of the deep red wine, holding the stem between her thumb and first two fingers, and swirled the liquid in the glass. She smiled indirectly at him. Grant noticed for the first time the good-sized diamond on her fourth finger.

"That's him. My husband. Some might refer to him as The Big *Cheese*," she said, emphasizing the word "cheese." As if Grant needed anyone to clarify their relationship. "He probably needs to prove to someone that he does in fact have a wife, I imagine." She looked at Grant and smiled. "But . . . I love him. We're lucky." She took a sip of the wine and glanced across the room.

She rolled her shoulders back again, as if stretching her taut muscles, being careful not to spill her wine.

"Have you lived in Portland long?" Grant began, feeling like an idiot as soon as the standard line left his mouth, forcing him into silence.

"I grew up here, moved away, and have been back for a while. My dad still lives just a bit out of town." She paused to give Grant a chance to jump in, but he decided he was done being a dork. "I like it. Once in a while Phillip and I argue about Portland. Sometimes he just doesn't get how much this town has changed, and if he does, it doesn't bother him."

She stopped and took another sip of wine, glanced around the room, and then back at Grant. "Like, can you imagine this street with these fancy apartments back twenty years ago?" She looked as if she had said something wrong. "I'm sorry. Of course, I don't even know about you. It bothers Phillip if I talk too often about being *native to Portland*." She put the words "native" in finger quotes. "He thinks I'm a snob." She smiled at Grant. "I apologize if you found that snobby." She laughed softly.

Before he could stop himself, Grant laughed. "Oh, hell, I know. That's exactly what Kelly says to me."

"Oh, you mean Kelly of this party Kelly?"

Grant nodded, trying to figure out what explanation he might offer.

"Another reason we seem to get along. Our men are both in this alter-work-world."

Grant blinked, but remained quiet.

"I mean, at least I assumed you weren't."

Grant tried not to take the comment personally. "I don't know how the hell so many people can afford these places. My teacher's salary barely gets me into any half-way decent place within the city limits."

"Oh? Someone with a real career," she said. "That's refreshing."

Grant scanned her face to see if she was ready to jab him about the three months of vacation every year and short school day.

"No, really," she said. "I honestly do think yours is one of the noblest professions. And I bet we'd find a lot of things to talk about regarding our city. I apologize but I do need to go find Phillip. He might fight me on the museum this weekend, if I'm not careful." Her smile told him she was teasing.

"Oh sure," Grant said. "Of course."

She stood up, slipped one foot back into a shoe, and bent over to locate the other one under the couch, "My name's Amelia." She reached her hand out.

Grant shook it. "I'm Grant."

"Nice to chat with you, Grant. Really. Maybe I'll see you around, Portland being the small town that it is . . . even with all the people." She smiled again and disappeared around the corner.

Grant finished his beer and carefully placed the empty on a coaster on the coffee table—he knew better than to create table rings. He pulled himself out of the couch, stretching his legs until he felt a cramp in his calf, forcing him to stutter a step backward. He walked to the adjoining room and scanned the mostly unfamiliar faces, primarily men holding glasses filled with alcohol. Thankfully, Kelly didn't allow smoking in his apartment, but Grant could see folks lighting up outside on the balcony. Joints most certainly these days, though it being legal didn't seem to change much in a town that already smoked so much weed, now a prominent aroma throughout downtown. He saw Kelly laughing outside with four other men before going to the front door, relieved he had no coat to claim.

GRANT WAS GLAD he had decided to walk this evening. Twenty blocks now in the dark cool air would help him get his head together.

He was troubled over his reaction to this woman, this Amelia. He hadn't felt such a quick connection to a woman since maybe as far back as Mary. *That's what it was.* Amelia reminded him of Mary. His Mary.

When Grant was a kid, he always knew he was different than the other boys he grew up with. Once, when he eventually grew the courage to mention it to his mom, she was dismissive.

"Every kid feels different," she said. "And besides, who wants to be just like everyone else?"

Years later Grant wondered if she had known all along. As he got older, his group of friends shrank: away from the boys he knew in elementary school who seemed to talk only about football or wrestling. He spent more time in the library and the choir room. He was drawn to quieter places with softer edges. And that's where he met the girl who turned out to be his best friend. Maybe the best friend of his life, he thought sometimes, sadly. He drank only one beer at Kelly's party, not enough to be drunk, but he now felt like sobbing.

Mary was brave and sometimes loud: traits that often turned him off back then. But Mary was also kind and sensitive, and she too loved English and choir, but also attended football games with him. By their junior year, Grant and Mary shared almost every class period together. At home his mother would frequently ask about Mary, she being one of the only friends Grant ever invited over.

"How's that Mary doing?" His mom would ask. Sometimes she would add, "We sure haven't seen Mary around here in a while. Are you two still friends?"

Later that spring, his mom threw out a not so subtle nudge as she asked him if he might be thinking about going to the prom. "Perhaps with Mary?" Grant's stone-faced head shake was warning enough to discourage his mom from repeating the same question his senior year.

Through their high school years together, though, Mary never invited Grant to her house, and he only once met her parents, briefly after a choir concert. "You wouldn't like them, Grant," Mary offered once when he had asked about them. "They mean well. They just don't understand things." And she ended it with that.

Instead, Grant and Mary hung out together at school, less and less at his house, but at the local ice cream or coffee shop. After a bit, Mary's girlfriends included him in activities as well, and although some of the guys teased him at first, asking the group "how the ladies were today," the guys soon tired of giving Grant the time of day. Sometimes, he wondered, if a few of them might have been a bit envious. Most of the guys he knew, especially the ones he still had to be around in the locker room during PE, only talked about sex and girls.

These were the same guys the girls laughed about when they shared ice cream at Baskin and Robbins.

"Can't you just see Jaime as a caged animal at the zoo?" Shelly said. "Drool dripping down his mouth as some sexy zookeeper walks by."

And then another girl might add, "Yeah, he'd have sex with any animal," and all the girls would laugh.

Grant would get a little uncomfortable when the conversation headed this way—surprised that girls could be as mean as guys—and would paste a stiff, fake smile on his face, shuffle his feet, and look at his watch. Sometimes, Mary would catch his eye and smile, which would make it worse and cause his face to turn hot. But usually by that time, Mary, seemingly always one with a social grace, artfully changed the direction of the conversation.

It had been Mary who initiated conversations about college during their senior year. "What are you thinking of doing next year, Grant?" she had asked one early October day.

They were walking out of the school after a late choir practice. Both lived within school boundaries of one of Portland's more highly regarded high schools, which, although Grant knew he should appreciate, sometimes created a higher degree of stress than what he could handle. A lot of the kids around him imagined going to college, one way or another. Grant knew both his parents, and certainly Mary's, expected their children to successfully make that their path. Grant's older sister Elizabeth, graduating six years earlier from high school, had also graduated from the state university, secured her teaching credentials, and was just beginning her first year as an elementary school teacher in a nearby community.

"I'm not sure," Grant replied to Mary that day. Although he had thought about it, the idea terrified him. In many ways, he would have liked to have skipped high school all together, but now as a senior, its security, and most of all, leaving Mary's protection and friendship frightened him.

"What about you?" he asked in return.

"Oh, you know. My parents." Mary snorted. "They have given me exactly one option. "One. Can you imagine that? You know, BYU." She looked at him. "You know, I've mentioned it before."

Grant stared at her as his mouth dropped open a tiny bit. *How did he not know about this?* They sat in silence.

"Well. I mean, what if you tried somewhere else? You would for sure get scholarships." Grant knew she had a top GPA and was considered a highly accomplished student.

Mary shook her head. "Oh, come on, Grant. Give it a rest." She sounded as if she was angry with him. "You don't really know my dad. There's just no way. It's always been the expectation for all of us." He knew she was referring to her four younger siblings. "All our life. It's not even worth getting into it with him. It's what we all do."

They continued walking along the sidewalk away from school. Grant stared at the cracks in the concrete, willing his brain to focus on them rather than allow the fear to build inside.

"I used to sometimes tell myself when I graduated I would take a big risk and change my path," Mary said simply. Grant expected her to sound angry again, but she surprised him by simply shaking her head. "But no."

The orange and yellow fallen maple leaves, now crackling at their feet, released a pungent odor Grant identified as the smell of autumn as they walked in silence.

"You know," Mary began. "Really, I know you don't understand but it's no surprise to me. I've known it all along. In fact, many of the kids in my Sunday School class will try to go there too." She paused. "Though most of them are too stupid to get in."

Grant had remembered back then how much Mary had disliked some of the kids who attended her church classes. And then, for a perfect fantastical moment, he imagined how perhaps he too could go with Mary to her school. His grades were good enough, he knew. But he knew it was a pipe dream. Other things would certainly keep him from that school; from following his friend and continuing to walk in her footsteps. Religion, family, sexual preference. All of it. She had been such a good friend. Maybe his only real friend. He knew he had loved her. Although it was a different kind of love than what he wanted it to be. His heart had started to beat too quickly back on that day he was confronted with their future. He had no idea how he would make it without her.

Mary had broken his reverie that afternoon by raising her voice and nagging him, almost like his mom. "So, Grant, you know, you probably need to start thinking about it." She got after him then, just like she had for signing up for some audition or joining the advanced choir. All these things he never, ever would have had the guts to do without her playful banter.

"Yeah," he had said simply. But, he knew he didn't have the bandwidth on that day, or the next, to imagine it.

BUT NOW, ALL these years later, walking home along the quiet streets from Kelly's party, still early enough not to be too fearful about being out alone, he missed Mary. He hadn't seen her in what, twenty years? She saw him once after she got married even before she graduated college. She faithfully sent his parents Christmas cards for a while, with pictures of the first kids that had arrived. She was living somewhere in Utah. But he stopped looking at them soon after: it was too painful. It wasn't that he wanted to marry her—God, he knew that. But he missed her. Still. He hadn't asked his mom but was sure Mary had stopped sending those cards long ago. He had never attended any of their high school reunions to know more about her or any of the rest of them, although once in a while he spied a seemingly familiar face in the crowds of Portland.

Already it seemed, after being lost in memories of his youth, he was at his apartment, and entered the code to get inside. He was surprised how quiet the building was for a Friday night. He climbed the stairs to the second floor, opened his door, and then closed it quietly behind him, not switching the lights on, but instead trudging into the small bedroom off the hallway. He dropped down to the side of his double bed, bent over to unlace his Rockports, and stripped off his socks. He only then realized how badly he needed to pee, walked back to the bathroom, and released an arching stream of urine into the toilet bowl, creating sounds of a cascading waterfall in an otherwise quiet apartment.

He caught a look at his face in the mirror above the sink, knowing he still looked like he was barely thirty, even though he felt decades older. He didn't snap his fly, and instead pulled off his Levi's as he held onto the side of the basin, leaving them in a crumpled pile on the tile floor. He should wash up but instead, like a sleep walker, he headed back to his bed to lay on top of the covers. He thought he heard the vibration of his phone, but ignored it.

He again retreated to the past. As it had turned out, back during that senior year, it didn't get much easier to think about his future as the term progressed. His mom would ask him, and he didn't offer her much to appease her questions or worries.

"I don't know, Mom. I just haven't had time to think about it," he'd reply.

"Well you need to, Mister. Life isn't going to just drop its answer for you out of the sky. You sit around too long and you'll miss it. Trust me. Just look at your dad."

"Oh, Mom. Give it a rest. That's not fair," Grant had said.

Although his parents obviously hadn't made it together as a couple and they never officially divorced, he thought his dad was happy. Happy but broke. The true journey of artists, he had told Grant. But Grant never was sure what it was his mom really wanted from him, other than perhaps going after something he truly desired. He didn't know how to get his mom to understand it wasn't so much that it wasn't worth fighting for something; he just didn't have a clue what he wanted.

Before he knew it, college application deadlines had come and gone, and he had submitted only one, on the suggestion of a school counselor, to his local community college. For some reason, after getting it done, he felt better. He had an option, even if Mary was disappointed in him. And if, in the meantime he either got more hours with his summer job or found something better, who knew, he had told himself back then. College wasn't for everyone, although he had never been brave enough to share that feeling with his mom. She had already lived through one man who she felt had ruined his opportunities.

Lying on his bed in the dark, exhausted, Grant closed his eyes. He finally had his wish to be alone in his apartment, eyes shut. He just couldn't figure out why he felt so sad. And so alone.

Chapter 8

Forging ahead
March 2016

IT HAD BEEN another long day for Amelia. It was only now, more than a month after her dad's death, she realized how staying busy was preventing her from accepting the pain and sadness she felt deep down. And although her co-workers supported her, perhaps only Phillip knew what Ernest had meant to her. Amelia repeated to others how Ernest had lived a long, good life—and she was starting to accept how much luckier he had been than so many others. People who died before their time, or after leading awful lives. Yet while she fully acknowledged the good life her parents, Ernest and Sharon, had shared, it didn't soften her grief. Sometimes she wondered if it was made worse largely because her parents were so loved, even if she regretted not always being there for them.

She brought her rambling thoughts to a close to focus on what lay ahead: she still had to figure out what to do with his house. Amelia was astute enough to recognize his house, so in need of work, and the remoteness of its location, complicated any hope for an easy sale. She couldn't imagine who in the current market would have any interest in buying it. Certainly not a speculator of today: if the town had once had a heyday, that era had long passed.

After being lost in worries and old memories for most of the drive, she instinctively pulled off the rambling Highway 20 into Arnie's Gas and Groceries. The gray day had melted into a dark, damp late afternoon, leaving the horizon invisible just beyond the few lights dotting the settlement. She had meant to pick up supplies before leaving town, only now realizing it to be just as well. She should say "hi" to Arnie sooner, rather than later. He may never admit the extent of it, being often a man of few words, but she knew how much he cared for Ernest.

Life would be one chair less and a bit lonelier for the old guys gathering on weekdays for coffee, hanging out in the back of the part gas station, part store, drinking bad coffee.

Amelia swung open the dirty glass door. "Hi, Arnie." She tried to sound cheery. She knew his vision had declined: she imagined once the glass door to be spotless, he seemed to be the kind of guy to care about things like that. As she entered, a rumbling of moving boxes emanated from nearby, and Arnie slowly rose from a squatting position.

"Well, Amelia. What a treat to see you." He brushed his hands together, as if to rid himself of the dust and grime that had collected on unwanted packages still sitting on the shelf, took two steps toward her, and stopped as if to steady his dizziness. "Can you sit down for a quick cup? I made a fresh pot . . . well, not too long ago."

Amelia wanted to get on with the chores that lay ahead of her, but knew she needed to take time with Arnie, even if she wasn't feeling sociable. "Sure, thanks. That'd be great." She followed him to the side of the store where a few chairs circled a rickety card table.

"Cream, right?" he asked.

Amelia anticipated fake powdered cream packets. She knew nothing much could help this coffee, its burnt smell already crept into her nostrils, an odd sentimental reminder of times long ago. She was certain non-dairy creamer would only make it worse.

"No, black is fine." She unzipped her parka, sat down, and pulled the coat away from her body, allowing the warmth of the shop to sink into her bones. She rubbed her hands together, hesitating around the diamond on her ring.

Arnie carried over two ugly plastic orange mugs and eased down across from her. He searched her face as he set one cup in front of her, and she understood he didn't know what to say.

"Sure has been a rainstorm. Did you just get in?" he asked.

She hesitated, hating to admit to her dad's closest friend how slow she had been to return to her dad's house. "Yes. Have had so much work. I'm, well, uh, sorry I couldn't get out before."

Arnie nodded.

"I'd hoped to be here last weekend, but, well. Anyway, I'm taking tomorrow off." She started to take a sip of the coffee, the greasy cup's handle slippery as she clenched it, but put it down before any of the scalding liquid met her lips. "Thursday too, depending on how it goes." She wondered if Arnie had ever been to the house? As good friends as Ernest and Arnie may have been, she wasn't sure their social life extended outside of the store.

They sat in silence. Amelia looked around the store. Arnie attempted to keep things in stock locals might need at a moment notice, and for all those times they didn't have the energy or time to drive into Astoria's big box Costco or the few other grocery stores along this winding Highway 30. The racks of junk food made her wonder if it was travelers through Westport rather than the ones living here he actually catered to. She turned back to Arnie. He continued to sip his coffee.

"How long have you been here, Arnie?" Amelia asked.

Arnie hesitated, and then sighed. "You mean here with the store, or here in town?" Then he offered a small smile. "Or here on earth?"

"Any of them," Amelia said, returning his smile. His crooked grin revealed a missing upper tooth on both sides of his mouth.

"I guessed you were just trying to get at my age, huh?" Arnie smiled again.

The few times she had seen him with Ernest, he had always been friendly to her. Now she felt badly she hadn't ever talked to him much beyond the weather. She strained to try to remember if he had a wife.

"I was born just down the street almost eighty-four years ago. Can you believe it?"

Amelia smiled.

"Heck. I can't." He looked like he wanted to say more, and Amelia waited, but he just took another sip of coffee.

"And what about the store?" Amelia asked.

"I took it over from a young couple who thought they'd live out their country dream. Here in the boondocks. To them, at least. Till the rain and I guess being kinda lonely. Especially in the winter. I'd guess. A lot of folks have a hard time in the winter, it seems. Maybe even lonelier. Gray and wet. You know," he offered, looking at her.

Amelia waited.

"Maybe it was more of a problem for her. The missus, well, you know," he said. "Anyway, maybe about fifteen years ago? After I retired from the mill in Longview."

"Is that how you met Ernest?" Amelia felt embarrassed she didn't know and could only guess.

"No, your dad and I didn't know each other then. Well, your dad didn't really work for the mill, although he had some contract jobs there. It was more after your mom died and he was pretty new in these parts. He pretty much kept to himself. I thought people didn't go out of their way to be around him just because they didn't understand him. But you know, that's how people can be." Arnie looked at his cup and rubbed the handle with his thumb. "I did though. Yeah. I did."

Amelia shifted in her seat. She didn't want to cry. She just didn't. Yet it was more discomforting than she had imagined, to be out here without Ernest. Before he had died, she would never have visited this town without him. And as close as they were, recently she struggled to accept not knowing all his stories. The details of his life.

"Thanks, Arnie. For being his friend. It meant so much. To him." She smiled at him, still trying to contain her tears. "And, to me too." She pulled her fingers through her hair.

Arnie took the last drink of his coffee. Amelia felt badly to leave more than half of hers. She didn't think she was so picky, but this cupful was awful.

"Times like these I wish I could have a cigarette," Arnie said suddenly. "You know your dad was one of the last of my good friends. He was a good man, he was. Not much new blood sticking around in these parts either. If they show up seems they are zooming into the city again. I hear 'em complain about not being able to get their messages on those crazy phones or wondering why I don't have wee or wi or whatever that's called. One actually asked me how I could live here. Can you believe that?"

This was getting too hard. Amelia pulled her jacket back on and zipped it up. She tried to signal her intention to leave, although the store was warm, and what lay ahead of her felt formidable. She stood up anyway. "Thanks for the coffee. What do I owe you?"

"Oh, heck. That's on the house. The least I can do."

Amelia took a few steps toward the door with Arnie following, then stopped and turned to him. "Oh, no. I have so lost my brain. I need a few groceries for the next couple days."

She browsed around, feeling lost in the tiny store with so few choices and fewer that were appetizing. She grabbed two cartons of yogurt, a bottle of juice, and a box of crackers. Maybe Dad has something left, she told herself, although she knew it had been at least a couple months since any new groceries had been brought into his house.

She went to the till. "Is the little restaurant on the corner still open for dinner? I couldn't tell when I drove in."

"Oh yes," Arnie said. "You should stop in and make sure you tell Molly who you are. She adored your dad. Always called him 'the man of few words.' Oh, and make sure you have pie. Berry."

DRIVING ALONG THE now darkened lane, Amelia wished she had left Portland earlier in the day. She pulled her car up the narrow gravel driveway. From her parked car, Ernest's house looked forlorn. Pitch black and empty. It hadn't occurred to her when she left town how dark everything would be out here, far away from the lights of the city, now in these still shorter days of early spring. She tucked the small bag of groceries into her overnight bag and reached back for her laptop. Habit, really. She couldn't imagine getting any work done out here. Now. She flipped on her phone's flashlight to guide her into the house. As she approached the door, she rested one armload on the porch, and retrieved the single house key under the doormat. As she shined the flashlight at the door, she spotted a folded piece of paper tucked behind the screen door. With her arms so full, she grabbed the crumpled paper and stuffed it in her coat pocket, before opening the screen and guiding the key into the door knob.

As she pushed open the front door, the cold and stillness stunned her heart: the absence of what had been before. She could smell mildew, but missing were the usual smells of her dad and his life, fried eggs or fish, and his Irish Spring soap, making it feel foreign. And empty. Their old family home had never felt quite right after Mama had died; and this, she knew, would be the same. Other than taking care of a few things after Ernest had so suddenly died, there had never been a reason for her to be here alone. Ernest had no pets, nor did he ever go away on trips after he had moved in. She settled her bags on the couch and turned on the thermostat, hoping it would still pump out heat quickly. Ever since Sharon had died, and Ernest had moved out here, the appearance of his home was simple and austere. Maintenance, though, was always something he paid attention to, priding himself as a fixer of just about anything.

Amelia's stomach rumbled, alerting her only then that she hadn't eaten most of the day. Generally, she was a woman who loved to eat, and while a hot cooked meal sounded appealing even now, she didn't have energy to seek out the town's one restaurant. Not tonight. She went into the small, drab kitchen, where the only fixture on the counter was a toaster. Ernest liked his eggs with toast. And marmalade. She turned on lights as she went, stashing her yogurt in the fridge, wishing she had thought to bring something appetizing. She settled instead on a can of Campbell's vegetable soup she found lurking with three other cans in the mostly bare cupboard. As she stirred it with a can of water into the saucepan, she snooped around the little kitchen. It didn't look lived in. She pulled the box of Triscuits out of the grocery bag, carried the warmed soup with the spoon over to the kitchen table, and ate right out of the pan.

A list. That's what I need. An overachiever who checked off every mark, usually a day ahead of time, Amelia grabbed the note pad by the telephone. Ernest had never agreed to buy a cell phone, and when Amelia hinted at buying one for him once as a Christmas gift, he insisted adamantly that he would refuse to use it. It had made her anxious to think about him, at his age, out on his walks alone without communication. "What if something happened?" she had asked him, which eventually did, although not while he was alone. Not while he was on a walk near the river. She stood back up to grab the pen by the phone, and sat back down to take a few more bites of the hot, bland yet salty, soup. Unidentified bits of vegetables floated within the brownish broth.

"Shoot!" She muttered at the pen's refusal to work. She reached into her pocket, thinking maybe she'd be lucky enough to find one there, she'd been known to make permanent ink marks in clothing that caused Phillip to shake his head at her and her quest for efficiency. But this time, all she found was a scrap of paper, the one that had been tucked into the screen door. She read it.

"Dad?" was all that she could summon, barely as a whisper. And then she started to cry.

Chapter 9

Found

DAMN. HOW DID she sleep in so late? Sarah had hoped to wake up early to give herself alone time of, if even, just a few moments, to sip her strong coffee and relax in her soft chenille robe. Time to think through what next to do. Maybe there simply wasn't an answer, she told herself, angry that this tenacious dart of worry and dread penetrated her being most minutes of the day. People get old. Life changes. *It's not as though it is my fault.* For after all, she has many other challenges in her own life, she reminded herself like a broken record. And truly, she and Gloria had never been close. Ever. Not like other pairs of daughters and mothers she knew or imagined, who shop, go to lunch, and trade their innermost secrets. Never that.

Instead, Sarah hurriedly brushed her teeth in the shower, nagged by the fleeting thought that she was terribly overdue for a teeth cleaning, her hair wrapped in a towel to keep it dry so she might get to the shop in time for the start of her shift. She is just too old for this job, she repeated to herself often, although the thought expelled a vision of Betty. Dear, old Betty, who must be close to seventy, dressed in her outdated fashions of shoulder pads and frilly collars, proud to emulate the horrid fashions of the 1980s. But her attitude. Betty's damn attitude: if only Sarah could harness that. Betty was the one to consistently smile authentically, rather than force the fake version Sarah felt obligated to produce whenever she was on display at work. She knew she owed it to Betty to be more patient, for no matter how Betty acted or dressed, Sarah would always have a soft spot in her heart for her. For it was Betty who glued her shattered pieces together back on the afternoon Sarah's own world burst apart those many years ago.

When confronted with that emotional train wreck back then, Sarah acknowledged how long there had been signs. Popular parenting books and seminars sounded their alarms: The "five warning signs that tell you your child is screwed up," or, "how to keep your kid on the straight and narrow." Its clarity, when it hit, made her feel foolish. But when what in yesterday was the unthinkable happened, Sarah was fully unprepared, without any extra umph for any new life challenges.

LIFE HAD JUST happened to Sarah, not one to plan ahead and craft her future. She was eager to leave Gloria behind, immersed in parties, friends, and occasionally attending classes. Sean seemed perfect. He was there when she wanted him, and he never exerted too many of his own demands, although eventually, his inability to make a decision or a decent living led to the demise of their relationship. Before that, though, she was thrilled to land full time work, first as a bartender. It was only in hindsight later did she recognize she selected it precisely because it would bother her mother to have a bartending daughter. Lucky for Gloria, the job lacked benefits, leading Sarah to eventually find work in retail, where it eventually developed into a job with benefits. Not great pay, so-so benefits, but a package nonetheless—and something that could lead her to, she told herself then, the dreamy fashion job she had once imagined.

One night after a few too many drinks after work, while still bartending, she and Sean decided they should tie the knot. The next day, at a lunch break, they went to the justice of the peace, each taking a co-worker with them. Sarah barely knew the co-worker she invited—a man she occasionally relied on for recipes of more unusual drinks like a Rum Martinez or Commonwealth. When she told Gloria on the weekend, she just about exploded: an unusual act for Gloria of the calmly controlled emotions. Years later Sarah admitted, only to herself, that her decision to marry in that manner was a juvenile-like revenge aimed directly at her controlling mother.

Not long after tying the knot, both she and Sean wondered if they had done the right thing. As time passed, they acted more like roommates who had sex, not two life partners. Then she got pregnant. Sean demanded she get an abortion: he made it very clear he was not "dad material."

"Hell, Sarah," he yelled. "I'm not even husband material. You know that."

And as much as Sarah knew he was neither husband-like nor could she imagine him as a father, and that ending the possibility of a baby might be the right decision, she couldn't do it. She told Sean for the first three months she was still thinking about it. Before she knew it, her inability to resolve the matter in a short time-frame eliminated the option. Sarah never regretted it, she always told herself—when Alison was little.

When she couldn't hide the pregnancy from Gloria any longer, she was surprised that her mother couldn't help but be beside herself with happiness. Gloria saw it as another opportunity to provide her grandchild, a granddaughter as it turned out, what she had never felt she'd been able to provide for her kids. Once Alison was born, Gloria turned into a fairy godmother of sorts. Sarah had to admit Gloria was good at it: she was often there to help manage the working mom gaps, especially once she and Sean split up. Sean never moved very far away, and was always there for a phone call, but he kept his bargain that he really would never be dad material and sealing Gloria's prophesy that he was basically a "no good."

Sarah never believed he was a "no good," even when she and Sean were in the worst of it; he was just a man who would never be enough of an adult to have an intimate relationship with another adult, much less parent a kid. She shouldn't have been surprised, although she was, when he told her once he hardly could wait till he and Alison could just go and hang out and have a drink together.

"What dad says that?" Sarah had asked him.

And Sean looked at her with a smug expression. "I know. Told you." As if he was so pleased with himself for being right from the start.

Once Alison entered high school, things began to change. Undertakings that Sarah had told herself, then, were normal for teenagers: staying out late at night, lying about where she was going, skipping school. After all, Sarah too had done those things. She had struggled to engage in school or understand the importance of completing academic work, even more than Alison. She was busy with work, taking on increased responsibilities but without much salary increase, as many of the longer-term company employees eventually departed. She was lonely without a partner and lacked a network of good friends. Most days she could hardly wait to get home to have that first evening drink. Before she knew it, she couldn't make it without two drinks each night. Some nights she told herself she deserved three. She must have known she had a problem as she made sure to hide it: from Sean, from Gloria, and, as much as she could, from Alison. She loved her daughter, but told herself it was normal for a sixteen year old to be away from home much of the time; reluctant to admit the privacy gave Sarah the freedom to do what she wanted.

One Friday night when Alison was a senior in high school, Sarah was at home with her feet up after a typical long work shift. She'd had another day of training a new hire, one she still remembered as being particularly dense as she tried to learn how to properly assess inventory on the computer. She was mostly through her second beer, watching a sappy tear jerker movie on the Hallmark Channel about a woman whose husband just died in a car accident. Alison had told her she was with her friend Christine, at Christine's house. The home phone rang, and a woman identifying herself as Christine's mother blurted out that Alison had just been admitted to the emergency room at Emmanuel Hospital.

"Oh my God. What? What happened?" Sarah worried a lot about car accidents and young drivers. Even though Alison didn't have her own car, many of her friends had access to one.

"I don't know the details," the woman said, her voice flat and cold. A stranger. "Christine asked me to call you. She took her there."

The rest of that night was mostly a blur. Sarah had known, even then, she shouldn't be driving. She called Sean, but he didn't answer his phone, and so she drove, tipsy and scared, unclear on directions. She drove in circles, first near Lloyd Center, before realizing she was off track. She was a mess when she arrived at the emergency room and parked sloppily between two parking spaces, trying to force herself to slow down her breathing, still imagining a horrific car accident. Instead, she learned that her daughter, her innocent seventeen-year-old daughter, had overdosed. Alison had combined an exorbitant amount of hard liquor with some left-over pain pills the girls had found in Sarah's own medicine cabinet. Sarah later learned from Christine that the two had experimented mixing the pills and alcohol before. Alison begged to do again.

"It was just the best high," Alison had told her friend. The almost overdose was the start of the end of the two girls' relationship.

At first, as Alison came to, she was embarrassed, apologizing over and over. But before long she became defensive. "It was just a stupid mistake, Mom. Everybody screws up. I'm sure you did. It won't happen again."

Sarah did believe her. Or at least, she wanted to believe her. At first.

Sarah never told Gloria about the hospital episode. As panicked as she was to see her daughter lifeless when she first stumbled into the hospital room, she was fully grateful when she learned Alison would be okay. She didn't want to bring Gloria into it and Alison begged her not to as well. When Sean knew she was out of danger, he quickly dismissed it as one of those tough lessons you got when you were a teen.

They moved through that frightening bump, Alison graduated from high school and enrolled in community college, supporting herself with a part-time waitressing job. She couldn't afford to live anywhere but home with Sarah, and Sarah believed, she *so* wanted to believe, that everything was okay. *What college student doesn't drink?* She had no idea, at first, that Alison was experimenting with other drugs as well. First pot, like all the kids, but soon progressing to more addicting substances requiring costs beyond what Alison's meager budget would have been able to cover.

What Sarah never forgot was the phone call she received from Gloria one day when Alison was twenty-three. Gloria rarely invited herself over to Sarah's house. In anticipation of the visit, Sarah felt an ominous dread. Something was happening, and she tried not to let her imagination soar by jumping into diagnoses of cancer, financial duress, or worse, if there could be a worse. But it was worse. Gloria showed up, perfectly dressed as she always was, slacks with a matching wool jacket, but clasped onto her purse and sat rigidly on Sarah's old dumpy couch.

Gloria told Sarah that she—Sarah's own mother—had learned Alison had a drug problem, and no matter how much Sarah begged, pleaded, and argued, Gloria would not tell her any more detail. Instead, in her business-like manner, Gloria unemotionally reported to Sarah arrangements she had made for Alison in a residential treatment center.

And what Sarah still couldn't admit to or forgive herself for, was how furious she was with Gloria then, more furious with her than she was worried about her daughter. An unforgivable fury to have Gloria handle her parenting issue without inviting Sarah to be part of the discussion, or initiate a solution. Gloria calmly informed her daughter that Alison was not allowed to have contact with them for at least two weeks, and her whereabouts not to be shared. That statement was the most crushing blow of all.

A DECADE PASSED after the intervention, ups and downs, hope and lying, leaving Sarah feeling as if she were on a roller coaster: one day believing Alison could create a future of clean living, only to have the vision shattered by an event making any such reality nonsense.

Advice that Sarah now hung onto these many years late—Alison, now in her early-thirties—came from an unlikely source. Sarah's unsatisfactory solution, up until this point, was to refuse to speak with her if she was high, but she wasn't so naive to believe she was always a good judge of telephone sobriety. As much as she loved her daughter, she knew Alison to be a great deceiver. In the break room on the phone that afternoon of the unsolicited advice, not only could she tell that Alison was high, but she begged her mother for money. Again.

"Mom. I promise. Just this once. I just have to make rent," Alison cried.

Sarah knew, more reminders would make no difference. For the first time, she hung up on her daughter. She held it together until she had set her phone aside, trying to contain herself. Instead, she bawled. It was a slow day on the floor and she prayed no other employees would walk in as she struggled to pull herself together. But, as she tried unsuccessfully to sniff back tears, wiping her eyes on her sleeve, a figured appeared in the doorway.

"Sarah," Betty said.

Sarah didn't look up—she knew that voice—but instead dropped her face despairingly into her hands. *Of all the people to see her like this. Betty.* The employee who kept on ticking, like the everlasting bunny. She even looked like a bunny, she thought distractedly, visualizing the floppy collar scarves that often hung down from Betty's neckline.

"Dear, dear," Betty began.

Awkwardly, Betty sat next to her on the couch and put her skinny arm around her. And rather than the reserved single arm hug that some might offer, Betty fastened both arms around her, pulling her close to her chest, almost as one would do with a small child, smothering Sarah in her scent, reminiscent of putrid roses, surrounded by the beating of her birdlike heartbeat. Sarah tried to pull away, but although smaller than her, little Betty was surprisingly fiercely strong, and held her ground.

"Shush, now," Betty said. "It's okay. Let it out. Life is like this sometimes. You've just got to let it out."

Sarah, reluctantly at first, and then, as if it was all she could do, gave in. She gave in to her tears, she gave in to the force of Betty, first with big gasps through which she could barely catch her breath, developing into softer sobs eventually forming tiny hiccups.

"There, there," was all that Betty said. Over and over.

Sarah felt strangely comforted, as if the world outside was a million miles away. Her body softened into this hug of a woman who, she felt badly, she had relayed comically to Sean.

"Betty?" a voice called into the room.

Swiftly, the efficient Betty they all knew and sometimes feared, piped up. "Laura, get back to work, now. This has nothing to do with you. Please cover the tills on this floor for now. Show me you can earn your pay today."

Betty's sudden change in temperament caused Sarah to pull back from the hug enough to stare her in the face. "Wow," was all she could say, surprised out of her tears.

"Oh, now. You got to keep the new ones on their toes. You know that." Then Betty was quiet. "Now tell me, let's talk about Alison."

"What? How long were you listening?" Sarah began.

"Sarah, Sarah." Betty pulled her arms back and created a little distance between them on the couch. "Do you think I was born yesterday? I guess I'd take that as a compliment, but I know better."

Sarah simply stared at her.

"We've been working together long enough for me to pick up what's up with your daughter. And I tell you, it's a long path. Or at least it can be for us unlucky ones."

Betty went on to talk about her brother, an alcoholic who was now suffering from advanced liver cirrhosis, but he refused to stop drinking. At that moment Sarah began her new promises to herself. No more money, ever, to her daughter. Not as long as she wasn't committed to a life without drugs. She wondered what would happen if she was ever truly tested: if Alison found herself so broke she was forced to live on the street. Although she wasn't a praying kind of woman, she prayed this time would never come.

ON THIS MORNING, these few years after receiving the advice, Sarah pulled herself out of the shower, the steam fogging the mirror and stealing her reflection. The hot water sprayed down on her so long the water now had cooled in the pipe, even though it wasn't supposed to in her apartment complex. She dried her body and coated it with her favorite citrus smelling lotion, attempting to repair her incessantly dry skin. She'd happily take a couple of zits again if only her skin didn't feel so scaly and taut all over her body. She wiped down the mirror with her towel and moved back to within a few inches from it, forcing herself to look at the reflected old face. When did all the wrinkles appear? More than just a few crow feet. But worse than the lines were the dark bags under her eyes. She stepped back two feet and began her daily ritual of moisturizer, hastily laid foundation, and mascara.

"Oh, to hell with it," she said, ignoring the hairbrush as it sat lonely on the counter. "It just doesn't really matter anymore."

As she hustled out her front door, she ignored her vibrating phone. She waited a minute to let her car warm up, attempting to dismiss the worry she felt at the strange noise her car had recently started to make. She looked at the phone to see two missed calls, one that had come sometime the previous night. The more recent one was, of course, Gloria. She quickly redialed, placed the phone on speaker, and listened to the rings, paying attention to the parked cars around her as she pulled out of the lot.

"Hi Gloria. You called?" Sarah took a deep audible breath as she listened, pulling her own car onto the street and guiding herself to the freeway entrance.

"No, not today. I told you we'd do it on Sunday. I work today, remember?" Sarah shook her head and issued another quiet sigh. "No, today is Friday. How about I call you later after work? Okay? I'm just kind of late. Okay, bye."

She attempted to turn her phone off, yet keep her eye on the road, and dropped the phone into the gap between the car door and her seat. Ignoring the phone, she hoped Gloria would hang up first.

"Oh, fuck it," she said to the morning.

It wasn't until after she locked her car at work and hustled into the store did she remember the other missed call and voicemail, but she firmly tucked her phone back in her purse for later.

"Today I will be nicer," she pledged softly as her affirmation for the day.

AMELIA ENTERED THE cafe and looked around. Fewer than ten tables were spread out before her, most of them empty. She felt uncomfortable not to know who she was looking for, or what she might look like, and she hesitated at the sign telling her to wait to be seated. A young woman came over to her, holding a menu.

"One?"

"Um, no, there will be two. Do you know if anyone is waiting for someone?" Amelia asked, nervously laughing as she realized her statement was both nonsensical and unnecessary, given the emptiness of the café.

"No, I don't think so," the girl said anyway, and set off as if Amelia should know to follow her.

Amelia sat down, but kept her coat on to help her chilled body recover from Ernest's cold house, even though she'd cranked the heater during the long drive back into town.

"Coffee?"

"Yes, please. That'd be great," Amelia said to the waitress, eyeing the hole in the knee of her dark wash jeans and the multitude of silver bangles on both arms. The girl sported one small tattoo on her forearm which Amelia couldn't see fully. "With cream please."

Amelia peered at her watch, noticing it was already ten minutes past the agreed upon meeting time. She pulled out her phone and checked her emails, not able to ignore work—even on the weekend—wondering why she couldn't break this habit. Nothing was that important at work. It's not like before, she reminded herself frequently, back in the days when sometimes it did seem, or at least she believed her immediate response was important to keep the planet turning.

As she was mindlessly deleting spam, she heard a bell hit the back side of the door and felt a rush of cold air come from across the café. A woman, looking rushed and disheveled, struggled with the door handle with one hand as she gripped a box in the second. Their eyes met, and the woman, looking flustered attempted to give Amelia a quick smile. She came over to the table and stumbled on a corner of the carpet.

"Shit," the woman muttered. The box began to slide, but she caught it as it rested on her foot. She neared the table and said a bit louder, "Amelia?"

"Yeah, I am. At least I was; this week's been a bit odd. You must be Sarah?"

Sarah nodded, juggled the box in her arms, and dropped it on the table. The two other coffee drinkers in the café looked up.

Sarah unwrapped her plaid, worn scarf from her neck. "I'm so sorry, I'm late. Life is out of control." She hesitated. "Not quite the impression I hoped to make." She gave an annoyed smile.

"No worries." Amelia was fascinated by this woman's appearance. She was sloppily dressed in jeans and a sweatshirt and it looked as if her hair had traveled directly from her pillow to this moment. "I absolutely know what you mean." She held up her coffee cup by the handle. "Cheers? Is it too early for a drink instead?" She laughed.

Sarah pulled at her hair and rubbed the ends of her short strands between her fingers, giving off a nervous smile. "Well, let's just add all of my bad traits to this impression. But it's generally always too early for a drink for me. These days." She gave a wistful look. "Don't tempt me."

The waitress appeared, surprising them both. "Coffee?" she asked brightly.

"Yes please," Sarah said. She looked at Amelia. "Coffee is one of my main food groups, though."

Amelia smiled at her. *She liked this woman. Regardless of her unconventional manners.*

"Will you be ordering anything to eat?" The waitress poured coffee into the empty cup, fully bored by the morning's conversational opportunities.

"Could I just have an order of toast?" Sarah asked.

"Nothing for me," Amelia replied. "Thank you."

They sat quietly for a moment, sipping coffee.

"You must think this is so weird. I have to tell you I don't know why I am so obsessed with this. This whole deal," Sarah started, almost as if she was talking to herself. She unzipped the top of her hoodie sweatshirt, and Amelia noticed an outline of a ribbed tank top below, nipples pushing against the sweatshirt. It struck Amelia that she hadn't been braless in public since her teen years at least.

"Wait. I'm sorry." Amelia searched Sarah's face for some hint. "I really don't know what you are talking about. I mean, other than your note asking me to call you. I'm assuming it must be about my dad. But, again I have no idea."

"Oh, yeah. I'm sorry. I'm just racing." Sarah rubbed her hands through her short hair, gave it a quick once over with her fingers, and pushed down a clump from the back that was sticking up. She looked out the window. "Yes. At first I couldn't figure out why you called. I mean I thought Ernest would be a man. I mean. Well, you know, where I left the note. At least I thought the name was a man." She looked down at the table and pressed her fingertips to her forehead, as if she was pushing back a pain. "Oh, fucking God. I can be such an idiot."

Amelia took a deep breath. "Ernest is my dad." She paused. "Well, was my dad. He passed away earlier this year." The admission still felt strange and sad: to acknowledge her father had died.

"Oh, I'm so sorry. I didn't know. I didn't even think about that. I'm so sorry." Sarah took another drink of coffee. "I just don't know what to say." Sarah said.

"Well, did you know him? Why did you stop by the house?" Amelia felt uncomfortable to sound so rude. It was so unlike her for her words to come out so accusatory to this stranger. And yet, she couldn't seem to help it.

Sarah gazed at her, then opened the box and extracted two letters. She handed them to Amelia, leaving the green bottle in the box.

The waitress returned with an order of wheat toast, with butter and jam. "More coffee?" Sarah nodded, and the waitress filled up both cups.

After quickly scanning both notes, Amelia looked more carefully at the one signed "Ernest," staring at it for what felt like a very long time. She wiped tears from her cheeks.

"Darn it, Dad," she whispered. She looked up at Sarah. "I don't cry. Really, I don't. I'm so sorry." She used a napkin to dry her nose and eyes, before rummaging into her purse for a small package of tissues. "What is this?"

Sarah remained silent.

"I miss him so much. And reading this letter. It sounds just like him. It's almost like talking to him. Again." The silence was interrupted as the door to the café opened and a young woman came in and ordered a drink to go at the counter. The whirring sounds of the espresso machine filled the space, allowing the emotions of the moment to waft in the gap of the conversation.

After studying the letters again for several minutes, Amelia resolutely set them down on the table. She pulled out a fresh tissue from the packet and wiped her eyes, her black eyelashes mascara-free. She wrung her hands together, as if warming up her fingers.

"I'm confused," Amelia said. "Who is Annie? And why did you try to find Ernest?"

Stuttering and hesitating at first, Sarah shared what she knew about Annie and about how she couldn't stop wondering about why Annie and her family disappeared from the house, and how she worried about what had happened to the girl.

"But you're right," Sarah said. "I mean. Well, I don't know. I mean, why should I care so much? It's so weird. This girl shouldn't mean anything to me. I know it's just plain weird, but I just can't stop thinking about her. I just keep feeling like I hold something that gives a clue, only I don't understand the clue. And I don't even understand why it should be important. I just thought, I guess, that if I could find Ernest, I might understand the story and know what to do next. But now . . . I guess I'm more confused than ever." She gave Amelia a weak smile. "And you must think I'm even crazier than I really am. Or just some fucking idiot."

Amelia couldn't help but release a small smile to this odd woman. Tears formed in her eyes and she turned to the wall, embarrassed. She dried her eyes with the crumpled tissue and looked down at her lap.

"Oh fuck. I'm such a fucking idiot," Sarah said.

Amelia gave her a sharp look. Sarah sniffed and brushed tears from her eyes.

The waitress came over to the booth. "I'm sorry. Can I get you anything? Is everything okay?"

Amelia gave her a serious look. She hesitated. "No. The coffee is so terrible it's upsetting."

The young waitress looked horrified. "Oh, I'm so sorry . . ."

Amelia broke into an awkward, unsteady laugh peppered by hiccups. "Oh, honey, I'm sorry. I'm just teasing you. The coffee is great. Really. We're okay. I mean, we're not but we will be. And it has nothing to do with you. Or your coffee."

The waitress gave her a quizzical look. "Um, okay. Thanks. "Whatever you say," she added under her breath. "More coffee?" She remained expressionless as she poured the coffee, but her hand shook and she spilled a few drops on the table. As she walked away she looked at the clock near the door and shook her head.

"That was terrible," Sarah said.

They suppressed a laugh, followed by an onslaught of youthful giggles, dwindling into sobs and sniffles.

"I can't believe you did that to that poor girl," she whispered loudly.

Amelia wiped her eyes with the crumpled napkin. "I know. I'm so sorry. That's the kind of thing my mama would have done and my dad would have been so embarrassed he would have had to leave the cafe. It just flew out of me. I really don't know where it came from. I'm so sorry. It was really mean." She continued to stifle her laugh. "I'll leave a good tip." She picked up one of the letters. She stared at it, her finger highlighting the date at the top of the letter.

"He wrote this over a year before he died. I hadn't noticed. He never mentioned it." She looked Sarah in the eye. "We do need to know more. And what about this Annie? Do you think she never knew that he found it?

Sarah gave a small smile. "Or that she never knew somebody cared enough to write back?" She looked Amelia in the eye as she gathered the two letters together. "I think I have an idea."

Amelia sat up straighter and stared at Sarah. And then she smiled at her new friend, and nodded.

Chapter 10

Fortuity

THE NEXT DAY, Sarah proceeded with their plan. She pulled on her jeans and flannel shirt, sloppy as usual—well aware she usually didn't look much like someone who had yearned to work in fashion. She didn't much care anymore, knowing her life in a mall chain store was nothing like the industry she had great dreams of bursting into all those years ago.

She shifted her body into the bowels of her well-worn leather couch and searched for the website on her phone. She closed her eyes to think of the things she should be doing: emptying the junk out of her car, stopping at Goodwill, visiting Gloria.

Dismissing the burgeoning noise in her head, she got up, still barefooted, and walked into the kitchen to put the tea kettle on. The acrid smell of burnt toast returned her focus back to the moment—she watched a barely visible wisp of smoke rise above the blackened crumbs on the burner. She rummaged through the cupboard that was jammed with boxes full of old tea. So often she had tried to make herself choose it rather than coffee in the morning. But now, she forced herself to calm her thoughts. She pulled down her favorite mug from the cupboard, hand thrown and given to her long ago from a friend, a cup that was good at holding heat. She hated lukewarm drinks of any kind. The tea kettle whistled her out of remembering Kendall. Another friend from the past. So many years had come and gone since they had talked. She felt like a big baby when it came to remembering her friendship losses. She poured the steaming water over a bag of apricot tea, black to give her just a little zing, and went back to the couch.

She had to count on her fingers to figure out what grade a twelve -year old would be in as she settled back in the soft cushions and placed the steaming tea on the table next to her. She settled on seventh grade, not that she could be sure. Middle school, she knew, not like junior high in the old days. She was glad to be living in the internet age, giving her the ability to track down teachers—or almost anyone you wanted—even if it was all rather creepy. She was surprised that a town Newberg's size would have two middle schools, further complicating her search. But finally. "Hell, yes. *Oh, the powerful lift to her mood by this simple find.* Ms. Marquam was listed adjacent to an email address. She scribbled down the school's street address and added its phone number for good measure. Setting her phone aside, she thought back to herself all those years ago.

"Yes, Annie. Seventh grade was the shits," she muttered. She closed her eyes to remember back. Harder, yet, to let herself remember, was Alison's seventh grade year. That was probably when it all started, she now suspected.

LATER THAT AFTERNOON, Sarah neared the school parking lot where kids loaded onto buses and shrill shrieks echoed in the street. Nearby streets teemed with cars, some parked illegally, to pick up a kid or two. Little bodies streamed out of the building, and she wondered how on earth they could belong to middle schoolers? Their brightly colored backpacks consumed some of the smallest figures, sagging down to their knees. Yet opposite the little ones were some students with figures looking as full-grown women. *What a madhouse.* Through her unrolled windows the raucous sounds of high pitched voices pulsed her brain, reminding her vaguely of times, decades ago now. Although she rarely was able to pick up Alison this early in the day, unless it was an emergency doctor appointment. Being around so much energy forced her to pay attention to the crosswalk and crossing guard, until she squeaked into a parking spot over a block away. As she walked toward the school, she passed parents braving the crowded and over-energized school property, a few tagging little ones along.

God, they are so young. Sarah realized she must look like a kid's grandma, even though she wasn't, and probably never would be. Or, and she hesitated, she hoped she wouldn't be, for any potential child's sake. She slowed her steps as kids continued to stream out the front door, realizing too late in the game how she could have timed this better. At least by working on Saturdays she was able to offer to Amelia her ability to fit this into a weekday.

Sarah sat down on a green painted metal bench just outside the front door. Paint was scratched off the supporting posts. Skateboard antics, probably, she figured.

"Come on, John!" a young woman nagged.

She was scowling but her voice amplified a forced lightness. Her body was weighed down by a napping toddler, her pudgy lip stretched as it smooshed into the fabric of her coat, a stream of drool hanging from her chin. The toddler's left hand cupped the collar of her mother's shirt, ever so slightly. Sarah caught the mother's eye and attempted to give her a gentle smile.

"It'll get better," Sarah told her softly. She hoped her expression wouldn't give away the lie she just told.

The woman looked at her and slowed her step. The toddler's face crunched against her shoulder as she dreamed through the schoolyard din.

"It better," the woman said, shaking her head. "I won't make it otherwise." She gave a tired smile. She stopped as a little boy the color of vanilla wafers with bright red hair grabbed her hand.

"I don't want to wait here longer," he said.

The woman shook her head *no* and yanked his arm to keep him tighter to her body. At that moment, an older boy came out the door and strode ahead of them, wordlessly. Sarah knew this look. *Too cool for parents.* The woman—holding the toddler who was now waking and fighting to burst out of her arms, and grabbing the pulling arm of the red-haired boy—just looked away as she followed the older boy. Sarah watched them walk into the distance, reminded how quickly she had forgotten some of those earliest days with her own daughter.

The parking lot quieted—the yells from pubescent kids dwindling, and the last of the buses pulling away as brakes screeched, emitting the putrid smell of diesel. Sarah slowly got up and stopped to massage her back. She followed the sign to the office that flashed a reminder "all visitors check in here." She entered the doorway to the office where a middle-aged woman in a pastel cardigan moved paper on a desk surface overloaded with paperwork mountains. She didn't look up.

"Um, excuse me?" Sarah said.

The woman slowly raised her head, an impatient expression on her face.

"I was hoping to see Ms. Marquam?"

"Is she expecting you?" the woman asked as the phone rang next to her.

"I don't think so," Sarah said. Wondering if she should lie. "I really just need a minute. Um, I sent an email but I didn't hear back."

"Just a minute," the woman said as she answered the phone, but just as quickly hung up. "Are you a parent? Or a grandparent?"

"No, I just have a question for her if I may."

"Well, I think she's here," she said as she looked at the board on the wall. "It doesn't look like she's checked out yet. She's just down the hall that way." She nodded a direction. "Room number ten." She gave Sarah another look, as if dismissing her, and then stared back at her paperwork.

Sarah walked down the hall, passing rooms seven and eight, and as she passed room nine, she spotted a woman ahead of her closing and locking a door. The woman looked up at her as she let go of her key. Her lanyard dropped back onto her chest.

"Hi," Sarah said. "My name is Sarah. Well, I don't know if you got my email?"

Ms. Marquam looked at her as she adjusted her overstuffed bag on her shoulder. "I'm sorry. I've been really swamped and sometimes my email box gets a bit backed up. Do I know you?"

"Um, no, but I can explain if you have a few minutes?"

"You know, I'm really in a hurry." Ms. Marquam flashed a smiled, as if she wanted her to know she wasn't a rude person. "It's just that I have yet to pick up my son on time at daycare this week and need to prove to them that I'm capable of it. Last thing I need now is for Henry to get kicked out." She tried to smile again, as if it would be ironic for a teacher who expected kids to follow school rules not able to obey them herself.

Sarah imagined how middle schoolers would find this teacher's youthfulness fun and motivating as she admired the simplicity of her outfit: a jumper, turtleneck, and low-heeled boots.

"I'm so sorry," Sarah said. "I know I should have called. Can I just walk you to your car? It'll really only take a minute."

"Of course. Sure," Ms. Marquam replied. "I'm Heather Marquam, by the way." She started to walk toward the office.

"Yes, I know. I've kind of tracked you down." Sarah hesitated, knowing she sounded creepy, yet bewildered by how else to begin this odd conversation.

Heather pushed open the office door and poked her head in. "I'm heading out Margie," she called inside the door. "Could you sign me out, pretty please?"

Margie looked up from her desk. "Sure," she replied without emotion or smile.

"Everyone's so overworked. It's tough some days," Heather said.

"Yeah. Tell me about it," Sarah muttered.

"So, what is this about? I know you don't have a student in my class." Heather sounded hurried, but also skeptical.

"Yes. I mean, no, it's not about that," Sarah stammered. "Well, it's about a student you had. I mean, well, I guess it would have been last year? But. Well, I'm not sure. Or the year before? Her name was Annie. I'm sorry but I really don't know her last name."

Heather stopped walking. "Is something wrong with Annie?"

"Oh, I'm sorry. No, no. I mean, well, actually I don't know. I mean, I don't know Annie. I'm just trying to track her down." She realized how much she sounded like a nut case.

"I'm sorry," Heather said, more guarded and official as she continued walking. "I really can't give out private information about a student."

Sarah thought she might cry and scolded herself for being such a wimp. She hesitated in an effort to calm the sobs she knew were about to gush forth. "Oh, I understand. I'm sorry. I mean, um, I'm not explaining this very well. I'm sure it all sounds weird. I'm not a psycho, though it might sound like it." She silently berated herself for being such an idiot and took a breath. "Trust me, I'm only trying to help her. I just need to get her a message. I only want to know how to reach her." She looked at Heather, and determined that she had no intention to speak further. *Teachers, of all people, were warned about weird folks who tried to kidnap kids or use them to get back at their exes.* "Okay. Is there any way you can put me in touch with her? I do know how special you were to her."

Heather walked across the parking lot, her face softened. As if she couldn't help herself, she smiled. "Annie was one of my all-time favorite students. I truly miss her."

"Oh no. Is she okay?" Sarah started.

"Oh. I really don't know, but I bet she is probably doing fine." Heather stopped and gave Sarah a firm look. "I can't talk to you without knowing who you are or getting her parents' permission. I'm really sorry. I'm sure you mean well. You should just know that I believe that kid will make it no matter what the world gives her." She looked away, as if remembering something. "And I hope to God she gets some good. She deserves it." She looked Sarah in the eye. "But again, I've already shared too much. I don't know who you are or what you want." She put one of the keys from her lanyard into a car door. "I really need to go."

"Oh, but please, could I call you? I think you will understand and I need to get something to her. Please, it really, really is important?" Sarah bit her lip to try to prevent herself from crying. *Why was she being such a baby about this?* She had so many other things she should be attending to.

Heather stopped what she was doing, and looked at Sarah curiously. "Okay, maybe. Why don't you give me your phone number? I'll try to call you. Really, I will. Is after nine at night too late? Life is pretty crazy from now till Henry gets to bed. And if I don't reach you tonight, I'll try to over the weekend."

Sarah sighed. Hopes dashed. Again. Instantly, the weight of her body made her feel as if she was sinking into the ground, like the wicked witch as Dorothy threw the bucket of water. She wanted to curl up somewhere nearby. Give up.

"Sure." Sarah tried hard to sound cheerful as she pulled a pen and piece of paper from her purse, faking her overwhelming disappointment. "That would be great." She gave Heather the paper and stepped away from the car so to allow her to put her bag in the back seat, crunched down on the floor below a car seat. "And thank you. I want to talk . . . I mean, I really look forward to talking."

Although Sarah kept her phone next to her each evening, the call didn't come until the following Saturday night. She was alone, another night when Tony said he had business elsewhere. She was already in her sweats, nodding off to a romance novel she was reading in an effort to take her thoughts away from present day. She wasn't much of a reader. The call made her jump, and her heartbeat quickened.

"Hello, this is Sarah" she answered to the unrecognized phone number.

"Yes, Sarah, this is Heather Marquam.".

"Thanks so much for calling. I know it all might have seemed weird." And she began to explain the situation. After listening to Heather for a few minutes, she grabbed her notepad from the table and jotted down a few notes.

OVER A WEEK later, the phone rang again with another unrecognized number: not Gloria, not Tony, not Allison, not Amelia. Sarah answered it and put it on speaker. Just in case she needed to write anything down.

"Hi, this is Sarah," she said.

"Hi, Sarah. This is Mr. Anderson. I am returning your call. And your emails." His voice was cool and tinged with annoyance.

Sarah took a quick breath and attempted to silently release it. "Thanks, so much for returning my call. I know you are busy and my message might have sounded a bit weird."

"Well actually," Mr. Anderson replied sharply, "I don't have access to voicemail. All I received was your name and number. I did get your emails, though."

Sarah wondered if he too thought she was psycho. Maybe Heather had warned him about her.

"I understand that you are concerned about Annie M.'s wellbeing? Do you know her or have reason to believe she is in harm's way?" Mr. Anderson asked, sounding very official. Unemotional. Robotic.

Sarah pulled at her hair. She knew she had one chance to sound reasonable. "Oh, no. No. Nothing like that. All I really want is to get her a message. I'd really like to talk to her. I mean, uh, that would be best."

"I understand that. But given the circumstances, I don't think we can arrange that," Mr. Anderson replied. "At least not through me. Um . . . Annie seems to be doing fine, I checked in on our records here before calling you. All of our students' interactions are confidential, you must understand this. We don't want to promote something that might risk her own well-being." He paused. "You understand that, right?"

Sarah slouched down and banged her head on the top of her chair. She took a deep breath, fighting hard to keep herself from crying. *Why was she crying over this when she had ceased to cry over her own daughter?*

"You just don't understand," she said, identifying herself as whining. "It's just that . . . well. I mean, I really want to help her. And I have something that might make her happy."

"Maybe you should tell me what you are talking about, if you would," Mr. Anderson said, his voice evoking the tiniest bit of interest.

Sarah shared the whole story, trying to keep it as direct as she could. At first, Mr. Anderson occasionally interjected, as if trying to speed her along, but the more she spoke, the more his interest seemed genuine. She told him about the package, Ernest, and the notes.

"I just think it would be comforting for Annie to know that someone answered her note. That cared about her. I was thinking, if it was me, it might make me happy. Even though it's sad that he died."

Sarah waited for what she hoped would be a positive answer.

"Okay, I'll consider all this," Mr. Anderson said. "I am not aware of any troubles. Of course, we've got a lot of kids in our school, but I did once meet her when she was a freshman and, as far as I know, she's doing well in school. But I can't connect you with her; I'm really sorry."

"But . . . you know. I mean, it's just that I'd like to be able to tell her all this. I mean, I think it would make her feel good. Maybe give her hope about people. Well, maybe. I just mean, someone taking the time to reply to her." Sarah hesitated, as if she knew she might be jumping to conclusions. "And maybe someone should know about what she said about her dad?"

"I don't think you need to worry about her safety. I will double check as I can," Mr. Anderson said.

Sarah could tell he was holding back, and it bothered her. She knew how large classes were, even back when Alison was in public high school, and although she didn't know what kind of a teacher this Mr. Anderson was, she just felt he was missing her point. Annie could be lost in a sea of high schoolers. She closed her eyes. *This wasn't what she imagined.*

"I'll tell you what," Mr. Anderson said. "What if you mail or drop the package by the school? With the letters. I would be happy to return them to Annie. Would that help?"

Sarah thought about it a moment. "Yes, I guess. Really that's all that I needed."

Convinced she wanted far more than this outcome, she wanted to be the one to do the right thing for someone and this was finally a chance. Her chance. She wrote down the school address, thanked the teacher again, and put the phone down. *Why did she feel so disappointed?* She looked out her window and watched the dark green uneven branches of the tall Douglas fir outside the apartment complex arch back and forth in the wind. She picked up her phone.

"Hi, Amelia, it's Sarah."

Chapter 11

Out of the blue
April 2016

IT HAD BEEN his sister, Elizabeth, who eventually helped him imagine what his "big thing" might be in life. How *he* could make a difference. After withdrawing from community college before the first day of his first term, he jumped at a chance for a barista job. Coffee was creative, he told himself, embarrassed years later to admit to a friend how he had imagined learning enough to enter the world barista championships. He had read about such events in the *Willamette Week*, a photo identifying a young Portland barista as a previous contender. He had naively told himself back then, he would meet *interesting people*, different than those he was stuck with in high school.

Grant slowly let down his guard around others; no longer feeling such a need to hide behind what he thought had been the expected facade of his teens. He saved money, found three new friends to join him on a trip to the Oregon coast and hang out with. Jeff was his first almost boyfriend. Grant for the first time learned the truth: that not all gay men were extroverted hair dressers or hung out only in bars late into the night. This too, was comforting. To understand he didn't need to fully recreate himself to fit into the world. But, in the end, Jeff required more time and energy than Grant could muster, and they spent less and less time together. And before long, Grant's days in the coffee shop dragged. He spent more time at the library and bookstores, using his free time to read and search, without any clue as to what he was looking for.

One day, sitting at Powell's City of Books, ironically having paid for a cup of coffee rather than waiting for a free one at his own workplace, he met a girl named Sharell. The coffee shop of this iconic Portland bookstore was always so crowded, people felt lucky to find an empty chair; and everyone, the regulars at least, expected to share tables with others they may never have met before, and may never see again. Tables surrounded by shelves of books, inviting book lovers to get lost in the red room or the rose room or rooms named for a handful of other colors, upstairs and downstairs, in the midst of thousands and thousands of books.

Grant pushed out a chair adjacent to a young woman, certainly in her teens. As he sat down, shy to make eye contact with strangers, he looked instead at the tattoos snaking up her arms, wishing it was summer with more skin exposed to reveal the full design escaping beyond her lower arms and neck. Tattoos were common, although he hadn't been brave enough to add one to his body yet, but for some reason, he couldn't take his eyes off this design: colors of the rainbow in a formation reminding him of wilderness, rivers, and trout.

Soon enough the woman glared angrily at him. "Got a problem?" Her eyes shrank together and her lips pursed into a mean frown. A dimple in her cheek showed through, contradicting her expression. It was a voice full of impertinent nastiness, though, which made Grant wonder how long he had been staring at her, throwing him off guard.

"Oh, I'm sorry. I was, um . . . just looking, well, admiring your artwork." He hoped she didn't think he was trying to come up with a dreadful pick up line.

At first, the woman continued to stare at him without changing her expression, as if she was trying to figure out if he was serious or just another loser teasing her. The right side of her mouth slowly crept into a small, lopsided grin. She had a small gap next to her right incisor, making her look even younger.

"Yeah. My boyfriend is a dammed original tattoo artist. Though my last boss didn't seem to think much of it." She pulled her top up a bit in the front so the top of her bra no longer showed, and then down in back over the gap of skin that appeared between the ass of her jeans and her back, covering up boldly crafted lime green leaves. "Not that I care. Really," she added, not fully convincing.

Grant was so absorbed in wondering how much of her body might be covered with tattoos he no longer knew what she was talking about. He forced himself to look back at his coffee, nodding, while he removed the plastic lid with his thumb and forefinger. He observed how the barista overdid the temperature on this Americano. Wisps of steam escaped the dark liquid. He wished he had gotten a real cup, rather than paper.

"I'm Sharell," the girl continued, friendlier. "You don't look familiar? So many of the people hanging out here, well, they are. You know. Returnees, basically. Sometimes I wonder if any of them sleep in the stacks," She laughed, a grizzled laugh for such a young person. Grant could tell smoking had already left its raspy mark. "I actually thought about trying it. You know. Sleeping in the stacks." She looked around the room. "It could be cozy. But then I figured, knowing my luck, I'd get arrested. I can't risk that again. Just now."

Again, Grant simply nodded. He felt immature and unworldly next to this young girl.

"I mean, I'm here a helluva lot. At least I have money for the coffee, I guess. Well, sometimes. But I have a few friends that show up here hoping someone might buy them a cup." Sharell smiled knowingly.

"Uh, yeah." Grant responded. "I don't get coffee out very often since I work in a shop. I'll be first to say it's ridiculously expensive."

"Well, these FooFoo drinks people buy. Triple vanilla whatever banana double shot putrid crap. They shouldn't be allowed. Just give me a goddamned cup of caffeine is what I say." Sharell looked back at the front page of the *Willamette Week* plopped on the table in front of her, and traced her pointer finger to outline an image, but not turning the page.

Grant opened the book he'd pulled off the shelf, not intent on buying it, but he knew none of the salespeople could tell or likely even cared.

"That looks boring," Sharell commented.

Grant looked up at her. *Who the heck was this girl?* She couldn't be more than sixteen, not only talkative but opinionated. He still wasn't comfortable interacting with people who had an edge to them. He had always thought his mom was one of those types, but since he had moved out on his own and encountered edgier, and what seemed to him, ruder people, especially those demanding coffee—often while holding a conversation on the phone—he had to admit his mom was rather soft. And his dad? The emperor of kindness, often, to his own detriment.

Grant didn't know what to say. Instead, he muttered something incoherent about art history. But he thought maybe someday he'd have the courage to travel to Italy and Europe to see the real art of the world for himself.

"Do you know the time?" Sharell asked. She must be bored with Grant's inability to talk, and he found himself wondering where it was a girl like this might have to go. Nothing school-related, it didn't seem.

"Almost four-thirty. Got a big evening?" he added, without thinking.

She sneered at him. "Smart ass." The dimple showed through again.

Grant was surprised. "I'm sorry—I didn't mean anything. I just . . . never mind." He started to put his coat on. Now he was glad he'd gotten his coffee to go.

"Oh, I got a thing down at Outside In."

Grant gave her a quizzical look.

"Oh, you know. The place down the street that tries to help fucked-up kids like me." Sharell rolled her eyes. "There's an old guy there. He's helping me figure out something I want to do. Pretty much if I don't show up I've fucked up another something."

Grant simply nodded. Growing up on Portland's east side and mostly unaware of downtown, he was learning how much had been hidden to him from life in this city.

"See ya. Enjoy your *art*," she said, emphasizing "art," shrugging and making a snobby expression.

Grant nodded to her. He pulled out his phone and read a text from his mom reminding him about dinner on Sunday night. At least she was a great cook. He did a search on his phone, closed the book, and looked around for staff before deciding to leave it on the table. He only had half an hour before his shift started. At least the other guy working the coffee shop that night was decent company. He quickened his pace, once leaving Powell's, toward 13th Avenue, and then south. It was a nice afternoon, and a bit of a walk would wake him up even more than the caffeine before his six-hour shift, followed by the mechanics of closing. On his way to his final destination, he peered through the windows of Outside In, noticing the sign advertising "volunteers needed."

"THAT WAS PRETTY much it," he told Amelia the second time he ran into her, sharing how it was when he first thought he might get into teaching. He had recognized Amelia across the coffee shop, and although he wouldn't have interrupted her, she had waved and signaled him over to her table. If he hadn't grown up in Portland he would have thought this was too coincidental, but he knew it was in many respects, still a small town. She told Grant she was waiting for someone and suggested, since all the other tables were full, that he sit with her.

"I'm early and my friend's always late," Amelia said. "I figure it probably gives us time for one cup of coffee. If you want."

"Oh, no coffee for me. I just stopped in for the bathroom." Grant rolled his eyes at his apparent lack of social life. "Jake's a friend of mine." He nodded to the man at the till. "We used to work together."

"So, then what?" Amelia asked, propelling him to finish his story about what happened after meeting Sharell.

"Well, after volunteering for a while, I realized how much I enjoyed the contacts. Kids I had been so scared of not long ago, and well, I don't know. I guess I was just enough older to see through their crap. And maybe what they really seemed to want."

"Good for you. I don't have much experience and am pretty inept communicating with teens. Kids too, if I were to be honest about it," Amelia added with a bewildered expression. "So, do you still volunteer there?"

"No, not these days. I'm so burned out with my counseling job. Sometimes I wonder if I'd be where I am today if I hadn't been so innocent about teens when I made that decision. There'd be no way." Grant hesitated and looked down at his hands, and then back at Amelia. "Sometimes I wonder if I'm just not as patient as I was back then. Or maybe just hardened to the stories, I'm not sure."

Grant noticed Amelia was distracted by the jingle of the bell on the door. She waved to someone.

Grant stood up. He hadn't taken off his coat, not intending to stay longer than just a minute. "I've gotta run." A woman hurried over to the table. He noticed she was breathing heavily, as if she'd been running, hurrying for some time.

"Hi, Sarah. Look at you, you're earlier than normal," Amelia said with a smile.

"Haha. Hello to you too." She laughed.

As they shared a brief hug, Grant could feel the connection between them, and how quickly he felt in the way. He stood up, accidentally knocking the table with his waist, spilling water out of Amelia's glass.

"Oh, wait, Grant," Amelia said, putting her hand on his arm. "First, meet my friend Sarah."

"Hi." Sarah wiped her hand on her jeans and held it out.

"Hi." Grant shook her cold bare hand, noticing short fingernails with chipped red nail polish.

"I'll see you around again, maybe," Amelia said as he walked away.

Grant nodded, distracted, as he tried to determine why Sarah's voice sounded familiar. Surely, he heard it somewhere around this town. In the end, it was a small world.

Chapter 12

Hope Resurrected
May 2016

GRANT MET ANNIE later in the afternoon on a Monday. The day had begun as any other start of the week. *Why were Monday's always the hardest day?* Some might mourn or begrudge the end of a relaxing or exciting weekend, but Grant knew that wasn't his issue. It was the hope that something different would happen. That he might feel as though he *was* really making a difference in this sea of tardiness and truancy and excuses. These days he often felt as though his empathy savings account amassed earlier in life—now routinely sapped by kids without direction, support, or money—was draining before his eyes. Slipping through his fingers as if evaporating in air; without improving lives he once thought he could help change. As the early hours of Monday became late morning, inching toward the end of the day, he recognized signs predicting another endless week. He anticipated the rest of his days to be chocked full of referrals for kids misbehaving, or smoking, or simply not making the grade. Kids that, in the end, didn't show any interest in cashing in on his banked empathy.

When Grant had asked Annie's home room teacher about meeting with her, he learned that her English teacher had recommended Annie meet with him for help in planning her life after high school and it had been buried under other higher priority requests. It made him wonder how many kids he never saw who might have benefited from counseling because the request was lost, never rising to his attention, or making it into his appointment book.

He saw a mix of kids. First and foremost, those who simply kept getting into trouble, followed by a handful of kids whom some teacher thought he could inspire into changing their ways, and then, a third of the kids in the school—those with last names between the letters H and O—who asked for help in planning their future. Annie would have fallen into both of the final categories. And now, on top of that, he had made a promise to the nearly hysterical woman who had emailed him so persistently. He was not surprised, after speaking to her on the phone, to find she emailed two more times after dropping off the package and being told to leave it at the main office.

Grant was certain it was only because students may share confidential stories that he had a real office with doors, sure that most of the staff sitting in cubbies made more money than he. He got up and left his door ajar, knowing it was intimidating to some kids to knock on a closed door. The politer kids worried they were interrupting something, while the bolder troubled kids took it as an excuse to mosey on, often back to what they weren't supposed to do in the first place. He wasn't surprised that some of those who had been batted around so much in their short lives didn't have enough self-confidence to believe they were worthy of such an interruption. When he got back to his desk, he saw a girl peek in at him, and then feign a knock when she noticed him looking at her.

"Hi," Grant said. "May I help you?"

"I'm Annie McDonald. Ms. Glover told me I had an appointment with you?"

"Yes, come on in," he said as he went to the round table with three chairs, squeezed into his corner, while reaching out his hand. "Nice to meet you, Annie. I'm Mr. Anderson."

As he shook her hand, Grant noticed how slight this girl was, and how nervous she appeared. Although her eyes crinkled as she formed a smile, her shaken hand trembled. Grant went to partially close the door.

And that, as simple as it seemed at the beginning, was his first meeting with Annie. He couldn't have imagined then, how at the moment Annie entered his office, a girl might recharge his interest in what he had once been so excited about in the first place. And as happens often in life, he would never know the impact he made in that moment on this one person.

AS ANNIE WALKED home later that day, the notes tucked into the outside pocket of her backpack, the bottle and packaging still stashed in her locker, she recalled that day four years ago as if it had just happened. She hadn't thought about it much, at least not since the phone call. Back then, for a long time she kept hoping the package would arrive, but after her family unexpectedly moved, she pretty much gave up. At first, though, after putting the bottle in the river, it was about the only thing she could focus on.

A solitary raindrop struck her nose, its wetness causing her to peer up into the sky as if to predict the weather. A great cloud was passing over, blue sky nearby, and as she forced herself to return to present time she focused on the playground near her house. She looked at her phone to confirm the time: she had at least an hour before her mom would even be home from work. *Definitely time for a pit-stop.* She plopped down on a park bench and hauled her heavy backpack off her shoulders, crammed with calculus and English textbooks, and so many spiral notebooks. Not far away she saw two kids playing on a play structure with their mom, or maybe a babysitter, watching nearby, talking on a phone. At moments like this, Annie couldn't believe she wasn't a little kid anymore. Now she was able to think about college ahead, even if her dad still insisted it was a pipe dream.

But at this moment, she knew, she had to follow her memories on a journey back in time to the exciting days when she planned the bottle's voyage. Back then, she had even gone to the library to download a map of the river; examining every crook in it, anticipating the turns her bottle might make. She somehow believed that if it could only survive the dump over the big falls, and then make the turn into the Columbia River—her note might make it all the way. To that kid in Japan, she had figured back then. She laughed at herself, thinking about how unlikely it would have been for the bottle to travel clear across the Pacific Ocean. Back then, though, she believed it was possible. It had all started with a story she had written for Mrs. Marquam. All about two girls who ended up becoming best friends for the rest of their lives.

For almost a month, back when she got the idea, she had tried to find a bottle. Her dad drank beer in cans. She had even asked him once, hoping maybe he might buy bottles instead, but he said cans were cheaper. She also figured she probably needed something bigger than a beer bottle anyway. She wondered now how she knew it needed to be bigger; if she wanted to assure her classmates as to her true nerdiness she should ask her physics teacher to show her how to determine the volume of a bottle needed to stay afloat in a strong current. Maybe it didn't matter, she now thought.

But back then she told herself that the whole thing was meant to happen when Mrs. Buck asked her to clean her house one day, kind of like those stories she'd read about that always ended perfectly. It wasn't something she would normally do, but Annie's mom encouraged her to help out since Mrs. Buck had fallen and could barely get off the couch. As young as Annie was, even then she suspected it was because Mrs. Buck felt bad for her family that she offered to pay her to help her out a few times. Annie had always liked her, especially when she made homemade caramel apples at Halloween, the brown stickiness staying in her teeth even after brushing them.

After scrubbing the toilet one day, she took the waste basket outside to the garbage can next to the garage. As she opened the lid, she couldn't believe her luck. There sat a green bottle. It had a pretty gold label and stuck its nose up between other pretty gross-looking things, but Annie held her breath and reminded herself she had just scrubbed an even grosser toilet. She felt like she was stealing, even though she knew it was just garbage, and so at first, she closed the lid and glanced around to make sure nobody was watching her. Then she reopened the lid, pulled the bottle out, and put it on the ground.

Since Mrs. Buck was stuck on the couch and Annie didn't think she was expecting any visitors, she figured the bottle might be safe for just a bit. But as she started to head back into the house she got nervous and ran back to ferry the bottle across the driveway to under an overgrown scratchy hedge that reached all the way to the ground. She took the waste basket back inside and tried to be normal and polite to Mrs. Buck as she finished wiping up the counter. She wasn't accomplished at cleaning, her mom always complained about how she needed to pay better attention and not be in such a hurry. But she finished the job and went back to the living room to say good bye. Mrs. Buck was fixated on *The Price is Right* on television. She did look up at Annie and motioned her toward her. Annie knew Mrs. Buck wanted to give her a hug. She looked so sad. Annie knew the right thing to do was to sit down with her for a bit, but she couldn't bring herself to do it, and instead gave her a quick hug.

"Just let my mom know anytime you need something else," she told Mrs. Buck, trying to smile.

She still remembered how, while she waited for the school bus when she was younger, Mrs. Buck would pass her on early morning walks, always asking her how she was and wishing her "a very special day."

"Thank you, dear," Mrs. Buck said. "Can you hand me my purse?"

"Oh no. You don't need to give me anything," Annie had said, although she knew it was just a formality.

"Annie, yes," Mrs. Buck said.

So Annie handed her the purse, smiled, and said thank you. But it made her feel sadder, not happier, although she didn't know why.

"I'll see you again," Mrs. Buck replied, after handing her a ten-dollar bill and leaning back against the couch. Her eyes drifted back to the television.

Annie got up and stepped out through the front door and screen. She was glad it was evening, and she was immersed in darkness. The dark didn't scare her like it did other kids. Somehow, it made her feel safer because she knew nobody could see her. She thought it was like being invisible, giving her a special cloak of protection. And now, it was exactly what she hoped for, for what might a neighbor think about a twelve year old kid carrying a wine bottle down the street? They'd say something like, "A chip off the old block." She knew her dad was an outsider who people gossiped about in this little town; at least that's what her mom said. She was wearing her brother's navy jacket, which hung down extra low anyway, and was perfect at providing a bit of room to hide the bottle. And she skipped home, delighted to find the solution to her challenge.

But now, these few years later, sitting on this bench, she felt like shouting, *Wow! Just wow!* What nobody else knew, not even Mr. Anderson, was that she already knew the bottle had been found by the old man. Out of the blue, he had called her, telling her that he fretted that maybe she would never know he found the bottle. She knew she'd remember that call for the rest of her life, or at least she sure hoped so. She was so glad she had included her phone number. The man had told her he was afraid the package wouldn't get to her because he remembered, after he had mailed it, that he left off the zip code. He hadn't remembered if someone at the post office had added it or not.

The only reason she was home the day she had received the old man's phone call, was because she was sick. She had a bad stomachache and it was frightening for her to imagine throwing up at school. She had known it was a lucky break, because on a normal weekday there wouldn't have been anyone at home to answer the phone, with her mom and dad at work, and they didn't own an answering machine. So, Annie had answered the phone and this old guy said his name was Ernest and that he had found a bottle. He had sounded so excited, as excited as she, and told her how he felt it was meant to happen—for him to hear from a kid like her.

It was kind of eerie—she knew most people wouldn't understand or believe it, especially since she was kind of shy—but the two of them had talked on the phone for a while. It was almost like they knew each other before, even though she knew that was impossible.

Ernest had asked her about Mrs. Marquam and about her dad: he was really interested in what she had written in her note. He told her he had a daughter too, and that her letter reminded him of something his daughter might have written and sent. He also talked about how astonishing it was the bottle had traveled through such challenging conditions; and he said it reminded him of life. Ernest had told her just like in life you don't always know what's going to come because of something you do, and how he thought little things happened for a reason. How sometimes you didn't even know the little things that happened set bigger things in motion. The old man said a lot, and she vowed to remember it forever. Maybe, she imagined then, some day she might even write about it.

But on this day these handful of years later, the return of the bottle and the note he had written were beyond belief. Now she was given not just the letter she wrote, but Ernest's response, which said even more than what she remembered he had said on the phone. It was something she could hold in her hands and read over and over. She found reading it now, at sixteen, was even different than if she'd received it when she was younger. The old man said some things that made her wonder if he might have known her dad, even though she knew that was impossible. It all just made for the best day ever—even better than the best birthday—something that was her own special secret: to have the package with the bottle to have found her so many miles away from where she first put it in the river. And while much of it she would keep a secret, she just knew now was time for her to talk to her mom about bits of it.

Annie didn't tell Mr. Anderson all of this, because it felt private. But he seemed to think the parts of the story that she did share with him were cool. He also asked her about what she planned to do after she graduated and he told her that was what he was there for—to help kids plan things out. Annie hadn't understood there were teachers whose jobs were to talk about things like that, but when she left Mr. Anderson that day, she set up an appointment for the next week to talk about her options. When she told him her family didn't have enough money to pay for college, he told her that shouldn't stop her from researching colleges to find the best place for her. And Mr. Anderson talked to her about dreams, and the difference between fluff dreams that only expanded in your head, and those you just might make happen. Although she knew there were scholarships, figuring them out was overwhelming, and her mom was too worn out most days for Annie to ever talk about her future.

"Just get through one more day," was her mom's motto.

Annie's phone vibrated. She had been so lost in thoughts. She read the message from her mom. "Home in 30 minutes." She looked at the note from Ernest one more time, folded both notes carefully, and placed them in the zippered pocket of her backpack. She noticed that the little kids had already left, and she put her pack on her back, and headed home. She smiled. It was her big secret.

Chapter 13

Bonding
July 2016

SHARON MAY HAVE entered the room that first time with Ernest like a tornado, but she approached motherhood as a CEO, Amelia told Sarah during one of their coffee dates on a Sunday morning. They had become regulars, and although at first, they met over an unspoken pretense of connecting with Annie, before long they migrated on to other compelling conversations. After all, Sarah told Amelia she had never heard back from Mr. Anderson after she dropped off the package, although they both held out hope they would sometime learn more about Annie.

They returned regularly to the coffee shop with the bell that jingled on the back of the door, where they were often served by the waitress named Kim with the silver bangles creeping up her wrists. Kim became less wary and friendlier with each cup of coffee they ordered.

"You should try the blueberry scones," Kim said to them on this particular morning. She sported large silver hoop earrings and a wildly colored t-shirt shouting Bob Marley.

"Sure, I'll try one," Sarah said.

Amelia shook her head but smiled at Kim.

As the waitress hurried away, Sarah asked quietly, "Isn't that second stud in her nose new? I don't remember it."

"Yeah, you might be right. I'm not sure I remember."

Just then Kim brought the scone on a plate, and set it in front of Sarah. As Sarah broke off a piece of the pastry, royal blue juice dripped onto the plate and the aroma of blueberry, cinnamon, and sugar lofted above them.

"Thanks," she said to Kim. "Yum. Have a bite, Amelia?"

"No thanks, I'm good." She hesitated. "I'm avoiding gluten, but more and more I'm regretting it. It seems like a stupid thing to do."

As Kim refilled their cups, both Sarah and Amelia discretely examined her right nostril, the stud surrounded by visible redness.

Sarah watched Kim walk to another table. "I just think it'd be uncomfortable when you blow your nose, or get snot stuck in around the backside of the stud."

They laughed.

"God, I'm old," Sarah said.

Amelia smiled, catching Sarah's eye.

"Okay, please carry on," Sarah added.

"Oh. Well, I was only saying how my mama and dad were so ready to be parents," Amelia said, continuing to share stories her parents had relayed to her. Her mama's favorite story described how slow her dad was to catch on, at first, when they went out alone together that first time: how he needed to be reminded it *was* a date. A wedding was planned not long after, surprising her dad that he could be so spontaneous and shocking Sharon's own parents. Ernest leveled once with Amelia about how he knew his own mom, Amelia's grandmother Helen, worried about the marriage at first. "Yet, she knew how good Sharon's dad—your grandfather, Amelia, Jackson—had been to both my dad and me, and in the end accepted our marriage," he had told her when she was younger.

She added how she believed in the end her grandmother was simply worried about being left alone.

Sarah wetted her finger and ran it over the blueberry juice lying sticky on the plate, and licked it.

"I know people say opposites attract," Amelia said. "I have never believed it. But my parents are, well, I guess were. I mean they were a testament to what I mostly don't believe. For everybody else. That opposites can make it together beautifully."

Amelia told Sarah about how her dad loved to claim that the only reason her mama wanted to marry him was because he was the only man who would ever let her talk so much. "The best part was how every once in a while he could think fast enough to get in a zinger. Oh, did my mama laugh!" Amelia smiled at Sarah. "That was the best."

Sarah bit a nail, hesitated, then clasped her hands together on the table. "Well, the opposites I know—me and my ex—had no chance in hell of ever making it together." She released her hands and took a drink of her coffee. "You were lucky."

"Maybe." Amelia paused. "The thing is, I'm so sad at them being gone that sometimes I feel like I forget all the really good things we had in our lives together. Do you think that loving people so much makes it even harder when they go?" She looked up at Sarah, worried the comment might jab at her, or glorify her own past at Sarah's expense. "Afterward, I mean. Maybe if you don't love people so much in life you won't hurt as much when they are gone?" She looked away from Sarah, down at her coffee, and then back at Sarah. "I'm sorry. I don't mean it like it sounds."

Sarah nodded. But Amelia wasn't so sure she understood, or agreed.

ANOTHER WEEK, SOON after, they vetoed their usual coffee, and, instead met to walk through Forest Park. It was a beautiful dry Sunday morning, and Amelia felt lucky to find a parking spot; the park filled with walkers and runners and families stealing time together. As usual, she waited for Sarah, this time on a bench near the parking lot. It didn't bother her anymore that Sarah was always late. Instead, recently, she forced herself to avoid her phone and email, close her eyes, and inhale deeply. She knew she should meditate, but it was still hard to keep thoughts from infiltrating the space.

She closed her eyes and inhaled deeply to try to identify the fragrance of blossoms just now launching into bloom. The aromas reminded her of her mama—how much she loved to put out pansies and dianthus in her flower boxes, even before the yellow triangular shaped daffodil petals unfolded in the yard. When Amelia still lived at home, Ernest always teased her mama: if she'd wait a bit longer she wouldn't have to worry about the slugs eating them. But not Sharon—she planted too early every year, usually having to replant anew to replace the ones ravaged by slugs, leaving petal-less stems and slime.

"Hey, Amelia."

Amelia opened her eyes and spotted Sarah walking toward her.

"Oh, hey. Sorry. Have you been here long?" Amelia asked.

"Oh, I just got here. I was lost at first. I got confused on the one-way streets. Well, and it's busy. Parking, you know. Anyway, sorry." Sarah combed her hand through her hair.

Amelia stood up and gave her a quick hug. "It's fine. I was just relaxing. I think the sun is trying to pop out. It was reminding me of Mama."

They started walking.

"I've been here a few times. We can head this way," Amelia said.

They talked for a few minutes about the week and their respective jobs.

"Well. Tell me more," Sarah said. "I mean about Sharon. I mean, your mom."

As they walked, maple and Douglas fir trees on either side, ferns still glistening with morning dew, Amelia told Sarah how desperate Sharon was to have a baby, taking more than three years to get pregnant, followed by a miscarriage and two more years until she carried Amelia. "I guess after working so hard at it, Mama felt like it was her one chance to try to create perfection. A perfect pregnancy. A perfect childhood with a perfect girl—me—who would grow up to be a perfect woman!" Amelia looked at Sarah and put her hands on her hips. "Not a great recipe for a perfect mother-daughter bond, though." She dropped her hands and continued walking.

They walked a bit further in silence.

"Wow, Amelia," Sarah said. "I just assumed you had an easier time with your mom. Well, certainly than I had with Gloria. I'm sorry. I mean, not to get it before."

"It's taken me forever to come to terms with how I always felt she controlled my life," Amelia replied. "Well, to be honest. I'm still not sure I'm there. She needed so badly for everything about me to be perfect. I never forgave her. I don't think I fully understood it when she died. And it makes me angry at myself because she's dead. I mean when will I ever let go of that, I wonder?"

"Oh, Amelia." Sarah placed her hand on Amelia's shoulder as they walked along.

Amelia sensed that Sarah wanted to offer something more, but instead stepped behind her.

"I realized, eventually. I mean, it took me forever but all Mama ever wanted was for me to be the powerful woman in the world that she, although she tried, never felt she could fully become. But we never talked about it while she was alive." Amelia hesitated. "And I've never talked to anyone else about it."

"Really?" Sarah asked, surprised. "Not even Phillip? You too seem closer than any couple I know."

Amelia stopped walking and gazed into the tops of the trees below them. Then she looked back at Sarah. "I don't want to burden our relationship with this. I don't know why I can't mention it, when he is so good to me and we talk about almost everything else. I think I just avoid that part of the equation." She sighed. "I'm embarrassed and angry with myself I guess . . ."

Amelia watched Sarah move closer to her again, imagining she might hug her. She felt Sarah's desire to want to help, and knew she must be disappointed Amelia was keeping her distance, but she was afraid she would break down and cry if she allowed Sarah to touch her. Instead, she kept moving her feet on the path. She didn't want to cry. *She must not cry.* They walked in silence. One massive Douglas fir towered above them, and the ground crunched beneath their tennis shoes. Occasionally a sweaty runner passed them, and the croaking of frogs in the nearby wetlands were masked momentarily by heavy breathing.

"It's just . . ." Amelia began. "I just wish I realized all this before she died. You know."

As they continued to walk, Amelia shared more about her childhood and growing up. She told Sarah how, although she was never shy and had to fight some of her battles, her mother had always been there for her—maybe too much. Eventually, as she got older, Amelia hid things from her mama, although it wasn't easy given how over-involved Sharon was in her life.

Amelia related about a time as a fourth grader when she heard two girls talking about her in the school bathroom. "Don't say anything bad about Amelia. Her mom will come after you just like she did Eric." And then the two girls giggled and whispered something Amelia couldn't hear. She remembered hoping they wouldn't recognize her feet hanging down behind the stall door. She had been stunned and embarrassed.

She had no idea, although she knew her mama visited school often, and wouldn't let her ride the bus home like the other kids.

Sarah interjected with a quiet laugh. "Amelia, your mom must have loved you so much." She hesitated. "What a character."

Amelia looked at Sarah and, still teary, laughed. "You know, I've always been so angry about it, I seem to forget that part."

Amelia continued to relay how, although Sharon worked a full-time night shift for so many of those years, she was usually around to help get Amelia to school and pick her up after. Sharon was always so nice to the few friends Amelia had that came to her house: girls who gave Amelia a chance, who thought she was smart and fun to play with. After the time she had told her mama about Eric's teasing, she believed the boy just got bored and stopped. She would never have imagined, back then, that her mama would have gotten involved.

"Pretty much, after overhearing the talk in the bathroom . . . well . . . I stopped telling Mama a lot of things," Amelia said. "I was just so embarrassed—if you listened to her you'd think she thought I was a genius."

Once, when she was in kindergarten, Amelia thought she might have a little brother or sister. At least, that's what her mama said. But not long after, Sharon picked her up after school, her eyes red, face swollen.

"What's wrong, Mama?" Amelia had asked as she climbed into the Ford sedan.

Sharon pulled the car over to the curb. "Your daddy and I are gonna just have one girl—and that's you. And you will always be the world for us."

"But, Mama. What about baby?" Amelia couldn't understand: she had already named the baby. Baby Davy.

"The baby decided our family wasn't right for him," Sharon said, looking Amelia in the eye. And then she gave her a hug. "But you are our child, and we are very lucky, and you are all we need." She sat back up, rubbed her eyes, and signaled to pull the car back into traffic and home.

Later, as Amelia made her way through high school, it became more unbearable. "You know," she told Sarah, "it's strange, but it all would have gone better if she hadn't always made such a big deal about my straight A's. Dad would always remind me how B's are really good and he only got C's and B's in all of high school, and Mama would quickly remind him that would never happen to me." She glanced at Sarah.

Sarah rolled her eyes. "Remind me never to ever tell you about the star pupil I was. Hell, it's good your mom never knew me. Sorry, but my school life was totally different."

Amelia let out a half-hearted laugh, but continued telling Sarah about when the time came to apply for colleges, Sharon was almost unbearable. Amelia secretly asked her dad to come to the high school presentation about applying for college.

"Honey, I don't know anything about this," he had said. "Your mama will be a much bigger help."

"No, Dad. I think it'd be fun just for you and me," Amelia said.

Amelia told Sarah about how she tried to play to her dad's sense of fatherly love, not sharing the truth of the matter. And after, when they returned home after college night, and Sharon, having worked late, sat and waited for them with a late dinner in the oven, Amelia knew she might not be forgiven.

Her mama cried. "Amelia. I have been waiting so many years to help you decide what happens next."

"Oh, I'm sorry, Mama. I didn't want to bother you," Amelia lied.

Her mama was the first to point out the good private colleges nearby. But then, at almost eighteen, Amelia tested her courage and stood her own ground, receiving an almost full scholarship to an east coast school. Even then, she noticed how her mama couldn't seem to balance her satisfaction for what she had achieved with her disappointment in being left out of the process, only to realize too late that her only daughter would be thousands of miles away.

In those later years, Amelia learned by phone about the time her mama now spent with girl-friends, laughing and talking for hours. Amelia's dad let her know he was sure it was fun for his wife to have friends who better appreciated her loud spinning of stories than he. They never travelled much and worked long shifts.

"But they sure loved each other and were happy with their evenings together no matter what they were doing," Amelia said. "My dad adored Mama and stayed by her side to the end. He seemed to know how he could never keep up with her when she got revved up, just like my grandfather Jackson. I know her jokes and storytelling were one of the things Dad loved most about her."

Amelia explained how close she and her dad were. "Even though we were a lot alike, Mama never put the same kind of pressure on him that she did on me. He told me after Mama died that all she really wanted was for me to get what I deserved and somehow she felt it her sole job to see that I did."

Sarah stopped to tie her shoe, and Amelia hesitated. *How can I keep spilling it out?* She took a deep breath and, feeling that Sarah was still listening, plunged further in, about how her dad knew but she didn't think her mama ever did, why she accepted her first job after college in Chicago, far away from home. She had told her mama then it was important she live in a big city so to learn more, learn faster: that she would never move up if she didn't learn from the best. Amelia knew this line she fed her mother sounded sensible, and it would strike Sharon in a way that fully explained her choice. Yet Amelia hadn't predicted how disappointed her mother would be when Amelia explained the job offer by phone just before graduation. It was long after Sharon died that Amelia learned how much Sharon had cried the night she learned Amelia had accepted the Chicago job.

And for the next ten years, other than her two weeks of vacation spent in Portland, Amelia communicated with her parents by phone, and in the end, email. Although Amelia always received letters in the mail, signed simply, "Love, Dad."

"Letter writing really worked for my dad," she said. "You might not have expected it, knowing his life in the trades, but it gave him the time he needed to process his thoughts. Not like my mama who could let you know just about anything anytime!" She laughed and looked at Sarah. "My mama was so funny. You would have loved her humor."

Amelia had risen up to an account manager position, supervising others, traveling for business throughout the United States to other company offices in New York and Dallas, and even once to London. She began to send her parents expensive gifts—like a fancy coffee maker or Persian throw rug, things they didn't need in their unsophisticated house and lifestyle. Amelia imagined her mama telling all her girl-friends about the luxurious and successful world her daughter was part of.

"Later my dad told me about how he had asked Mama why she never told me how much she wished I would move back to Oregon. It is still hard for me to realize how long I went not knowing how fake she was to me on the phone, all those years." Amelia turned to Sarah. "That she felt like after all those years of telling me to be the best I could be that she felt it would be hypocritical to tell me the truth. That my own mama couldn't tell me, couldn't admit to me, that she really just wanted me close."

"Oh Amelia," Sarah said simply.

"You, know, Sarah. I guess I just don't know if it is her or me that I can't forgive."

AMELIA FELT BREATHLESS, rambling on so, slowing her stride as she breathed in deeply. They walked for a while in silence. Amelia was exhausted by this sharing of so many details she had later learned from her dad, and she glanced at Sarah's face. She wondered if she was boring her. Sarah caught her eye, but didn't say anything. The next part of this story, Amelia knew, was even more difficult to tell. A part of the story she had shared with Phillip, but with nobody else. She wasn't sure she was ready to share it with Sarah. It was so hard.

They neared Balch Creek, the rippling water creating gurgles and splashes as water passed under a bridge and bubbled over rocks.

"Let's sit?" Sarah nodded to a bench next to the creek.

Amelia put her hand on the bench, noting it was dry, and they sat down. The rushing creek and scattered bird calls filled the air.

"So. Then it got even harder," Amelia said.

Amelia closed her eyes and began to tell Sarah about the phone call that precipitated her life tumbling down and falling apart.

"Hello? Mom?" Amelia had said one afternoon as her office phone rang, caller identification flashing.

"Hi, Amelia. No, it's Dad."

"What's wrong with Mom?"

Her father never initiated phone calls to her. He might get on the line, but only after Sharon told him he could.

"Honey, I just wanted to talk to you about something. Your mama doesn't know I'm calling."

"What is it? You've got me worried. And how did you know my work number anyway?"

As frightening as the moment had been, even now Amelia remembered how she had imagined Ernest smiling to himself. "I'm a bit more capable than you may think." But then his tone became serious again. "Your mother would be angry if she knew I was calling you. She's at work, of course."

"Well, what is it?" Amelia asked impatiently. "It's just unusual to hear from you during the week, or on the phone." She was usually the one to initiate a call at their prescribed time.

"Well," he began. "It's so hard to do this on the phone. Your mama had a test this week. And the news isn't so good."

Amelia tried hard to maintain a calm voice. "What test?"

"Well she'd found a lump." Ernest began. Silent embarrassment seeped through the phone line. "You know."

"You mean on her breast?" Amelia said, feeling a stab of nausea. She knew these weren't things her dad would ever feel comfortable talking to anyone about, especially his daughter.

"Yes," Ernest said simply.

"What do you mean?" Amelia asked. "What does it mean?"

"Well, we don't know for certain. And we won't for a few days." More silence. "Your mama didn't want me to call yet. She didn't want to worry you. It might not be anything, she said. And you know, your mama is tough."

"But what do the doctors say?" Amelia asked.

"I don't know much more," he said. "You know your mama. She used some big medical words. But I think we just don't know yet. She didn't want you to know yet. But I was thinking . . ."

"What, Daddy?"

"Well, I was thinking. I know you are really busy. You have such important work, and all. But I wondered if maybe you could come home for a visit? Maybe just for a bit. Maybe to be with her just for a bit."

Amelia remembered, now in telling Sarah, how she had opened up her calendar on her computer and looked at the week ahead of her, fully blocked with appointments and meetings. She had closed her eyes and imagined Mama. Her tough mama, sitting in an ugly rough worn hospital gown on a cold examination table. Just like all the same cold tables she administered her wicked jokes and efficient care to so many others, all those years. "Of course, Dad. I have a lot of meetings and things this week, though."

"I know, dear," Ernest said. "I understand. Maybe it's too much. I just . . . I just."

Amelia remembered how she had imagined her dad forcing himself not to cry. She had felt herself becoming undone. "No, Dad. I will be there. I'm just not sure when. I'll let you know."

Her dad let out a stifled sigh of relief.

"But don't tell Mama, okay? I'm not sure when I will be there."

"Yes, dear," he said. "In fact, don't you tell her I called. It'll be our little secret."

And now, in sharing this memory with Sarah, Amelia smiled. She quickly wiped the tears from her cheeks and told Sarah about her dad's fondness for "their little secrets." Usually, the most trivial. Like when he took her out for ice cream before dinner. Or the time she received a "C" on a Geometry mid-term that only her dad knew about. Of course, she got her grade back to an A by the end of the term. But never, she added, had they had a secret quite like this new one.

After several minutes of silence, Amelia said, "Maybe we should start back to our cars." She shivered and stretched her arms back into the sleeves of her sweatshirt. A group of kids came shrieking down the trail and one of them stopped only after her right foot sloshed into the creek.

"Sure," Sarah said.

THEY HIKED BACK up the hillside, a forested paradise on this morning—Oregon grape and salal edging near the dirt trail, and so many fir trees still smothered by English ivy.

"So, Amelia," Sarah began. "It must have been a relief when you moved back here? I mean after your mom was diagnosed and stuff." She wondered how much more Amelia would be up to sharing.

"Are you kidding?" Amelia stopped walking and gave Sarah a shocked look. She laughed. "You didn't know my mama. Good lord. Even Cancer, the Big C, couldn't make Mama give up being in charge."

They resumed walking. "Mama was so angry with my dad at first, when I showed up. She put on her stage act, emoting wildly with, 'Wow, look at this. Amelia just decided, out of the blue to visit us.' And then my dad was, 'Sharon. No. Come on. You're not being fair.' And then you should have seen the look she gave him. Wow. I'm not sure I ever saw her look at him like that before. I was really hurt at first, because I felt like I'd made this big sacrifice to get a whole week off work." She took a deep breath. "I'm sure I was being a martyr."

Sarah realized how much more complicated Amelia's relationship with her mom had been. It made her think maybe her own crap with Gloria was peanuts.

"There were so many calls and emails," Amelia continued. "And arrangements to make. But now, I guess I just wanted Mama to give me a little credit. To try. For her to be a little vulnerable for once. And I couldn't stand being mad at her. We didn't even know yet it was cancer, but still. So, in answer to your question, no, it wasn't great."

They rounded the final curve as the trail led back to the parking lot.

"And once Mama learned that things weren't looking so good I think she just made the decision she would do what she had to do to keep being the boss. She had been around so many cancer patients who kept fighting, no matter what. And my mama—she was a good caregiver, 'Nurse Sharon,' they called her, using her witty humor to keep them laughing."

Sarah had thought earlier Amelia might cry, but now she sounded resentful.

"Her patients so loved her," Amelia continued. "And, well, I didn't even know that. Not until after. That's the thing that still haunts me. There was so much I didn't know about my mama."

They stepped onto the parking lot, as if perfectly timed to the end of the story. Sarah looked at Amelia, and although she worried how upset she might be after reenacting this difficult time in her life, Amelia looked calm. They were back at the bench where Amelia had originally been waiting for Sarah, and Amelia took off her sweatshirt and set it on the bench. She stretched her arms to the sky before gathering the sweatshirt in her arms.

Sarah so badly wanted to fold Amelia into her arms. "I'm sorry. I didn't mean for this morning to be like this." Only then did she realize how long she had ignored her own cell phone, fully losing track of time: not once thinking about Gloria and the myriad of issues that may have arisen during her excursion. She looked at Amelia for some sense of how she was feeling.

"It's okay." Amelia dabbed at her eyes and then slid her hands across her face. She shook her head, causing her hair to flow across her face, and pushed the stray strands out of her eyes. "I'm good. You know, it's hard . . . It feels right to share it. I should be apologizing to you. Or . . . maybe thanking you. I mean, really." She pulled her keys from her sweatshirt pocket. "Thanks, Sarah. Truly, I mean it." She gave Sarah a long hug.

"Let's come up with a time next week, okay? I'll text you. I hope Gloria is okay," Amelia said.

Sarah nodded and pulled her own keys out of her coat pocket. Her heart pounded and her armpits felt wet. She was dizzy, and stood still for a minute, not remembering at first where she had parked her car: she was filled with mixed emotions. Finally, she spotted her car and looked back at Amelia, who was now backing out of the lot, and gave a quick wave.

Sarah walked to her car, unlocked the door, and sat inside. She felt such loss in parting with Amelia, and feeling like she should have said more. It had been years, perhaps decades, since she had the girlfriends of college days. But even then, the last thing they'd talk about was family, or anything particularly meaningful. Never like this.

After a few minutes of staring straight ahead, wondering what it all meant, she pulled out her cell. Three missed calls.

"Fuck," she muttered.

Chapter 14

The salty air
September 2016

NOW THAT ANNIE was seventeen, she had traveled by Greyhound more than a handful of times. On this early fall weekend morning, she reveled in her solo adventure. *She could be traveling anywhere in the world.* She had almost three hours—a hundred and fifty minutes, she told herself—alone, to look out the window, contemplate, or write. These days, she wished she had more free time to write her own thoughts, not the staid, mind-numbing essays that stilled her creative juices, yet were required for term papers and college applications. The bus minutes, punctuated with bumps and sharp turns, also prepared her for the visit she knew could still be uncomfortable. It was clear to her how she needed to make the trip, even though her mom disagreed, saying it wasn't worth her time. Resolving her relationship with her dad was the one confidential detail she had once shared with Mr. Anderson, and although he was careful not to give advice, she could tell he supported her to take it on, even if her mom told her to give it up.

"You know, Annie," he had said during an appointment the previous spring, "there are some things you can't do-over in life."

She had wondered then how much this teacher knew about her life, her family. Mr. Anderson was one of those teachers lots of kids liked, but just as many talked teasingly about behind his back.

"I bet down the road, maybe when you are as old as me," He gave her a goofy look, stooped down, and shook his hands as if he was really old, and covered his teeth with his gums, "that you'll be glad."

Annie *liked* how he sometimes seemed like such a dip, and then laughed at himself. He wasn't like some of the other teachers who hugged their power as if it was a cloak they only removed on special, personal occasions. They didn't talk about this topic again, but when her dad invited her the first time for a weekend soon after, Mr. Anderson's comments influenced her decision to visit.

Now, as she sat on the worn, upholstered bus seat, empty seats next to her and across the aisle, she stared out the window as they pulled away from Portland's bus station, away from the high-rise buildings and fancy bars and coffee shops. A chilly rain drizzled down, creating blurry blobs outside her fogged-up window. She hoped a peek of blue sky would bubble into the horizon by the time she arrived at her destination. Her mind drifted back to earlier years when her dad was a regular part of her life. When he was part of all their lives. As she allowed herself to reminisce, she acknowledged the valuable writing minutes she was losing, but she couldn't seem to draw herself out of the memories from that one day, now more than five years before.

"You know, Annie, life isn't gonna give you anything if you don't go looking for it," her dad, Frank, had said to her that day. "In fact, you damn well better prepare for the worst. Mr. Nice Guy never gets anywhere." He had shot Annie a sad, surrendered look. "Trust me on that."

Even now, sitting firmly on the cushioned bus seat, Annie remembered her dad holding a beer can, still staring at her: she had hoped then he would turn his attention back to the TV instead of talking to her. The more beer he drank, the more obnoxious his ranting became.

"Really, Annie. Trust me on this," he repeated, louder.

Annie nodded back at him, ever so slightly, but her expression stayed the same. She had heard him say this so many times she had memorized the lines. She knew the story. Her grandfather, Grampa Joe, who had died when she was a baby, had been a teacher, and, according to her dad, too nice of a guy. He spent most of the money he earned, trying to dig people out of their problems and was soon spotted as the guy to turn to for help. As Annie grew older, she sometimes wondered how much of this story was true, for whenever her dad began to share it, her mom would say, "Oh Jesus, Frank. Give it up." And then her mom always left the room. Every time. But her dad would continue to drone on about how he swore he would never do that. Then he'd add that, in fact, life owed him something to enjoy a better one.

Even at twelve, Annie had known how hard it was for her dad to hold down a job. He spent an awful lot of time talking about how *he* was going to make it big. She believed him for such a long time, even when she wrote the note in the bottle. Sometimes she wished she had kept track, back when she was little, of all the different "big deals" he talked about, never following through with any of them.

"Just you wait, my Annie," he would say back in those days. "One of these days, your mom and the whole world is gonna look at me. They'll say, 'Damn, we should have believed in you, Frank.' They'll all be begging me to forgive them for this or that." Her dad laughed. "And you know what? Maybe I will. Maybe I will." He might look out to the distance. "Wouldn't that be something?"

Annie had known, even then, that he didn't expect her to reply to his exclamations; he mostly seemed to like to hear himself talk.

"You mark my words, my Annie," he'd add. And then he'd turn back to his beer or television, or once in a while, the stack of crumpled papers he kept in an old brown file folder, wrapped with an overstretched thick rubber band.

Back then, when they all still lived in the house by the river, Frank moved stiffly, especially after work, even though he was only forty-five back then. He was like an old man to her, moving like the old guys she noticed in the supermarket. Her mom worried out loud as to whether he would keep bringing in a pay check, whether he could keep his warehouse job. All day long he moved big heavy boxes and pieces of equipment, sometimes using a fork lift, but not always. He popped pills. "His medicine," he called them, claiming they were his "health pills" as they always made him feel better. And whenever the topic of this medication arose, Annie's parents would argue. And her dad would yell.

"If you damn well want me to keep paying for all the crap you and these kids need, you better leave me alone!" He'd shout, adding how the pills were the only thing that made him feel better. Sometimes when they'd argue he'd add it wasn't his fault he was "screwed out of" the insurance money he deserved from getting hurt at work. And then he'd repeat how the pills were the only thing that really were a *good* thing. If her dad happened to notice Annie listening, he would add, "besides you, Annie, my love." Back when Annie was little, that special comment made her feel better, but the older she got, it only irritated her.

It wasn't long after that particular discussion when she was alone at the house with a day off school, a teacher's workday. Her dad was at work and, since her mom had started picking up odd cleaning jobs here and there, she was out of the house as well. Annie couldn't recall why her older brother and sister were away, but she did remember how she knew it was a perfect time to snoop. Usually her dad kept his brown folder with the rubber band cinched tightly around it close by him, even taking it in the car as he headed off to work. But on this day, the folder sat tucked near the TV in the living room. Annie cautiously crept over, pulled it out, and opened the flap quietly as if someone was around who might notice. She took it over to the heater vent down on the floor: her favorite place to curl up against the wall, a pillow behind her back, to read. For just a moment she closed her eyes as the warm air deliciously floated up inside her sweatshirt, warming her back and stomach.

She opened her eyes and looked through the packet to learn what it was her father immersed himself in: a story about $10,000 buried in a coffee can near something called the Astoria Column. She carefully unfolded copies of old articles printed from the internet. The origination of the papers surprised her because she didn't think her dad even knew how to use a computer, or had access to a printer. She had begged her parents to buy a computer. "Everybody has one!" she would say. "How am I supposed to do my homework?" Her mom would remind her about the computers at school. "And by the way, isn't that what libraries are for?" Sometime later her mom would soften and add, maybe, when Annie reached high school they might be able to figure it out. The folder's contents shocked her, and she wondered if just maybe her dad was onto something.

Back on that day, Annie looked through the dog-eared and tattered articles, some more worn than others. There were so many pages. Not all of them were about the Astoria treasure, but all were about hidden gold or money. After looking through the worn sheets, she tried to remember how they had been arranged, put them back into the folder as she found them, and hoped her dad wouldn't remember their exact order. Although she was confused about what it all meant, she was also relieved. And the hopeful part of her filled with a slice of excitement: what if there was something to this? She was relieved it wasn't something worse. Her dad always carried the file around, protecting it as if it was so private. Sometimes she wondered if it was pictures of naked women like what her brother had told her. And that had creeped her out.

Later that night after dinner, her dad finally got home. Annie was on high alert: paying extra attention to him and what he was doing. She watched as he quickly examined the room, immediately grabbing the file, letting out a sigh of relief. She caught his eye: something she was doing less often. Up until the previous year or two she and her dad still had fun together, joking around a lot. Now, at twelve, she knew how some kids at school had dads who were mean: they yelled at them or threatened to hit them. She hadn't worried about that happening with her dad. But she didn't like how sad he was all the time and how much he complained. She just couldn't listen to him anymore. Sometimes she actually felt bad for him when her mom yelled or swore at him, and then stormed out of the room.

On the night after learning about his file, she watched her dad eat the food left on the extra plate as he stood up at the counter, with the file next to his plate. Most nights he said that sitting hurt his back more.

"How's my Annie?" he asked, as he caught her looking at him. It was her night to do the dishes and she busied herself putting the soup bowls into the dishwasher.

"I'm fine," she said simply. She felt curious about what she'd read, but she couldn't admit to him that she had been snooping. That, she knew, would infuriate him. She stole a look at him out of the corner of her eye as he pushed his plate across the counter toward the sink. Then grabbed the file that rarely left his direct control.

"Well that's good, my Annie." He went to the refrigerator and opened it.

Annie knew without looking that he was seeking his first can of Budweiser. Most nights he had two or three, except when her mom yelled at him. Then he might stop after the first.

She put his plate and the final bowl in the dishwasher, rinsed out the washrag, and did a quick wipe of the counter. She knew her mom might complain later that she didn't clean up very well, but tonight she didn't care. She watched her dad take the beer and head over to the easy chair against the far living room wall. He stumbled at first on the carpet before he got to his chair, and a bit of the beer dripped onto the worn, stained carpet. She was glad her mom wasn't here to yell at him and start another civil war.

Annie worked up her courage. She hung the washrag against the sink, dried her hands on her jeans, and cautiously went into the living room. She sat down in a chair near her dad, trying to act nonchalant. Her dad was absorbed in his reading but after a bit looked at her.

"What do you want?" he asked gruffly. True surprise showed on his face, making her feel guilty at how often she and her brother and sister kept their distance from him, or ignored him. Ignoring his pain, his complaints, his worries. And some nights, his drunkenness.

Annie took a breath. "What are you reading about?"

"Nothing you need to know about, little girl," he said, then laughed in a fake way, as if to tell her, "no big deal."

Annie continued to sit motionless, willing herself to exude a no caring expression.

Then, her dad's expression changed. As if he suddenly wanted to talk. "Well Annie." He looked around the room, as if to make sure nobody else was present, and leaned closer to her. "Yes." He looked at her intensely, and his eyes shone strangely. "Oh, yes, my Annie. You will understand. My smart girl." He looked through her now, as if he was thinking about something in the distance. "I just know it's there."

Annie looked at him, at first, as if he was a crazy man. "What?"

"This is my time. Finally," he almost yelled. He sat back, picked the beer can off the table next to him, and took a long swig. He set the beer down and looked outside with a long sigh. He looked toward the doorway, as if he was afraid he might be heard. "So much has been unfair. But now. It'll be worth it? I'll show them." Redness seeped into his cheeks. He burped, and Annie smelled the gross aroma of beer mixed with potato soup.

"What, Dad?" Annie asked, not trying to provoke him, but doing it anyway.

Her dad gazed at her with crazed eyes, like pain and excitement all mixed up together. "Every time I just about catch up, shit just gets thrown my way. But I keep pulling up and looking. Knowing there is something there for me." He took another big drink of his beer and set it down on the coffee table. "And now, my Annie. This one. I just know. This one is it." He sat back, took a breath, and smiled broadly at her. "It's our little secret. You have to promise not to tell anyone."

Annie stared at him. She had not often seen her dad this excited, at least not in a long time. It worried her that her mom didn't know anything about this secret. She began to feel responsible—maybe it was all a fantasy? He'd had others along the way; supposed opportunities that none of them had learned about until after the bubble had burst. Her mom said if he spent as much time as he did dreaming about the big deal, just working hard on his real paid job, they'd have enough money to do what they wanted by now. To that, Frank would shake his head, call her "ungrateful" and leave the room. But now, Annie was curious. *What was he so excited about?* Her heart beat faster. *Maybe there really might be something to this. Finally?*

"I even have the librarian down in town looking at this for me," he said. "She thinks I've really got something going."

Annie didn't say anything, although she worried that now even the local librarian would think her dad was a weirdo. Maybe she even joked about him with her husband or friends, other people in the community, or with kids at her school. His story did explain the computer print-outs. She hoped the librarian didn't know it was her dad.

"Just think what Monica will say when she learns. Oh, she'll be sorry, let me tell you," he said, as if talking to himself. "Twenty thousand dollars isn't the hugest jackpot, but boy will it prove to her I wasn't crazy. It'll buy us a couple of years before paying back those loans. Who knows, it could even be way more."

Annie wondered if maybe this wasn't his first beer. It seemed like he wasn't really even talking to her anymore. And again, for a moment she allowed herself to imagine that maybe, just maybe, there was truth in this. Maybe something good really could happen for her dad. "Shh. Remember. No sharing. "Promise?" He didn't wait for an answer. "That guy I saw at the library was supposed to be some big history bigwig. Ha! He didn't know what the hell he was talking about. I just feel it in my bones. What a joke he was." He looked Annie in the eye. "But you know. Well, yessiree. I think after a while, he realized there really is something there. And you know what? He realized I was going to get to it first so he just told me it was nonsense. Yes, I'm sure of it." He drained his beer.

Annie had heard enough that night. She needed to be alone, in silence, to think through it all, never before seeing her dad so wound up on something that wasn't either a complaint about work, her mom, or the pains in his body.

"I've got to go do my homework," she said.

"But don't you want to know more? "There's so much to tell." He looked around and dropped his voice. "I can trust you, Annie. And I can use you too. You are so smart."

"Okay, Dad," Annie said. "I mean, maybe later. I've got to do my homework." She stood up and the soup and bread turned uneven somersaults in her stomach. She saw the hurt on his face. "Thanks though."

"Okay, whatever." Her dad opened his file. "There are probably treasures buried all over this damn state. You just have to be the one to stick with it," she heard him mutter as she walked out of the room.

Annie went to the bedroom she shared with her sister, wishing she had a way to get on the internet. She'd search for it during recess the next day and tried to put it out of her mind. Until then.

A BABY CRIED in the back of the bus. She turned around and leaned into the aisle to see the chubby red-cheeked toddler, face stained with slobber and crumbs. She smiled at the woman holding the baby to let her know she didn't find the cries annoying. She sat back squarely on the seat and looked out the window—the bus weaved along the windy road climbing the coastal mountain pass, tall firs bookending both sides of the pavement. She scanned the bus occupants, only ten or so besides the driver, all heading to Astoria, or some area nearby. She checked her phone to confirm she had another hour before arriving, so she unzipped her backpack and pulled out a spiral notebook. After zipping it up, she unzipped it again to pull out a granola bar. She stuck the backpack on the vacant seat next to her, removed her pen from inside the spiral binding of the notebook, and looked outside again.

"Now," she thought, as she cozied herself more comfortably into the seat and pulled her feet up to sit cross-legged. She opened her notebook and began writing.

The braking of the bus caused her to look up an hour later: sixty minutes that flew by as if mere minutes. She stuck her notebook and things back in the backpack and jammed the unopened granola bar into her pocket. She pulled her cell phone out of her backpack and stuck it in her jacket pocket too. She had now been to Astoria several times, including that very first time on a school field trip to visit Fort Clatsop and learn about Lewis and Clark, staying on the hard gym floor of a neighboring elementary school. Now she recognized the long green bridge she knew crossed the mouth of the Columbia River, but looking as if it dissolved into moisture laden clouds. She hoped maybe she could cross it someday.

Annie took a deep breath and inhaled the fishy saltiness of the coast. Her heart beat more rapidly. Even though she was nervous, she was also excited to have two days to explore this town, certain she would have some time alone. Time to wonder along the Riverwalk shouting hints from long ago, days of steamboats, ferries, Chinese laundries, and capsized fishing boats. She grabbed her backpack as she readied herself to be among the first to get off the bus as it pulled up to the small building, hardly much of a station like the one in Portland. Probably safer, too.

"Dad, I'm here. Okay?" she said into her phone as the driver set his brake and opened the front door. She replaced the phone in her coat pocket, stepped off the bus, and looked around, then went toward an older couple waiting by the curb. She hoped her dad would be on time, this time, as she opened her lungs deeply to fill with coastal air, its dampness seeping through her pores, invading her cells.

Even though she complained about her dad's move to Astoria two years ago, she liked this town. Her mom referred to it as backward. Annie remembered the first time she came to visit her dad—recklessly imagining finishing her last year of high school at Astoria High. It didn't take her long, though, to realize such a decision would devastate her mom, and she would have gone crazy living with her dad for such a long stretch. Now she could admit to herself that her dad probably would never have agreed to that arrangement in the end.

"Hey, girl. Over here." Frank had pulled his car next to the curb and was yelling through the open passenger window.

Annie put both arms into the straps of her backpack and walked over to the beat-up Toyota. As she opened the back door and heaved in her backpack, she ran her finger over a dent on the side of the car. She slammed the back door and climbed into the passenger seat.

"Hi, my Annie," her dad greeted her with a smile, hands still on the steering wheel.

"Hi, Dad."

"You hungry? I don't have much in the fridge," he said.

"No, I'm okay. Mom made me a lunch for the bus, and I didn't eat it yet. I'm just kind of sleepy." She noticed how her dad was growing a beard again. Or maybe he hadn't gotten around to shaving. Its black uneven stubble made him look like he needed to wash his face. *Ugh.* "And Mom said to make sure you get me to the station for the twelve-thirty bus on Sunday. She doesn't want to have to go to the station late at night. Again." She looked at her dad. "Please."

"Yeah, yeah. I will." He gazed at her with the look he always gave when Annie mentioned her mom. Then he forced a smile. "Glad you could come. Do you have much school work?"

"Not much, just some essays for my English class. And some college application essays." She hesitated telling him about those, but he didn't say anything.

Silence closed in on them as the car jerked between the few stop lights in downtown Astoria, something rattling underneath its body. The car's heat warmed her cold toes and fingers. She hadn't realized how chilled her body was from sitting on the bus.

"Hang on a minute," he said as he pulled into a 7-11. "Sure you don't want anything? We can go out to the café for breakfast if you want."

"No, I'm fine."

Frank slammed the door, and she saw him pull a package of Camel cigarettes out of his pocket. He took a few steps, stopped, and then pulled out a cigarette. He looked up to the sky as he lit it, taking a couple of long drags as he took his time getting to the door of the store. He took a few steps, stopped again, took another drag as he looked out to the bit of the Columbia River visible from the parking lot. He snuffed out the cigarette, waited a minute for it to cool, and tucked it into his coat pocket.

"Oh gross," Annie said. *Whatever.* He seemed to be smoking so much more the last time she had seen him.

Her dad came back with a small bag, a six-pack of beer, she knew without looking. *Whatever.*

"So, tell me," he said, after he started the car and backed out of the lot. "What would you like to do tomorrow? I only have to work a few hours but not till later in the afternoon."

Annie knew what he wanted her to say, but instead she replied that she didn't really care.

He gave her a wistful look, as if he was about to say something, and looked back at the road.

Annie gazed out the window. She knew that he knew these days, different from before—that she thought his searching was ridiculous. She had taken some time those years ago to learn more about the history of the treasure, and back when she put her note in the bottle she got caught up in his excitement, studying the old Oregon stories about hidden gold and treasures. But now, she saw the stories for what they were. She tried to tell her dad it was all a wild goose chase, but he only got angry with her. When he chose to move to Astoria she even told him it was stupid, and he stopped talking to her for a while, but after a bit she simply accepted she couldn't change his mind. It was hard for her—she cared enough in an odd way for him and didn't want him to devote his life to this idiotic dream. But she realized no matter what she said, she couldn't steer him away from this grand, although delirious, stupor.

She knew he felt as if this could be their thing to do together, and even her first trip to Astoria he had driven her up to the Column; showing her the various places he imagined it to be buried. Last time he had talked about renting one of these metal detectors, and she felt strangely curious what had become of that idea, but knew better than to raise the topic. She couldn't help herself, though, and against her better judgement, asked him the usual question.

"Did you find anyone new to talk to about it? You know. The treasure?"

Her dad half smiled. "Funny you should ask." He looked at her with the broad smile of her early childhood memory. "Do you remember me telling you about my new friend Charlie?"

Annie wasn't sure if she remembered the guy and hoped it wasn't the drunk her dad talked to late at night at the corner bar.

"I'm not sure, Dad, maybe." She regretted asking the question.

"Well, as it just so happens, he talked to a guy a while back who was related to a man who once actually saw it. No lie."

Annie shook her head. It was impossible not to smile at him when he was animated like this, especially knowing he was sober, for the moment. He stole a look at her, out of the corner of his eye. She was pretty sure her dad knew his gig was up. He laughed anyway.

He pulled the car up to the apartment building. Annie opened the car door and hopped out, pulled her backpack over her shoulders, slammed the door, and again fingered the dent. She looked out at the Columbia River, picturing how her bottle could have followed this body of water to Asia, to Japan. And she followed her dad up the stairs.

Chapter 15

A truth
November 2016

SARAH SAT IN the breakroom, elevating her feet during a rare fifteen-minute respite. She knew she would be interrupted when the floor got busy, or when the new hire came to her with more questions. Sarah tried to be patient, but recently she wanted to shake the girl and ask, "Can't you for once, just fucking figure it out yourself?" She held a paper cup of coffee, even though she was trying to cut back. She encouraged herself to sip water, before often slipping back to her "just today" need for more caffeine. She should rejoice, though, on this Saturday—two free days ahead. Although, gone were the wide-open days of her youth as the increased time spent with Gloria allotted few excess minutes. These days, her weekend highlight was the time she got to spend with Amelia. Sometimes, it was almost the only thing that kept her going.

Something new was going on between her and Gloria, though she couldn't yet put her finger on what it was. Gloria—the mother whom she had always battled, from as far back as she could remember. Now, perched, feet up on a chair, a single memory from long ago, snapped into focus. Gloria's fortieth birthday. Sarah shook her head: impossible to believe how, Gloria, then, had been a few years younger than Sarah was now.

She was a fifteen year old who was perpetually disappointed with her mom, and had recently decided to call her "Gloria." Sarah had been angry and unforgiving at how her mom continued to put up with her demanding husband by passively accepting his angry comments, late nights, and other women that Sarah knew existed, even if Gloria pretended otherwise. Once, Sarah wondered if her dad finally hit her mom—she spotted a bruise on her face one day, poorly covered with makeup. She thought he had clobbered her as a threat to put up with his lousy self for the rest of her life. *Put up and shut up.* Sarah couldn't understand, then, why Gloria didn't simply kick him out of the house.

Now, Sarah pondered all of this—her own fiftieth birthday not that many candles away. Sitting on a couch stealing a few minutes away from a job she disliked, she finally admitted to herself: she saw it all differently. She recognized how her fifteen-year-old self could not have understood how difficult, almost impossible, it might have been to make that change then. How much courage it would have taken Gloria to leave her husband.

On that never-to-be forgotten birthday, Sarah returned home from school to find her mom wearing her sparkly dress, nylons, and heels. *Ugly*, Sarah had thought. As she entered her family's modest middle-class home through the kitchen door, picking up mail that had been dropped on the floor, she could only see her mom's back. Gloria sat at their kitchen nook, talking on the phone, looking out the window that faced into a vacant lot behind their house.

Damn, Sarah thought then. She had forgotten to get her mom a birthday card.

Her mom then carefully seated the phone receiver back on the hook, its dark green cord hanging down to the ground. A cord, back before cordless options, Sarah would pull taut to create distance from family members, as she struggled to find privacy in their chaotic household.

"Hi, Mom."

Gloria hesitated, and then turned to her, not looking her in the eye. Black mascara smeared deeply, creating dirty streaks marking her cheeks. The skin under her eyes was swollen and red.

"Hi, Sarah." Gloria stood suddenly and shook out her dress, as if attempting to shoo away disappointment. "I hope you had a good day." She walked through the other kitchen door to head up stairs, avoiding passing in front of Sarah. "I'm just going to take a quick shower. Plans changed," she called back to Sarah.

Sarah knew in her teenage heart how she should follow her mom upstairs, but instead, she froze. She knew her mom: Gloria would not break this barrier, always one to shield her kids from the evils of her world, and more recently, her own disappointments. Unsuccessfully, the older she got.

Rather than feel empathetic, she was infuriated by it all: how her mom never let her guard down, not even with her own daughter. Sarah had known she should feel sorry, but instead—the whole deal, even the disappointed birthday, made her angry. She couldn't help but blame Gloria for what life seemed to dish out to her. She knew she should be the one to try to make the night special for her mom, but she couldn't. She simply couldn't. *Besides, it wasn't her fault that Dad had messed things up. Again.*

Sarah had plans with her friends. Gloria would be okay, she convinced herself. *She probably didn't even want her daughter around.* Sarah remembered making a promise that she would never tolerate being treated that way by a man.

Her phone vibrated. She forced herself to ignore it, peering instead at her watch. It had already been fifteen minutes, although nobody had interrupted her. *To hell with it—just a few more.* She left her feet up. Her ugly black sensible shoes, the only pair she could now find to keep her ankles from swelling when she was on her feet all day, stared back at her.

Sarah closed her eyes, her thoughts returning to her senior year, two years after that infamous birthday. The day she began to call her dad, David. That day started out like any other. When Sarah left the house for school, Gloria, who worked for a friend as an office secretary, hadn't yet left for work. Later in the afternoon, Sarah returned home from school, carrying a backpack full of text books she would never crack over the weekend. Two full Hefty black plastic bags rested near the trash can outside the back door. Sarah opened the door to find her mom making dinner in the kitchen, an unusual act on a weekday. Gloria chose to be home in the morning as her way of making sure her kids went to school, but worked later. Sarah found ways to skip class anyway, walking on to a coffee shop or catching a bus to the mall.

Sarah cautiously greeted her mother while Gloria stood at the stove, testing the tenderness of cooked potatoes.

"What's up, Gloria?" Sarah asked. Although her mom had complained at first when Sarah called her by name, eventually she accepted it, muttering once it could be worse. Sarah hadn't been so sure.

Gloria pulled the fork out of the potato, set the cover back, and adjusted the stove dial. She turned to Sarah.

"Your dad is gone." Their eyes met. Gloria turned back to peer in the oven, releasing heat with smells of what Sarah knew to be, up until that instant, her most favorite meal, meatloaf. Catsup coated the loaf's top as the dark edges began to pull back from the pan.

Sarah starred at her mom, her head involuntarily shaking. "What?" She was stunned. Her shoulders quivered, and her body went cold. "What do you mean?" Although she had hoped her mom might leave her dad, she had never imagined that David would leave her mom. Leave them. All three of them.

Gloria continued to stare into the oven, until she stepped back to pull two stained canvas potholders out of a nearby drawer. Then she fully opened the oven, letting the door hang down from its hinge, and slid the hot tin of meatloaf out. The cooked catsup looked like dried blood and the aroma gave Sarah a sudden urge to vomit.

"I don't feel like talking about it," Gloria said, simply. "Do you want to shower before dinner? I made your favorite."

From then on, she referred to her parents as Gloria and David. Sarah saw David only once during high school, at her graduation. Two years later when Grandma Cooper died, most of the family sat together on the same row in the church. Sarah cried because Grandma Cooper was always kind to her. During the service Sarah searched her dad's face out of the corner of her eye, hoping desperately to see him shed tears. She wanted to believe, not only that he would show emotion in the death of his mother, but that perhaps, somewhere deep inside, he had some feeling for Sarah's mother. He sat dry-eyed on the wooden pew through the memorial.

Later, when the service was over, as friends shared condolences with family members, her dad sought her out, gave her a hug, and asked her how college was. Sarah remembered how stiffly she had stood as he put his arms around her shoulders. She remembered feeling removed from the moment, wondering what someone might think about them if they didn't know their history. Then, Sarah pulled away, looked him in the eye, and answered, "It didn't work out." She had badly wanted, at the time, to tell him more, but she didn't know where to begin. And before Sarah knew it, he had moved away to talk to her Uncle Bob. Later, as most people were making their move to leave and Sarah had retrieved her coat out of the church cloakroom, she watched her dad hug his new wife.

Sarah had other friends whose parents had divorced who worked hard at parenting together, even though they had split. Not David and Gloria. Gloria didn't mention David again, and he was never active in their lives. As Sarah got older she thought how weird it seemed: how could anyone have shared two kids, lived together more than fifteen years, and then just be gone? She knew at some point the two had to have talked together, later learning first-hand how divorce was not only expensive, but time-consuming. But even to present day as she slumped on the couch in the stale breakroom, she had never known any details about a settlement. Gloria's protective shield between her and her kids was like armor. Counterfeit protection, she thought.

"Hey, Sarah!" She reluctantly pulled her feet down from the chair and tried to get her body to rise, her lower back dissolving into its usual discomfort. She groaned and rubbed it with both hands.

"Yes?"

Amy, the new clerk came into the room.

"I'm coming," said Sarah, standing up.

"Oh good," Amy said. "Um, it's just that. I'm sorry. I just can't get the till to open again." She looked at Sarah, her voice breaking into sobs. "I keep trying but, I don't know. I don't want to mess anything up."

"It's alright," Sarah said. "Shit. Stop. It's not a big deal, really," she labored to add, kindly. "It's a dated system, trust me, and fucks up royally." *She had to stop swearing so much.*

Amy smiled at her, perhaps surprised by this old woman who so freely let loose the word *fuck*.

"Come on," Sarah said, as she joined Amy at the door and led her back to the floor. She took a quick look at her watch: two hours to go.

LATER THAT NIGHT, Sarah sat with Amelia, meeting in the evening in a bar instead of their usual daytime coffee date or walk. Sarah arrived before Amelia: another contradiction to routine.

"Wow, look at you!" Sarah said as Amelia plopped down in the booth opposite her.

Amelia wore a fitted jacket, slim trousers, and a starched, collared shirt, although it was Saturday and, unlike Sarah, she rarely went in to work on the weekend. Sarah tried not to be a wannabe about Amelia and her virtually perfect appearance: clothes, personality, looks, marriage, career. She was so confident.

Sarah had been slow to admit she had developed this crush, chastising herself. *She was a grown woman, after all.* She couldn't tell if it was intimacy she yearned for, or something else. A solution to her loneliness, friendship, or a formula to copy. Most weeks she counted the days until she knew she would see Amelia again, much like she had in her younger days with a newfound boyfriend.

"Spending Saturday at the office?" Sarah asked. She wondered why Amelia had suggested a Saturday night, unlike their usual Sunday morning. "Where's Phillip?"

Amelia pulled her jacket closer to her chest and shoulders, as if she had just sensed the chilly air of the restaurant. "Oh, he's back in New York again. It's almost spring line and busy. He begged me to join him this time—he doesn't do that often. But I've got so much on my plate at work right now, I figured it'd be a good time to catch up." She picked up the drink menu. "Besides. Well, I thought we could have a date." She smiled.

Amelia's smile sent shivers down Sarah. *How was she so lucky to meet this woman?*

The waitress stopped in front of them. "Are you eating too?" she asked holding out two menus.

Amelia looked at Sarah, and then back at the waitress. "Yes, but can I start with a glass of your red house?" She looked back at Sarah.

Sarah hesitated. "Whatever IPA you have on draft is fine." She hoped this wasn't a mistake. "Maybe just a glass." The waitress walked away. "What the fuck. Can you just make sure I don't have a second?"

"Uh, sure," Amelia said softly. She dropped eye contact to look at a couple passing their table, made a comment first about how cold it was outside, and then asked Sarah about her work day. A few minutes later, the work and weather chatter petered out, as it always did when they spent time together.

"So, continue," Amelia said, as she relaxed back into the booth. A smile spread across her face as she reached her arms out wide. "I love this."

"What?" Sarah said.

"Oh. I love learning about you. Talking . . . you know." She sighed. "Anyway, last week you were telling me about your dad. I mean, David."

"Oh, yeah, that," Sarah said. "Let's wait until the drinks come."

"Okay, I'll use the restroom," Amelia said. "Do you know where they are?"

Sarah pointed to the left. She tried not to stare as Amelia stood up, smoothed her slacks down, and walked away from the table.

Sarah sighed, rearranging her shirt and scarf. She struggled to uncover whether this feeling was the power of a heartfelt girlfriend—a relationship she had wanted forever, without knowing she desired it so—or if it might be more. She was mesmerized as she watched Amelia stand up, sit down, and move through her motions. She shifted in her chair in an effort to disrupt this new feeling, one she had begun to identify as the "reverie of Amelia." She didn't remember ever feeling this way toward another woman. She didn't think it was the same as an intimate lover—not like her distant friend Susan who dropped her long-term boyfriend for her former college roommate. It wasn't as if she wanted to get in bed with Amelia, although it was easy and rousing to imagine how such a pursuit would begin. She forced herself to think about Tony. Their sex. His handsomeness. She was lucky to have him, she told herself over and over: or was it only the echo of his words in her ear? For so long. Instead, all that came immediately to mind was the fight they'd had that morning. And a haunting fear only recently beginning to rise in her as she watched his face color with anger, reminding her of David all those years ago.

"Who the fuck is this woman?" Tony had asked her the night before, when Sarah mentioned she and Amelia were getting together again. "Is she some fucking dyke or what? Amelia this and Amelia that!" he said in a high, fake voice, as if to imitate a high-voiced woman. "You gonna tell me you're having sex with her? Or maybe you are just begging. Even a dyke wouldn't have you."

Sarah had stared at him. Forcing herself to stay calm. Not to react: not to cry or yell as she attempted her own self-talk—he wasn't worth it, even if they had earlier been having a nice evening. Mostly. *He had probably had too much to drink, and he didn't like it when she told him she needed sleep because of work the next day.* Another excuse.

"You know, Sarah," Tony had said. "You're just a sad fuck," and he had slammed her front door, heading home early.

The waitress was setting down their drinks when Amelia reappeared at the table. "Did you decide on anything?" the waitress asked, while scanning across the bar to anticipate others' needs, another overworked food server.

"Um, I'll have the soup and salad special," Amelia said, sitting back down.

"Tomato basil or roasted chicken rice?" the server asked.

"Uh, the chicken, please," Amelia answered. "Thanks."

"Me too," Sarah added.

"Ah, Saturday," Amelia said.

She stretched her legs, and Sarah caught a glimpse of her bare feet. She already knew that soon Amelia would slip her feet up underneath her after having dropped her flats to the floor. Every time Amelia did this, Sarah wondered how she managed it so effortlessly, having tried it once alone at home and finding it both uncomfortable and impossible. She wasn't flexible enough to get her feet under her butt, and it made her back hurt. She told herself Amelia was probably also a regular practicing yogi.

"Oh!" Amelia said, as if the thought only then occurred to her. "You don't work tomorrow either, right?" She smiled at Sarah and touched her hand.

Sarah felt the warmth of her hand. Might there be any hidden meaning, she wondered? She looked up at Amelia and gave her a questioning smile.

"Well, I mean you get to sleep and do whatever you want," Amelia added, as if reading Sarah's smile. "Although I imagine it's a day you spend with Gloria."

"Oh, yeah. Don't remind me now," Sarah said, trying to laugh off her disappointment, a mere puddle leaking from a pool somewhere deep inside. Expecting to see Amelia this evening had helped her get through the last part of her Saturday shift, making it drag less than normal. She had even brought a change of clothes. Saturdays at the store were mayhem with the store advertising sales that weren't true discounts, yet still brought in crazy shoppers craving bargains.

"Yeah, thank God. We have a bigger than usual sale this weekend, so I'm lucky I only had to work one day of that madness. Maybe by Monday the merchandise will all be sold. Or stolen." She sighed. "I have a bad attitude." She almost added how it might be fun if Amelia stopped by to see her at work. As nice as it would be to have Amelia break up her day, she knew she would be embarrassed for Amelia to see her as a salesclerk in a department store. In a stale, falsely lit mall, filled with teenagers and old people. Amelia whose husband worked in an expensive fashion industry,

"So, Sarah," Amelia said, changing her tone. "Tell me more about your mom—Gloria. I mean, why things seem so difficult between you and her." She hesitated. "I mean, if you feel like it."

Sarah took a gulp of her beer. She knew she should savor it. She felt its soothing effect on her as it moved down into her gut, warming her insides and causing an imperceptible attitude shift. She tried to remember how long it had been since she had allowed herself to have one, and momentarily lost track of their conversation as she wondered if she would regret it.

"Well. It's pretty simple," Sarah said, taking another drink, this time a sip. "I basically never forgave her." She had long ago stopped her internal dialogue of this topic, summing it up instead with that exact conclusion. "Here was our mom—Gloria– pretending to be this 'strong woman' to me and Ted. My brother. Oh, and he's a royal fuck up. Acting like she was the Queen of Sheba." She stopped suddenly, realizing she didn't even know who the Queen of Sheba was. She hoped it didn't make her sound unintelligent—maybe it didn't make sense? "But really. I knew. She was so fucked up. She tried so hard to pretend. But, she would not let us into her world. That's what it really was. I should have moved on and forgiven her. But, shit, she had given herself to David—let him use her up."

Sarah paused. She tried to avoid swearing around Amelia. But she couldn't do it when she talked about Gloria. "But I just couldn't figure out this fake front she put on for me. Her daughter!" She took a break in her rant. She gulped another drink of beer and then lightly pushed it away. *Damn. I don't want to do this.*

"It's okay, Sarah," Amelia said gently. She gave her a look that fluttered Sarah's heart. Sarah tried to stop the tears that filled her eyes.

"Remember the stuff I had with my mama. Really. And at least yours is still alive. I have to live with what I never did."

Sarah felt encouraged. She took a deep breath, hoping to still her racing heart. "Yeah, but really. I don't know what is better. Because, knowing the way Gloria has been and how she pretended so much in all those years. And yet, now I can't get mad at her because for the first time ever she seems vulnerable. I don't think she tries to pretend like she used to; it's almost like she knows she can't hide her little maneuvers so well. Or maybe she's just tired of it." She paused, not sure if she could admit some of this to someone like Amelia. "Back when Alison had her first drug issues." She swallowed to choke back the pain. "Hell, you should have seen Gloria. She just fucking wanted to handle it. Told me not to worry." She took a breath to calm her speeding words. "She wouldn't let me in!" She focused on relaxing her voice. "She 'knew this and she knew that,' Gloria would tell me. She tried to take over even in my dealings with *my* daughter, and be the one who could fix and control everything." She looked at Amelia, and shook her head. "I'm sorry. But I guess, you asked." She wiped at her eyes. "That's the other thing I never forgave her for."

Amelia wordlessly put her hand on top of Sarah's, like before, as it rested on the table.

Sarah's tears dripped onto the table. "Gloria pretended she was this strong woman, all these years later. Not letting me in. Instead, acting as if she was saving me. But she is the one who fucked up her life so royally and she wasn't strong enough to make the move. Except now. I don't know anymore. It's not all that simple like I've always told myself." She leaned back against the booth, but keeping her hand on the table under the warmth of Amelia's hand. Silent. Out of words and emotion.

Amelia let out a sigh. "Wow. I'm sorry. I'm so sorry."

Sarah wasn't sure if Amelia was sorry for what had happened or sorry that she had asked. It didn't matter to Sarah then, as the warmth of Amelia moved through her fingers and up her arm. She didn't want to move. She wondered what might happen next.

Sarah tried not to sigh as Amelia moved her hand to straighten up in the booth and then to smooth back her hair. Then, as if they had no more room to share pain, their conversation led to other subjects. Amelia shared more about her job, and how she was at a turning point in her life: she wanted to do something different. She needed something more, but didn't know what that was. She talked about her marriage, and as Amelia talked, her love and respect for her husband percolated through her laughter as she shared this or that story. Sarah could see how much Amelia loved him. Amelia asked about Alison, but didn't pursue it seeming to sense Sarah wasn't interested in talking about it.

Amelia had a second glass of wine with her dinner, but Sarah forced herself to ask for a glass of water. They began to chat about the people around them. Not gossip, just pretending about the lives those around them might have. They realized, with apparent surprise, that they were among the only over forty crowd in the bar now as the clock hit eleven-thirty.

"Yikes, Sarah, I probably need to get home," Amelia said a full hour after they had paid for their separate checks. "I'm so tired."

"Yeah," Sarah said. Tired as well. Disappointed, too. Amelia had finished her wine almost an hour earlier, but took a drink out of her water glass.

"So how about next Sunday again, okay?" Amelia asked. "Maybe a walk, if the weather is good."

"Sure," Sarah answered. "That'd be nice." She silently acknowledged how many hours there were in seven days, full of boring and difficult details filling those dragging minutes, until the next visit.

Amelia stood up first, rearranged her blouse and jacket, and grabbed her purse. "I parked near your car. Ready?"

"Yeah," Sarah answered as she jammed her arms into her coat and put her purse over her shoulder. She followed Amelia, noticing a young couple still sitting at the bar, the girl mooning at her young date.

An almost full moon glowed behind a few hazy clouds, but no rain showers were in view. They stood in the parking lot—Sarah felt her heart beating through her layers of clothing and watched as Amelia extracted her keys from her purse, their minutes together lapsing.

She took a deep gulp. "Amelia!"

Amelia looked at her. "What is it, Sarah? Are you okay?"

Sarah began to cry, threw her arms around Amelia, and pulled their bodies close. "I just want to be with you. I mean. Longer." She sobbed, not sure what she meant. Sharing similar height, she nudged her face against Amelia's bare neck and brushed her lips against warm skin.

Amelia pulled her head back, surprised, Sarah's arms still holding her. "Sarah, no. I mean—I adore you. But, but. Not this. Not like . . ."

Sarah had rarely seen Amelia at a loss for words, and pulled herself away, embarrassed. "No, I didn't mean it," she said, not sure that she didn't, but worried she had wrecked any kind of friendship. "I'm just. I don't know . . . I'm just confused." She hesitated. "I'm so lonely. I'm so sorry. I don't know what I'm doing. Anymore." She dropped her arms from Amelia and wiped and then, covered her eyes. Her body trembled with sadness. Shamed.

"Sarah." Amelia hesitated. "Our friendship means so much—it has opened up a lot for me, and I need us to continue. I can't though . . . well. I can't cure your loneliness. Maybe there's a way to help you. I mean to get beyond it. Not tonight. But, somehow." She put a hand on Sarah's shoulder, but the intimacy of the prior moments had dissipated. "Let me walk you to your car—are you okay driving?"

Sarah wiped again at her face, and shook her head, as if to release her pent-up emotions. "I'll be fine."

They walked to Sarah's car. Amelia dropped her hand and stood back as Sarah unlocked her car and opened the door.

"I'm sorry, Amelia," Sarah said, unable to control the wavers in her voice, but keeping it from fully breaking. She got into her car. "I'll be fine."

Amelia put her hand up in an informal wave. "Night, Sarah, sleep well! I'll call you tomorrow."

"Night," Sarah replied.

She put her key in the ignition and when her music came on loudly, she shut it off, and, aware of Amelia watching, pulled her car slowly out of the parking lot. After a few blocks when she knew she was out of view, she pulled her car into an open parking spot, locked her doors, and began to cry. Unable to stop the flow of tears. *Always such a fuck up.*

Chapter 16

Crossroads

IT WAS LATE when Sarah got home. As she locked her car, she spotted her kitchen light shining through the window onto the bushes below. She always turned it off when she left her apartment. She should put up some blinds, she thought, noticing how visible her kitchen might be to someone outside. *Whatever.*

The glass of beer, imbibed hours ago, formed tiny pockets of lightness in her brain; surprising her since, thanks to steady drinking, she had built up tolerance to more than a six-pack in her past. She had been disappointed to have stumbled in having the drink, after six months of sobriety, and wished her lack of inhibition had ended with the restaurant conversations. Not her act in the parking lot. Mistake or not, she probably couldn't blame it on the beer or the effect of being inebriated.

Sarah twisted the key in the lock, pushed open the door, then slammed it shut. She pulled her boots off, standing first on her right leg and then her left. She dumped her boots to the side of the door, let her coat drop to the floor, and hung her purse on the outside of the closet door knob, then headed into the kitchen for a glass of water. Her stomach rumbled, and she considered making a late-night snack. Her nerves had kept her from finishing her dinner. When she spotted the gathering group of empty bottles on the counter, one of them lying on its side, she stopped. The bottle labels denoted a cheap brand she would never drink, even in her drinking days. *Fuck.* She moved past them and filled a glass she earlier left in the sink from the faucet, her hand shaking as she grasped the clear tumbler. She had fretted that sharing her extra key had been a mistake. She had been intending to find a way to take it back without creating a scene. *Damn. She was not in the mood for this.*

Before she'd had time to think about what she might do, she heard footsteps moving toward her.

"Home from your girlfriend? Did you finally get some?" Tony snarled a rough voice. As he stepped into the kitchen, he almost tripped on the throw rug, his foot stuttering on the floor. He grabbed the counter, jutting out his face and hips toward her, his mouth dripping nastiness. He rubbed his knee where he had knocked the kitchen cabinet.

"Tony, it's late. I asked you not to come over tonight." Sarah forced herself to stay calm, although she knew her shaking voice gave her away.

Tony's face was blotchy, and his eyes stared at her without full focus. His rage billowed out of him as if it had been building for hours.

"Oh, did she turn you down? Guess you just don't always get what you want, you . . . silly baby girl." Tony moved toward her. He grabbed her waist with both hands. Sarah could tell he too was trying to calm his voice, unsuccessfully. "Besides, I know you want me. Face it! I can forgive you, this time, for thinking about her. You can make it up to me. But I know what you really want is me." He moved his body so that she was wedged between his powerful legs, his knees digging into her. "I've been waiting all night for you, my silly bitch." Then he roughly moved his hands to grab her chest, hard, as if claiming his prize in a game of possession. Sarah tried to pull his hands off her and attempted to step away, but Tony's legs kept her pinned against the kitchen counter.

"Stop it, Tony. I'm tired. Please go home and we'll talk tomorrow." Sarah had never felt this scared by him before, and she tried not to panic. She had never seen him this riled up, nor had he spoken so brutally to her.

"Stop it, Tony, I'm tired," he repeated in a shrill voice, echoing her, just like her brother did when they were kids. His fingers dug into her chest and along her rib cage, and she wondered if bruises were forming already. As kids, her brother Ted never tired of repeating her comments back to her when she was upset, in a teasing echoing game.

"Go home," Sarah said more forcefully, trying hard not to cry or let her voice quiver. "I have to get up early tomorrow." She hoped in his drunken state he would forget that Sunday was never a work day for her.

"Well, I guess you should have thought about that when you made a date with your girlfriend. What is it, Sarah?" he asked. "Is she pretty?

Or does she just hold you gently, let you cry while she lets you suck on her tits?"

"Stop it, Tony. She's just my friend. What the hell is wrong with you?" She had never before seen him this jealous. He had begun complaining about the time she and Amelia spent together, especially when it interfered with time he wanted with Sarah, teasing her about her lesbo friend. But he had never gone this far out of bounds. She started to feel scared and wished she hadn't put her car keys back in her purse in the living room. She tried to push past him to get out of the kitchen.

He grabbed her by the arms and slammed her against the wall. "No! You stop it, you fucking bitch. I wanted you tonight. I want you now. I've waited long enough, giving up *my* Saturday night to sit around imagining you and that, that . . ." As he pushed himself against her, slamming her body into the wall again, she could feel his hardness against her leg. She felt as though she was going to vomit. He had never hurt her like this, although more and more he had surprised her by how quickly his temper flared over trite matters.

"Tony, please." She began to cry, although she hated to show him her tears.

"Oh, fuck those lady tears," he spit back at her.

She smelled the cheap beer on his breath. It was all her fault, she knew it. She should have broken off with him so long ago, but hadn't known how without upsetting him. Every time she seriously considered it, he would be so sweet. He'd bring her flowers or surprise her with an expensive dinner. Once, even astonishing her on an overnight to Cannon Beach in a most expensive, beautiful hotel. But right now, everything she once found so handsome loomed ugly in his features, mutating his face into one of an angry killer.

"Get away from me!" she screamed.

And that was it. She didn't care anymore. *She was done. Done.*

"Tony, no! Just leave! Please!" she screamed again.

Now she wished her apartment complex wasn't effectively soundproofed. She wished she had kept her phone in her pocket, although she knew she wouldn't have been able to battle his power to call out. She wished she was back in the safety of the restaurant. For a second she imagined being able to grab a knife left on the counter to threaten him, but wasn't sure she was bold enough, even if one was in reach.

He hit her. "Shut up you bitch."

Sarah pushed back with as much strength as she could summon, pulled one arm free, finally giving up strength to dig in with the sharp points of her fingernails, the ones she hadn't bitten off. She tried to claw at his face, only to have it batted away. Her nose was bleeding, and snot mixed in as it dripped onto her white button-down shirt.

"I hate you!" she said.

Tony slapped her again and laughed, his anger elevating to yet another level. He was an ugly stranger before her, bearing a weird sneer, as if he was reacting to some horrid violent movie. "You know you want me." He began to use calmer words now. "Come on, beg me. Tell me. Tell me!" He bent her arm back, still pinned against the wall, as if he'd packed everything he'd ever been angry about into this one act. "I'm not leaving without what I want."

And that was it. In a micro-second, Sarah decided. *No way!* If she didn't stop him now, she would be just like Gloria—putting up with the only loser she could get. *No more.*

"No . . ." she said, at first, softly.

Tony, still holding her right arm just below the elbow, twisted it backward, propping her up, and pushed her out of the kitchen. When they got to the entry way, Sarah now to his side rather than directly in front, her foot got in the way. Did she stick it out, or was it just luck? It was no conscious effort, just something her body knew to do. Self-protection. A moment when what could and what should, intersected together in space. A nudge.

Tony stumbled again, this time losing his grip on her arm, as he crashed to the ground. It all rushed through Sarah's mind, like one of those slow-moving film strips she remembered from elementary school.

"Damn you, Sarah. Help me get up," he cried. Now drunk—he was weak and helpless as a lost child as he pleaded to her, unable to regain his balance, a giant turtle overturned on its shell.

As Tony lay disoriented, Sarah grabbed her purse off the closet door handle and smashed her feet into her fake leather boots. Her mind sober, crystal clear. She grabbed the front door knob and opened the door wide as he looked up at her, disbelieving.

"Come on, Sarah. I need you. Come on back. I didn't mean it," he begged.

Calm now, Sarah looked back. "Get out, Tony. We're done." She stepped outside and shut the door. As she walked to her car, her hands still shaking, a chill settling through her bones, she took out her phone and dialed three numbers. "Yes. I need help. Now." She unlocked her car, got in, and locked it again. She sat in the dark, answering the questions asked of her. She kept her eyes fixed on her front door, imagining Tony snoring noisily on the floor. Her brain was buzzing, her skin shivering, and although her mind wandered, the flashing lights ten minutes later brought her back. She continued to sit on the firm, cool seat as she watched the police officer knock on her apartment door.

Chapter 17

Salvation

ON A WHIM Amelia tried to call Sarah at the store on Monday. She knew Sarah usually had Mondays off, but was working because of the holiday sale. Amelia was anxious: rebuffing Sarah Saturday night had upset her—but she had not wanted to interrupt Sarah's Sunday time with Gloria. In addition to the uncomfortable way they had parted that night, she knew Sarah was reeling from old memories she had shared about her mother. Although it was difficult for her to understand the deep resentment Sarah held against her mother, she empathized with her pain. She would be lying if she didn't admit, as well, how envious she was of every friend of hers whose parents were still living. Sarah included. Some days she missed her mama so much and regretted not working through the "hard stuff" while she was still on earth. More recently, the absence of her dad's solid support haunted her.

When Amelia called the store, Sarah's coworker, Betty, answered the phone. When Betty told her Sarah wouldn't be in for the day, Amelia's anxiety rose. She felt responsible. Perhaps Sarah took their uncomfortable parting worse than she feared? Amelia knew Sarah's finances were tight and hoped her benefits included paid leave. She had never meant to compound her dear friend's worries. Slowly, over the past months, Amelia had added an extra dimension to her life, brought on by this new, honest, albeit disorganized, friend.

As she sat alone in her sunny kitchen nook with the morning fading, Amelia tried not to stew or fret: after all, she had an entire holiday to herself! She had promised herself she wouldn't bring any work home from the office for a change, and Phillip was still out of town. She hadn't even yet changed from her pajamas, and tried to stretch into a few yoga moves to still her brain. No matter how she tried to clear it, she couldn't get Sarah out of her head.

She grabbed her cell and dialed, only to hear the recorded voice mail. "Hey Sarah, it's Amelia. I was just thinking about you." She didn't need to tell her she had tried to reach her at work, she told herself. Sarah seemed protective, and even embarrassed, about her job—something Amelia didn't understand. To Amelia, a job that you left at the door would be a welcome relief from the stress and worries she brought home from work.

Amelia set her ringer to audible and put the phone aside as she started a cup of tea and some breakfast for a lazier than normal morning. Almost two hours later she dialed again, still landing at voicemail. She knew Sarah kept her phone attached as if it was an extra body appendage, and she began to wonder if there was something wrong. She tried to make light of it; maybe Sarah was sleeping. Her brain told her otherwise, as she worried about the beer she had drunk, her heartfelt sharing about Gloria, and, the uncomfortableness of their final parting. She forced herself to hop in the shower, with her mobile on the bathroom counter, something she never did anymore.

More often than not these days, Amelia found herself letting calls that weren't work-related go to voicemail first, just to give her the opportunity to imagine her response, sometimes even with Phillip. He did the same with her: it was, in fact, one way in which they were very much alike. She knew how most of her friends didn't understand the relationship she and Phillip had, sometimes curiously questioning her. Usually, this made her feel even luckier. Lucky she and Phillip had found each other, all those years before. Two unusual creatures when it came to intimacy who had together figured out what it meant for their own winning combination: time apart, balance, mutual respect.

Their agreement not to have kids, even if the decision nibbled at her heart a little, was one way her co-workers who were parents, never fully understood her. How could she not want to be a parent? They wondered. It seemed especially curious to friends who knew about the happy childhoods she and Phillip had enjoyed. If she and Phillip were together while friends discussed their own kids, he'd give her his knowing smile. The two of them would listen to the challenges of finding day care, complaints about early Saturday morning soccer games, or later, what colleges their little angels got into. Other times, if she happened to be at an event when kids were around, someone might say, "But Amelia? You are so good with kids!" Amelia would simply smile. It didn't bother her any more, it only amplified the wonderful secret she and Phillip shared. For later, always, it was these same friends who enviously listened to her travel tales: even solo trips she had taken if Phillip was tied up. Or the spur of the moment outings on a late Friday when they both were in town.

The only reason she ever regretted not having children was that it prevented Ernest from being a grandfather. He, true to his nature, had never admitted to her it was something he missed. Now, he was gone. Gone. Her father. She still wanted to tell people when his name or stories about him came up, that he had only recently passed away: but it had now been more than a year. *How could that be?* She wondered as she dried off with a towel.

She stared at herself in the steamy mirror. *How could it be that she was almost at the half century mark?* If she peered at her face she could see it: the crow lines now permanently etched, whether she smiled or not. People often told her she looked "so much younger," as if it was so bad to grow older: though it did sometimes come as a shock. To be this age. It was something her mama always said, even as she got weaker and sicker from the chemo: that she would look at her reflection in the mirror and wonder, "Who is that woman?" But then, her mama would laugh. "No Regret" was Sharon's motto. Except, that is, for Amelia never having a grandbaby for her. Her mama never did understand her decision like Ernest.

Amelia broke out of her thoughts to look at her phone, hoping she might have missed a ring. But, no missed calls.

AMELIA WALKED ALONG the waterfront later that morning, having received only one call all weekend—from Phillip—when it finally rang. She grabbed her phone out of her coat pocket. "Hello?" Only to have it be a work colleague. She nodded as she answered two questions, and then returned the device to her pocket. There were bits of blue sky to the east, with clouds rising from the west. The morning sun had disappeared behind billowing gray. A good day, anyway, to walk along Portland's Willamette River.

She avoided walking under the bridges where she knew homeless people would be waking up; not that they frightened her, but on this morning, she didn't want to interject the smells of urine into its freshness. It made her sad but she didn't know what to do about it. When Phillip had visitors come to town, he apologized about the number of people they saw sleeping on the streets, but his reaction bothered her as not seeming fully empathetic. She'd say to him, "It's not like they are making the choice," only to have Phillip disagree. "Yes, Amelia, some of them do." And when they were alone they'd battle it back and forth, and Amelia would remind herself to get involved in that cause. Or maybe not that one, but something. Sometime. Maybe that's what she would do when she found the job she could leave at the office. She shivered as she moved past a noisy group of teens showing off on skateboards, emanating a cloud of marijuana, and thought about, even though she'd already showered, how comforting a hot bath would feel. The Sunday paper. Just maybe, another cup of coffee.

SARAH WAS THANKFUL for the navigator on her phone during moments like this. Directions were not her strongest suit. Her heart pounded, her head ached, and she couldn't think straight. Thankfully, the app took her directly to the address. Her heart leapt: a sophisticated condo. She sat in the car, taking in the neighborhood. She knew Amelia would have no idea how she found her, though she was at least smart enough to find what she needed to know on the internet. Although she hadn't been sure if Phillip and Amelia shared the same surname, again, it was easy to find out. She tried to stop herself from shivering and heaved herself up to the doorstep; pots with blooming scarlet geraniums on either side.

She stood for several minutes, shivering. Embarrassed to bother Amelia, and yet not knowing where else to turn. She knocked lightly. After a full sixty seconds, she got the courage to ring the bell. After no answer, she forced herself to ring again, her hand shaking. She was nervous and shifted her weight back and forth. The door opened a crack.

"Sarah!" Amelia cried out, throwing the door wide open.

Amelia stared in shock at Sarah's black eye, her right arm fitted in a splint and resting in a sling. The rest of her face was splotchy and swollen. Sarah began to sob as Amelia enveloped her in a soft hug, pulled her into the house, and shut the door behind her.

"I need you," Sarah sniffled.

Chapter 18

Conquering

AMELIA HAD ONLY been to Newberg once before while wine-tasting with Phillip as they explored the wineries around Yamhill, a rolling, rural county dotted with tasting rooms, most touting their labeled Pinot Noir, and acres of grape-covered climbing vines. As she pulled into the assisted living center, she was surprised how much larger the town was than she had expected—was it now considered a Portland suburb, she wondered? *No way would Ernest or Sharon have lived in a place like this.* Her mama had been gone so long now and she had been relatively young when she died, that Amelia couldn't imagine her as an elderly lady needing assistance. Although Sharon had been weak and required full-time help at the end of her journey, Amelia believed she would have put the brakes on institutional living, at any cost. Sharon had insisted, in the end, to rely on hospice at home rather than allow Ernest to request another in-hospital treatment, advising him it wouldn't make any real difference anyway. She wanted as much control over the quality of the time she had left, she had insisted to both much adored husband and daughter.

As Amelia entered through the front door, she spied an old woman sitting in a chair next to the door, a walker at her side. She smiled nervously at her but continued on to the desk, the woman following her with her eyes. Sarah had instructed her to merely sign in, but the young woman at the desk looked at her expectantly, as if privy to Amelia's secret thoughts—how alien-like she felt wading into this sea of old people.

"May I help you?" the young woman asked.

"Yes. I'm visiting Gloria Harris in apartment 215," she said. How strange, she thought, after a career spent arranging and facilitating meetings with powerful people, to be anxious to meet this one elderly woman.

"Does she expect you?" the young woman asked.

"Uh, I think so. She should," Amelia replied.

"Just sign in here," the woman said, pointing to a clipboard, the brightly crafted nametag on her lapel identifying her as "Kate." After Amelia signed in, the woman pointed to the elevator. "Just go up one floor to two and you'll see her apartment down the hall." And then Kate returned her attention to her computer.

"Thank you."

On Amelia's way to the elevator she passed three women sitting together. She was unable to tell if they were conversing, as they all looked up at her as she neared. Another old man sat alone with a walker next to him, farther past the trio. Amelia wondered how she would have been if either of her parents had ended up in a place like this? Would she learn to move comfortably between residents on her visits? Or would she remain as those who looked at their watch the moment they entered the tinkling door, letting go of emotions for the short visitations with those who once lived such different lives?

Amelia dodged into the stairwell next to the elevator, climbed a flight of stairs, and headed to apartment 215. The hall lighting shone brightly, oak railings embellished muted walls, an occasional generic print hung from the wall. A tune she vaguely recognized filled her ears, instrumental only, played overhead and broke the silence of the corridor.

Amelia stopped at the door, knocked, but received no answer. She tried again, louder. She could hear movement inside, and after what felt like more than a long minute, a sturdy looking elderly woman came to the door. She wore a matching green sweat suit and a pair of thick-soled white leather athletic shoes.

"Yes?" the woman said. "Is it time for lunch?"

"Oh, no. I mean, I don't think so." Amelia felt caught off guard. She had overheard Sarah phone Gloria, informing her she would have a visitor. She took a breath and forced a nervous smile.

"I'm Amelia . . . a friend of Sarah's? I'm sorry, I thought she told you," she added.

"Oh hello, Amelia. Did she? I'm sorry. I didn't know that you were her friend." Gloria gave a sudden, embarrassed smile and then stared at the floor. She looked up. "My brain just isn't working so good. Today."

Gloria had brownish hair with a perfect beauty parlor crafted coif. Looking closer, Amelia could see silvery ends poking through.

Amelia knew it was up to her to be perky and welcoming, somehow, in the light of everything else. Perkiness wasn't something that came naturally: not like it might to others.

"Oh—you too?" Amelia forced herself to think quickly in her effort to bring Gloria a smile. "I know what you mean." She gave a vaguely uncomfortable smile.

Gloria looked up, releasing a bare hint of a grin. Sarah had warned her how it was getting harder for Gloria to pretend everything was normal or status quo anymore.

"I'm sorry, dear, can you remind me why you are here? Do I have an appointment?"

Amelia could tell her presence was making Gloria uncomfortable, and although she wasn't fully sure why, having heard so many stories about Gloria made Amelia feel as though she was walking on eggshells: any sentence she blurted might be wrong. She regretted offering to visit her.

But after the moment passed, Amelia felt braver, accepting that it was up to her. "Perhaps I could sit down and we could get to know each other a bit?" Amelia peeked inside the door and looked over at the small kitchenette. "Shall I make us a cup of tea?" She rubbed her hands together. "It is still so chilly out there for this time of year." She was desperate to fill the silence.

Gloria's eyes brightened, suddenly pleased to have a visitor. "Oh yes, that'd be nice. Some days are just so boring. But let me do it. Come on in."

Amelia followed her the few feet into the kitchen area, mostly a counter against the wall with a mini fridge, sink, and small cupboard. Yet everything was bright and new. She was embarrassed to admit to herself that this was her first foray into elderly residential care—she had harbored images of dilapidated rooms, and old people muttering alone in the halls, which of course, she knew, did exist, if not here, then somewhere else, in another part of town. One without all the frills, housing people further along in age and destitution.

"I have Lipton or peppermint," Gloria said. "What would you like?"

"Peppermint is fine. Thank you." Amelia watched quietly as Gloria concentrated on selecting just the right tea cups, two different but unique designs from what she imagined must have been sets from long ago. She took two off the shelf, paused a minute, and replaced one. Then she took down a different cup.

"Please sit, dear. Not that there are many choices." Gloria gave Amelia a sour look. "I really don't get many visitors. Anymore."

Amelia took the few steps toward the living area, passing an open door leading into a separate bedroom, barely large enough for a twin bed, chest of drawers, and chair. But still a separate room, which she imagined might be almost a luxury in facilities like this with space a premium.

"What a nice view," Amelia offered, as she looked out one of the two windows into a landscaped area below with a small pond.

"Oh, what?" Gloria asked, as if lost in thoughts. "Oh yes, I guess. There's a bench they say I can sit on if it's not raining. Although I miss being close to the river."

Amelia had to remind herself about the fewer stories Sarah had shared, earlier in their relationship, about the house her mother had been renting near the Willamette. Not fancy, Sarah had said, but with a most surprising glimpse of the river at an almost affordable rent. Amelia imagined it to be too far for most folks commuting daily to Portland's inner workings, although she knew from co-workers how much the housing landscape had changed—so many newcomers—and none of the options affordable.

As Gloria poured the steaming water, Amelia arose from the flowered upholstered settee to help carry the cups over. Gloria handed her one, but insisted on carrying her own. Gloria wobbled only a bit, which Amelia imagined only added to her frustration at being forced by Sarah to leave independent living. But for the moment, Gloria seemed okay as she sat back in her armchair, resting her tea cup with the bag seeping next to her on an adjacent small table. Amelia set hers on her lap, warming her hands as she rubbed them on the cup.

Gloria sat quietly, disinterested, it seemed, to initiate a conversation.

"So, I believe Sarah told you we are friends?" Amelia started.

Gloria nodded vaguely. She was focused on picking up her teacup and blowing on it, cooling the weak-colored liquid.

"I have heard so much about you, I told her it'd be fun to meet while she is out of town." Amelia tried to sound normal, carefree.

"Oh, yes," Gloria said simply. "Where did she go?"

"I think it was to help a friend or something," Amelia improvised, "but I'm sorry, um, I don't remember exactly. She did say she'd be gone all week."

Gloria looked disappointed, but didn't say anything at first. "Well, good. I hope she is having fun. I don't remember her leaving town very often." Then she added, a bit more softly, almost to herself, "Stuck with me. I promised myself I wouldn't do this. Not my children." She shook her head, staring ahead blankly.

Lost in thought? Amelia wondered. She wasn't usually very good at small talk. She looked around at the walls, wracking her brain for something to say.

Gloria asked her how she knew Sarah. Perhaps it was at work, she suggested?

"No. Not that. You know though, it's hard to remember now. It was unusual, the way we met. And, really, a very long story." Amelia hoped Gloria wouldn't ask for details: she knew she was not very good on her feet at making up things, and it all felt too personal and recent to share.

"So where are you from, dear?" Gloria asked instead.

Amelia was taken aback. "Um, from Portland."

"No, I mean before that," Gloria offered. "Like a lot of the girls who work here are from Mexico. Or somewhere like that."

Heat rose to Amelia's face. She tried to still her voice and tell herself that Gloria didn't mean it the way it came out. She set her tea on the table next to her and controlled her shaking hand enough to keep it from spilling. She paused to steady her voice. But then Amelia was surprised out of the uncomfortable moment as her mama's voice rang in her ear. *Wait for the right time. It makes the difference. In the end.* She had been hearing Mama's laugh and voice for years, although rarely with such a direct message. She was still awaiting something to emanate from her dad. She had thought she had awoken to a dream about him once, but it was blurry, fading away too soon after waking. She wondered how long she might have to wait until she heard him too.

"No. My parents both grew up in Portland." Amelia tried to pull her thoughts together and do the good that she promised Sarah. She picked up her cup and took a sip of the now lukewarm tea. She craved a strong Americano.

"So, Gloria," she said, changing the subject. "What about you? I'd love to learn more about your early life. Where did you grow up?"

Gloria smiled and looked away, toward the pond. Then she looked up at Amelia and smiled again. "My dear, I have grown up mostly here. But sometimes I like to think it has been all over. All ancient history, really, and probably boring to most." She sighed. "My daddy was about the toughest guy you ever did meet. Not mean. Just tough." She sighed again. "And let me tell you. If he's looking down at me now, he is thinking about how I failed him. The sissy I have become."

And with that, Amelia began to learn about Gloria's early life.

Gloria's daddy, George, was a young man who believed the only way to find the adventure he sought in life and to escape the Oregon small town he was born in, was to join the army. And for every awful thing he had to live through those first few years, he also developed close bonds with the other guys around him. The buddies who meant everything to him. That's when he decided a career in the military was his ticket; it'd keep him out of Oregon, instead living in exciting places, maybe even other countries, he had told himself. If he ever applied himself, which even he doubted he would, he could get college paid for on the GI Bill he told his parents in his efforts to sway them to support his idea.

Gloria told Amelia how before too long after enlisting, George was shipped out.

"I can't remember the name of the place in Washington. Oh, I always forget." She paused. "But I'll never forget what Daddy always said—that it was Newfoundland he was sent to soon. Not even Canada back then." She hesitated, but soon added how she'd never forget the stories of how her parents met.

"My mother was proper and all, but met him at a dance near the base. Her name was Margaret, and my daddy always said he couldn't help but stare at her across the dance hall." Gloria continued to tell Amelia, with a dreamy, faraway look in her eyes, how her daddy was instantly smitten. He'd never had a girl before and she was a beauty who stole his heart right from the start. She, too, was a small-town girl, thinking, at least at first, as if swept up in the cloud of a new, exciting idea, that she wanted something more thrilling in her life rather than to follow forever in the footsteps of those in her small town. George and Margaret had a simple wedding and didn't even get away alone together overnight. Gloria winked at Amelia.

"But that didn't stop my mother from telling me how she knew nothing about sex their first night together. She told me this, years later. I was so embarrassed! I couldn't believe it back then when she told me. That it ended her life as a virgin." Gloria turned her head side to side, laughing. "Oh God I was so embarrassed, then."

Amelia smiled, a glimpse of a cantankerous woman seeped out.

Gloria continued with the story, sharing how, before her parents knew it, they were told they had to head back to the states, to a base somewhere in Texas. At first Margaret played bravely, saying how exciting it would be. But then, she cried all night, and although she had talked boldly about experiencing the wide world, she wasn't so sure she was ready to leave her parents and family. She came from a large clan with six siblings—her brothers and sisters all older, and who had spoiled her. The quietness of their base two-person apartment already made her uncomfortable. Although she was only a few miles from her family, it wasn't as easy to visit home as what she had anticipated.

Once moved to the base in Texas, Margaret tried to get active in base activities and met a few girl-friends, but her bouncy, pre-marital sense of adventure shriveled. Not long after, Gloria's brother Bob was born, as was Gloria eighteen months later. Both Gloria and Bob attended the base preschool in Texas. But by the time Bob was ready for first grade, Margaret begged to be closer to family. George, too, was beginning to tire of some of the army drudgery and made plans instead to join the Guard, figuring his mechanic skills might land him a civilian job working on machinery or cars, talking Margaret into mistakenly believing being geographically closer to his family would offer her what she missed.

It was their Oregon life Gloria remembered most, although she always loved the stories her father told her about the years he lived in Newfoundland and his young family in Texas, as if she too could claim a bit of that worldwide adventure as part of her story. And while her daddy was strong and tough, her mom continued to shrink inward, returning only once to visit her family in then, Canada. When both of Margaret's parents died before they had even reached their mid-sixties, Margaret was inconsolable. She blamed herself—and George—for being apart from them during all of her adult years. And in doing so, she pulled herself even further away from her only daughter, becoming mostly unavailable to her now growing children.

Gloria stopped talking suddenly, as if she was only in that moment, discovering something new. "It was then when I decided, I would be strong like my daddy!" She explained further that he was the one she would emulate. She had promised herself, too, that if she ever had children, she would do everything in her power to be there for them. To make them feel safe. At the expense of all else. And then, again, Gloria grew silent. She sat back in her chair, the weight of her body relaxing her into a slouch against the backrest. Exhausted.

A knock on the door interrupted them.

"Come in," Gloria called, struggling to sit up straighter in her soft chair.

"Gloria, it's almost lunch time," the young woman said at the door.

"Thank you," Gloria said, and the woman quietly closed the door. Then, with a dramatic change of tone, Gloria added, "Breakfast time, dinner time . . . you'd think we were animals on a feeding schedule." She turned back to Amelia. "You know, I never, ever thought I'd be in a place like this."

Amelia was caught without words, but nodded.

"Yes. I hoped to die—when my time came—doing something really adventurous and fun. Or at least in my sleep. If there was a handsome available man in this God forsaken place, maybe I'd try to get into his bed and hope that one more run might just burst my heart." Gloria snorted a laugh.

Amelia smiled in spite of her surprise.

"Would you like to join me for lunch?" Gloria asked. For a mere moment, she looked younger than she had when Amelia first arrived. "My treat. Only four bucks. But I'll warn you, it tastes like a one buck meal!" Gloria tried a half-hearted laugh.

"I'd love to, but I do need to get going. Can I take a rain check?" And she meant it, she promised herself. She had fully enjoyed Gloria, but the whole situation took a little getting used to, she allowed herself to acknowledge. Being in the room with Gloria was one thing; eating in a dining room full of old people still sounded intimidating. She knew, also, how overdue she was to check on Sarah. She had temporarily forgotten about everything else while Gloria had rambled. She wondered why Sarah had never told her any of these stories.

"Of course, dear. I'm sorry. Emily? Is that right?" She looked at Amelia a little confused.

"Close. Amelia," she said. "Can I walk you to your lunch, though?"

"How about we walk together to the front door. I'll make all the old ladies jealous when they see me with you." Gloria picked up a stretchy green key ring from her kitchen counter, placed it over her wrist, and opened the door for Amelia.

"After you," Amelia said, and then pulled the door closed.

"Wait, let me lock it," Gloria said. "You never know who's hanging around trying to get my cheap jewelry."

Amelia didn't have any idea Gloria would exude such a sense of humor, especially in the midst of her disappointments in life's almost final chapter. As they walked down the hall, Gloria nodded to two women ahead of them, one using the walker and the other holding the other's arm. Both women wore short capris pants and sneakers, their shoulders humped forward slightly.

"I call them the Bobbsey Twins." She smirked at Amelia. "They do everything together. Sometimes I wonder if they have to help each other pee, too."

Amelia smiled.

"Though," Gloria added. But it took her a minute to continue on, as if she couldn't both walk and talk. She steadied herself on the handrail along the wall. "Not a bad thing to have a good friend in a place like this. Better than not."

They made their way down the hall and waited in silence for the elevator. Once on, Gloria pushed two buttons. "Maybe you'll stay for dinner next time?"

"Uh, sure," Amelia replied.

"Yes, please do come back soon, Emily," Gloria said.

As the door opened, Amelia simply smiled. "Of course. Bye now."

The elevator door closed, and Amelia opened the door to the stairwell and headed back to the lobby. On her way to the front door, she turned to see a staff member handing out small cups to a few of the residents waiting at their side with a small cup of water. It took her a minute to realize he was doling out medication. *Double checking that they would take it?*

Instead of leaving, she walked around the larger room, be it a parlor or living room, she wasn't sure which. A distinguished older man sat in the corner. He looked at her. Amelia had never been shy, her mama had seen to that, though she knew she had never been nearly as bold as Sharon, inheriting instead, some of her dad's introversion. But now she felt shy. She didn't want to say the wrong thing. Her experience with old people had been limited, with her grandparents dying before she remembered them well, and her parents gone before they seemed old. Or at least, this old, she thought, peering down into the dining room from the balcony. Sarah had told her that there were a number of residents in their nineties, and even two women who were over one hundred.

To that Sarah had said, "God spare Gloria that!" Amelia didn't know what to say in response and had stayed silent, listening.

Amelia neared the old man, she felt a nudge. *Go on,* it commanded. She stopped close to him. "Hi."

She couldn't think of a good line, but was filled with a calm confidence, surprising her. She was instantly reminded of her dad. If he had been forced to live in a place like this she imagined he might have just parked himself in the corner and watched the energy revolve around him. A bit like he had done in a house full with Sharon and Amelia.

"Hello." The man nodded at her. His right hand rested on a cane, its wooden handle carved into a design. He shook the cane in welcome as he greeted her. His other hand shook slightly as well.

Amelia was emboldened. As she glanced down below the balcony into the dining room, she could make out the mostly gray and white heads of women. So many women. She took a chance. "What's it like living in a place with so many women?"

The man's expression didn't change at first. But soon, a very slight smile drew his lips upward. "You have no idea," he muttered. "Sometimes it's like a cackling hen house." Silver hair covered all but a slight bald spot in the middle of his head, and he wore a crew neck red sweater with khakis.

Amelia laughed. "Aren't you going to lunch?"

"Just taking my time," the man said. "Waiting till the elevator isn't flooded with them all. Sometimes it's better to get there late, and leave late. I have learned."

Amelia began to feel badly for him, imagining him evading the other residents all day long. "Don't you like any of them?"

"Oh yes." He smiled broadly with blue eyes that may have once been brilliant but now appeared almost milky. "My gal is just next door. You know, the memory area. It's just that visiting hours have ended. Well, until later." He paused for a moment. "I spend most of the day with her, reminding her of old days."

Oh God. A tight smile pasted onto Amelia's lips.

She stood up straighter and pulled her jacket closer. Then she put out her hand. "I'm Amelia."

"I'm Harold," he said. "Some call me Hal."

Amelia felt the warmth in his hand, and again a reminder. Of chats with her dad. Her breath felt short, and her face warm.

"Stop back and chat again. I'd like that. And call me Hal." He smiled at her, and then looked down at his watch.

"Yes." Amelia turned as her eyes filled. A new feeling, something she couldn't fully identify, flooded her. She walked without thinking back toward the now unattended desk. As she signed out, she noticed two stacks of fliers; one about an upcoming tea, and the other about volunteering. She took one of each and then dashed through the doorway, bells tinkling behind her, breathing in the flood of fresh air.

Chapter 19

Sustenance

THE NEXT NIGHT Amelia and Sarah sat at the dinner table, plates loaded with rice, grilled chicken, and sautéed vegetables—carrots, cauliflower, broccoli. In her time staying with Amelia, Sarah found her to be a brilliant cook. Forcing Sarah to wonder, again, just what it was Amelia couldn't do.

Sarah's face was no longer swollen, the shiner fading to the dark remnants of someone who was sleep deficient. Luckily her arm had only been sprained, and she could now make it through the day without a sling. She knew she should get back to work, but still felt self-conscious—her face showed too much that would need explaining. She wondered if she could risk calling in for one more day, without having to explain to her supervisor the real reason for her time off.

Just then, Sarah heard a key in the door. Ten seconds later in walked a most striking man. He carried a briefcase and hanging travel bag, and wore slacks with a sports jacket. She bet this guy didn't run around Portland wearing a parka and fleece jacket like most everyone else.

"Hi, Melia," he said.

Sarah smiled to hear this nickname she hadn't expected. As if her friend was this little girl. As he went over and gave Amelia a kiss. Sarah looked away, to pretend she was not disrupting the privacy of their home.

Then Phillip turned to look at Sarah and held out his hand. "I'm Phillip, Sarah." He spotted Sarah's splinted arm and instead gently touched her left shoulder.

Sarah tried to speak, but the kindness enveloping her prevented it without releasing another flood of tears. Tears she was uncomfortable shedding, especially in front of this man. "Thank you. Thank you so much. I'm so sorry to be a burden. I will be leaving in the morning."

Phillip gave her a smile. "I'll just change," and headed to the master bedroom.

"I'll be right back," Amelia told Sarah, following Phillip out of the room.

Sarah poked at her chicken, now losing her appetite. She was eternally grateful to Amelia; but now, being here with Phillip home, she felt like an awkward third wheel. She knew how little together time they got. She set her fork down and nibbled instead on the sourdough bread, fresh from a local bakery that Amelia said was her favorite, but Sarah had never heard of. She took a sip of her water and looked around the open dining room and adjoining family room, all of the walls painted a soothing tint of moss.

Amelia came back to the table and picked up her fork.

Sarah started to say something about the meal, but stopped when Phillip too joined them, standing at the table now dressed in a pair of black athletic pants and a gray sweatshirt with the logo "Boston University," on its chest. Okay, maybe he does wear fleece, Sarah concluded. Then Phillip picked up the empty plate awaiting his arrival and served his meal from the leftovers sitting at the stove. Sarah's mind was full with the single realization of how Amelia didn't jump up to serve him, something the old Sarah would have been expected to do for Tony. No, Amelia and Phillip seemed to share a relationship that she knew wasn't unusual, but foreign to anything she had experienced. Another sign of how far she had to go.

"You know, I was thinking maybe I'd head back home tonight," Sarah said hesitantly when Phillip sat down.

Amelia looked at her and arched her eyebrows. She put her hand down on Sarah's hand. Instinctively, Sarah looked to Phillip for a response. But he too looked concerned, not threatened, as Tony would have been. She silently chastised herself to remember how Tony would never be sitting here having a civil discussion in the first place.

"Well, it's closer to my work and . . ." She paused. "And you know. Um, you two should have your own time."

Phillip and Sarah both made noises of protest.

"Sarah. You are not in the way. In fact, I think it's great you've been company for Amelia while I've been gone. Oh, but, I mean, of course not that what happened to you." Phillip appeared disconcerted for an instant. "I don't travel again for over two weeks this time, and by then, we will really be sick of each other." He gave Amelia a smile and moved his hand under the table.

Perhaps on her leg, Sarah imagined. She wondered what that might feel like, with someone like either of them.

"Besides," he added. "Well, it isn't really safe yet, right? I mean doesn't the order take a few more days?"

Stunned, Sarah immediately looked at Amelia, not thinking she would have shared that intimate detail. She worried about how much this man knew about her, and what a mess she was. *What a royal fuck up she was.*

"Sarah, it's okay," Amelia said. "Please."

Phillip poured himself a glass of water from the pitcher on the table and took a drink. "You know, Sarah." he looked as if weighing if he really wanted to speak or what he should say. "It's not like I'm not aware of the assholes of this world. You don't need to protect him." He looked at Amelia, and she nodded to him. He turned to Sarah. "And you know, I hope to God, that you know. It's not your fault. Obviously. You must know that."

Sarah couldn't help herself. She began crying, right there at the table. She stood up quickly, covering her mouth, trying to excuse herself, but she couldn't choke the words out. She hurried into the bathroom. She could not absorb the kindness being offered to her. *She knew she had fucked up.* Deep in her heart, she knew it was her fault. There were so many signs along the way, and she hadn't been strong enough to stand up for herself. Just like Gloria.

She didn't deserve a friend like Amelia: A friend who had it all together. Everything: she loved her deceased parents, had a great husband, a fine job. She didn't have any screwed-up kids. She ran cold water and splashed her face, over and over. It stung the parts of her face still healing, and she told herself she deserved it. She dried her face, blew her nose on some toilet paper, and threw it in the waste basket. She grabbed another wad and stuck it in her pocket.

She returned to the table. Phillip and Amelia were talking about a problem with his buyer, although he stopped talking as she neared them.

"I'm going to turn in," Sarah said. "I'm awfully tired and have a long shift tomorrow. But, um, of course, thank you. I mean, really. I can't of course tell you how much I appreciate it. All of it."

Phillip and Amelia said goodnight, almost in unison. Amelia got up and carefully gave her a hug, stroking her shoulder for a moment. Sarah barely made it back to the guest bedroom before she sobbed again and lay on the bed. She tried to imagine, over and over, why people she still barely knew, would be so kind to her. And wondering what stroke of luck led her to them.

AMELIA HAD BEEN meaning to take on something like this for some time. So much of her life she had worked hard, creating a good salary and taking work home. She had thrived on it. Once. Especially as she watched others struggle balancing demanding jobs and the rest of their lives. It never bothered her, and unlike a few of her other kid-less friends, she had no regrets then. She had so much her parents never had—although they were content with their lives as a couple and family. But now, for Amelia, activities once rewarding or exciting, barely raised her interest. The marketing trips to NYC and Atlanta, and even the one to London. None of that appealed to her—more often feeling like a bother. She knew she could afford to take time off. The company she worked for probably wouldn't mind her working less and drawing a smaller salary, given the economy.

But she hadn't known what else she might do with her time; what would fill that emptiness. Her friend Maria, when they were on a red-eye one night returning home from LA, had listened to Amelia explain the hole she sometimes felt, suggested that she volunteer in a school, be a SMART Reader like she was. Amelia was more irritated than curious. A few minutes later, she reclined into her seat on the plane and closed her eyes, feigning sleep, wondering if Maria had heard a word she said. Did she too believe every woman without her own child yearned to create time with kids? She loved kids, really, she did. Hanging out with her friends' kids was fine, and she enjoyed it when it happened. That, however, was not what she craved. It wasn't what would fill this space.

After arranging for Friday off later that week, she drove back out to Newberg, anticipating the welcome of the jingles tripped by the opening of the front door. She knew she could have chosen a place closer to her home, but she couldn't get this one out of her head.

"May I help you?" the young woman asked at the desk. She didn't remember Amelia from the previous weekend.

"Uh, yes. I have an appointment with Marilyn? I'm Amelia."

"Oh, okay. Please sign in. And then you can sit over at that far table and she'll be right with you." As Amelia signed her name, the woman added, "It might be a few minutes as she had to take an urgent call."

Amelia nodded and as she headed across the room, she spotted the same old man, Harold, sitting in the corner. Her heart beat faster and her hands turned clammy. She put them in her pockets to steady herself as she walked toward him.

He was dressed in a gray cardigan sweater with a closed book on his lap, the cane resting against his chair. She slowly moved toward him, giving him a minute to notice her. She looked at his face to see if he showed any recognition.

"Hello, Harold," she tried. "I mean, Hal."

"Hello there, you pretty thing," he said.

Amelia was taken aback. She realized she didn't know anything about the people living here, or whether she should even be talking with them.

"Now, now. Just telling a pretty woman what she deserves to hear." He smiled. "I remember you, have we met before?"

Amelia nodded.

"Just thought I'd check. Even though I seem to remember better than most here, I'm not so sure somedays whether something really happened in life or if I maybe just dreamed it. You know, when you live as many years as I have, it's hard to keep track of everything."

"I imagine," Amelia said. "Yes, we met last Saturday. I'm Amelia. I'm friends with a woman named Gloria."

"Gloria? Hmm. Not sure I know her. But it's hard to keep track of all the biddies running around here." He looked her in the eye. "No, really. It is. Those damn women just have to prove themselves by outliving all of us." But he gave her a shy smile. "Actually, to be honest." He leaned in closer to her and dropped his voice. "The thing is, they all gossip. If I decided to, say, talk to one woman much more than another. You'd never believe the rumors that would start flying." He smiled, though, as if it didn't bother him all that much.

Amelia looked over toward the desk and saw that the young woman was signaling her. "I need to go, now, Hal. But I hope I see you again." She couldn't make out the title on the book cover, but it was hard bound and worn.

"Yes. See you around." He smiled at her as she walked away.

As she neared the counter, the woman held out a packet of forms that were paper-clipped together. "Sorry, I forgot. If you could fill out the first two pages, that'd be great. Might as well get going on it now." And, again, she signaled with her head to a far table just past the television.

Amelia smiled at Hal as she walked past him and sat down on the padded chair at the table. She took a pen out of her purse and filled in her details, vaguely taking in the soft music piped into the room, an elevator-ized version of an old Beatle tune.

She was absorbed in trying to put into words her reasons for volunteering when another woman, certainly more than twenty years younger than her, interrupted her. "Hi, Amelia. I'm sorry to keep you waiting. I'm Marilyn," and she extended her hand.

Amelia stood up, shook her hand and said hello. They both sat down.

"So, we're interested, of course, in both why you want to volunteer— of course we're thrilled. But also, what you think you might want to participate in."

Amelia took a moment to gather her thoughts.

"You see, we don't get a lot of volunteers but they are so appreciated," Marilyn continued. "Assisted living is difficult from a staffing perspective. We try so hard, but we do always seem to be understaffed. And then, of course, we have pretty high turnover. These days with some of the newer centers we all seem to be competing for not very many workers. You know, it's just not a job everyone is able or willing to do."

"Yes. I understand," Amelia said, although she wasn't so sure that she did.

"One of the things most people, whether staff or volunteers, aren't prepared for is the frequency of death." She looked at Amelia. "You just don't realize how close you might feel to someone that you may not even see very often. And then there are the residents who struggle so, with memory, pain, and frustration."

Amelia nodded.

"It takes a very special person to volunteer here," Marilyn added.

Amelia began to wonder if this was their way to weed out the Do-Gooders who wouldn't make the grade. "Well, um, I guess I'd like to try." Her smile faded. For the first time, she wondered if she had made a mistake.

"Oh, I'm sorry," Marilyn said. "I didn't mean to scare you away. It's just, once in a while we get these volunteers. Oh, I sound horrible, don't I? But people who really do want to do good, but they haven't fully thought about what it might entail. Like not everyone here will act like they appreciate you, for example. I happen to believe that deep down, at a human level, they do appreciate it. They just can't always show it." She hesitated again. "And not everyone is comfortable with that."

"Well, uh, can I ask what I might be doing?" Amelia asked.

"That kind of depends on you," Marilyn said. "We encourage people to try a few different things, maybe joining us in different activities, at first. And then, eventually, after a few months, you might find what it is that feels like a best fit. And really, honestly, the best thing you can do is just converse with the residents. That's what the staff never has enough time for. That is, with the people who like to visit. You'll see some of them don't. Or can't. You'll figure it out. Trust me."

In that minute, Amelia felt as if she was years younger than this woman, wearing a skill set of which she couldn't yet even identify the components.

Amelia was about to leave, after making an appointment for the following Friday to join in on a group activity, when she thought about Gloria. She looked at the woman at the front desk and found her occupied with paperwork and a computer. Amelia headed into the stairwell, upstairs through the second-floor door, and down the quiet, carpeted hallway.

"Come in," she heard through the door after she knocked.

Amelia opened the door a crack. "Hi, Gloria, it's Amelia."

"Is it time for lunch?" Gloria asked.

"Oh no. I mean, I don't know. I don't think so," she said, having lost track of time.

It would be odd to have your daily routine established by meal times, she thought. She opened the door fully and walked into the apartment. Gloria was in her soft armchair with the television on.

"Gloria, I'm Amelia." No response. "Um, do you remember me from the other day? "I'm Sarah's friend."

"Oh yes, dear. What are you doing here, Emily?"

Amelia decided to let it slide. For now. She had always liked that name, anyway. "Well I was just in the neighborhood." She didn't know Gloria very well yet, but wasn't sure how she'd respond to either truth. "And how are you today?"

"Same as yesterday, I guess," Gloria responded.

Amelia needed to remember to avoid that question. "What's on TV?"

"Oh, I'm watching one of those game shows. I forget the name. But you know, I guess along. Hoping maybe it'll be good exercise for my brain." She tapped on her head. She paused. "So, how is my Sarah? It seems like I haven't seen her in a long time, though I do think she called me yesterday. Or maybe it was the day before."

Amelia thought Sarah had told her she had called Gloria earlier on this morning, but no matter. "She's fine."

"Didn't she go out of town? Is she back yet?" Gloria asked.

"Oh yes, of course," Amelia responded. They were quiet for a while.

Gloria had muted the TV when they started talking. Now all Amelia heard was a ticking of a clock somewhere.

"My poor Sarah," Gloria began. "I really never was a very good mother to her, you know?"

Amelia began to feel uncomfortable. As if she was talking behind her good friend's back. "Oh, no, of course you were." She stopped when she realized she truly didn't know anything about whether she was or wasn't.

"Oh, yes. I could have been so much better for Sarah. But really, you just do what you can do. That's all we can do, I guess." Gloria looked out the window into the garden area below. "A rose is a rose is a rose," she muttered. She looked at her watch.

Maybe it really was near lunch, Amelia thought. She too looked at the clock on the table and saw it was quarter to twelve.

"Gloria. Maybe we could go out sometime. Would you be interested?" she asked, hoping it would be allowed.

"Me?" Gloria pointed exaggeratedly at herself. "Are you kidding? Get me out of here anytime. But better make sure you sign me out. You know. Otherwise they might report me as missing to the police." She delivered her raspy laugh.

"So, if we did this sometime, where would you like to go?" Amelia thought maybe she was a shopper, or would enjoy going out to lunch.

Gloria leaned inward toward Amelia. "Out for a beer. That's what I want. Don't get me wrong. It's not like I'm a drinker like my ex-husband. Or my daughter." She dropped her voice and gave an apologetic look. "I just miss going out to my favorite little pub and having a beer. Let's do that sometime. You and me. Okay?" She sat back in her chair and smiled. Pleased with the idea she had come up with.

The knock came.

Amelia knew without listening further, that it was time for lunch. She was catching on.

Chapter 20

Familiar beginnings
February 2017

"HI, AMELIA," KATE said as Amelia signed in on a Friday morning.

"Hi, Kate. How's it going today?" Amelia replied.

"Oh, you know. This and that," Kate said. "Oh, Gloria wanted to let you know she is waiting out by the pond this morning."

"Oh, thanks," Amelia said, as she glanced at the empty chair in the corner. She headed back outside through the front door and followed a paved sidewalk around the south side of the building. Looking ahead, she spied Gloria perched on the bench with a red and blue plaid car blanket on her lap, staring at the murky pond.

"Hi, Gloria," Amelia said as she approached. She didn't want to surprise Gloria abruptly as she appeared to be lost in a reverie of sorts.

"Oh, hi, dear. How are you, Emily?"

Amelia hesitated. "I'm fine, thanks. Um, you know, Gloria. I don't mind you calling me Emily, but just so you know. Well, my name is Amelia."

"Oh yes!" Gloria exclaimed. "I guess I just keep forgetting. I'm so sorry. That is so rude." She was silent for a while. "You know, Emily was the name of one of my best friends. Maybe that's, well. I don't know. I find names difficult to remember. Sometimes."

Amelia neared her and gave her a small half-armed hug. "It's so nice to see you, Gloria. And, you know, Emily is a beautiful name; it really won't bother me if you call me it sometimes."

They sat there quietly. Amelia wasn't always sure, even after these recent visits together, if Gloria understood the close friendship she shared with Sarah. She wasn't even sure if Sarah had told Gloria anything about them.

"Tell me about your friend Emily," Amelia began.

Gloria looked back at the pond. "Emily was my best friend. She died a long time ago, now. But sometimes I still feel like she's here. In fact, it's odd, but I dream about her once in a while. And when I wake up I feel confused about where I am and where she is." She gazed at the man-made pond, scummy algae gathering near its sides. "At breakfast I sometimes all of a sudden feel like I have been away for forty years because of the dreams I have. It's hard to jump back into my life today on those mornings."

Amelia took her hand. "Best friends are great, aren't they? I'm glad you still have your memories of her. What was she like?" She smiled. This was coming easier to her, and maybe for once that was enough. If Sarah had taught her one thing, it was to accept how she didn't always need to have all the answers or attend to life as a to-be-continued check-off list. Especially when it felt right, as this did. It wasn't the same, but learning someone else's life stories helped ease the pain of not knowing all those of her own mama's. And in fact, an occasional zesty comment from Gloria could have been straight from her own mama's mouth.

"Oh!" Gloria gave off a raucous laugh. "Now, my dear Emily was someone you didn't want to mess with. Actually." She almost giggled. "She scared my ex to death! She threatened him, back when David was being so horrible to us." She looked away from Amelia, out toward the pond, not noticing her blanket had fallen off part of her lap.

Amelia tucked it back over her, wanting to pull her sweatshirt down to cover the gap between her sweatpants and her top, but covering the bare skin with the blanket, instead.

"Emily was the one who knew David was out seeing other women. It made her so angry." Gloria was quiet for a moment, as if remembering details. "I was just trying to make ends meet and make sure our kids were okay. But wow, not Emily. She told me, much later, how she had the guts to show up at his workplace with a big sign." She laughed out loud. "I think it read something, wait. Let me think. Yes, it was 'David the Adulterer!' Can you believe that? I would have been so, you know, um, embarrassed, if I'd known about it when she did it." She stopped talking for a moment, as if she had run out of steam. "Especially since she could be a rather polite person. But, Emily was the one who helped me decide to leave David."

Amelia looked at Gloria, unable to hide her confusion. She had questions she wanted to ask, but didn't want to betray Sarah's confidence. "You left David?" She worried at first that Gloria would wonder how she even knew about David, but recognized Gloria to be full with her own remembrances.

"Well, I *actually* kicked him out of our house. Yes. I realized, for the kids' sake and my own really, that ass didn't deserve our house. Oh, excuse my language, dear." Gloria took on a new bold look as if pleased with herself.

Amelia wanted to understand all the details, but again, wasn't sure how much she could ask. "So, he left? Just like that, then? Maybe when Sarah was in high school?"

Gloria looked at her. "You know. There is so much I forget these days. But that, I don't think I will ever forget. Well, maybe. Some day. Later. But not now. Not yet." She hesitated and pulled the blanket higher up above her waist.

"Yes, Sarah and Ted were both at school. I called in sick to work. You know, I was making almost as much money as he was then. Well, David, I mean. Work wasn't going very well for him because of the economy and he was only on commission. I knew . . . I just knew, he wasn't heading off to work early, so we had it out." Gloria hesitated. "He seemed to want to call the shots and when I told him to leave for the sake of the kids, he said he was about to leave me anyway. That I was just a stick in the mud and didn't understand him, and all that. I knew, by then, that he had a girlfriend and spent a lot of time in her apartment, so it wasn't like I was throwing him in the street." She stopped for a minute, panting in her talk. "But that wouldn't have stopped me. Know that."

Amelia drew in her breath. "That must have been so hard. But, wow, Gloria. You were so strong to do that."

"I should have done it years before, really. But when Sarah came home, I still wanted her to have a chance with her father. I thought that, well, you know. I thought if she knew that he had just left, rather than me making him leave . . . I don't know. Uh, I guess I just thought maybe they might still have a relationship. You know." Gloria looked at Amelia. "They say the relationship between a father and daughter is so important. But they never really did. Have a relationship. Never."

"Have you ever talked about this? I mean with Sarah?" Amelia asked, trying to keep her voice even.

"Oh, no. It's too hard to. And it's all water under the bridge, now. It's all done. Doesn't matter. Don't you think?" Gloria said.

"Well, you might think about it." Amelia hesitated. "You know, it might be really good for Sarah to know that. To know the real story." She promised herself she wouldn't be the one to divulge this old story, as tempted as she may be. "So, Emily, then, was a good friend for sure. Did you stay friends for long?"

"Oh yes, at first. But then her husband was transferred. I think somewhere in California. Or. I don't remember now. We tried to stay in contact. But, you know. Well, it just wasn't the same. And then sometime later, I don't remember when. I heard she had died. I never really knew how either. But it made me sad, and once I learned she had passed away, well, it made me miss her all that much more."

Gloria's shoulders began to shake.

"Are you chilled?" Amelia asked. "Hey, maybe we should walk around the courtyard, you know, get our steps in?"

Gloria looked at her sharply. "Did my daughter send you? She's always harping on me to walk more these days." But she smiled at Amelia. "Okay, missy. You got me, let's go."

Amelia took Gloria's arm as they rose together and grabbed the blanket as it slid off Gloria's lap. She wasn't sure how much Gloria remembered about her friendship with Sarah, but decided it really didn't matter. For after all, Amelia and Gloria were friends. New friends, but friends nonetheless.

Gloria and Amelia, arm in arm, walked the walkway circling the pond. Although it wasn't the most beautiful body of water Amelia had ever seen, by a long stretch, there was something about it that was soothing. They walked in silence: Amelia had a sense that the conversation had, in fact, worn Gloria out. She found herself feeling more relaxed. *I can do this.* She was embarrassed at how much anxiety she had before about talking to Gloria, or other residents. She had talked to Phillip about it, and he had encouraged her to just trust in herself. And even though visits had difficult moments—a calm drifted in from afar, spilling over her during and after.

"How are you doing, Gloria?" Amelia asked. Gloria's steps were slowing.

"I'm fine, dear. I do like walking, it's just that sometimes it does seem like an awful lot of work." She paused and stared at the pond. Then she turned back to Amelia. "But if you are a spy for my daughter, don't tell her that last bit."

Amelia smiled. She clasped her hand more firmly on Gloria's arm.

"Gloria, I am no spy. I'm friends with Sarah. But I'm here as your friend, too. Honest." And by uttering that simple statement, it was so. They continued to walk a little longer around the outside of the building, but Amelia sensed Gloria was tiring. "Would you like to go back inside, Gloria?" She checked her phone. "I think it might be close to lunch time."

"Oh, yes. I imagine I should," Gloria replied. "Besides, I'm sure you have other things to do rather than hang out with us old things."

Amelia was beginning to understand Gloria's wry humor; and she wanted to be wittier than she sometimes felt she might be. She pretended she was communing her mama into the conversations.

"You know, Gloria," she began. "The only thing I can think of that I'd rather be doing than walking here with you is having a triple fudge banana split."

Gloria stopped, pulling Amelia to a halt. "Now you are talking, young woman!" She smiled broadly.

"Okay, it's a deal. How about sometime very soon you and I go and find the best hot fudge banana splits Newberg has to offer, okay? Deal?"

"Deal. Done!" Gloria replied.

When they came back inside, Gloria called across to Kate, "I'm back. Don't worry, you don't have to send out the search party. Not yet, at least." Then she turned back to Amelia and lowered her voice, but not soft enough that Kate couldn't hear it. "Somedays I'm surprised I don't have to sign out to go to the toilet. Talk about no privacy!" Gloria laughed her light chortle, not appearing to be fully offended by what she was complaining about.

Amelia walked her to the elevator, noticing that Gloria didn't ask her to stay for lunch. She sensed Gloria had reached her capacity for talk and was plain exhausted.

"I'll see you next week, Gloria, okay? And sundaes, if you're up to it."

"You bet. Bye, Emily," she said, just as the elevator door opened.

Amelia looked across at Kate, who gave her a conspirator's smile. She checked her phone to find she had one missed call from the office, but figured she'd return it later. Looking across the parlor—the space residents referred to that overlooked the dining room– she saw Hal sitting in his chair, looking in her direction. She was thankful she still had a few extra minutes before heading back to town and walked toward him.

"Well, well. Amelia Bedelia. How are you darling?" he began, a bemused look on his face.

Amelia stopped. Only her dad had ever called her that, going back to their early reading together of the books with the literal-minded housekeeper which encouraged Amelia and her dad once to pretend to plant lightbulbs instead of tulips just to tease Sharon. It was only recently Amelia remembered how much her mama had laughed over their joke back then: thrilled to find her family emulate her humor. She took a moment to regain her composure.

"Hi, Hal," Amelia offered, finally. "Do you mind if I join you for a few? Or are you off to lunch too?"

"Oh, please, do." He struggled to reach the chair next to him in an effort to bring it closer to her. "I'd get up if I were a real gentleman, but I'm sorry to admit I have graduated to a mostly old man schmuck. Just know that I'd do it if I knew I could without possibly toppling on top of you."

Not a line her dad would ever have thought up. Amelia reprimanded herself. *Stop comparing.*

"Thanks, Hal." Amelia sat down, and tried to think of what to say. "No lunch today?"

"Oh, some weekdays I eat with Vivian. Today it was a bit earlier than normal. She's tired. Needed to rest, so I came back up here." Hal looked sadder than he had the last time she had been in. "You know, she's not doing very well. That's what the nurse says. Keeps saying, really. And well, you know, I can tell." He looked back at Amelia. "I met her when she was a fifteen year old. Imagine! I'm not even sure I can do the math to figure out how long ago that was."

They sat together, quietly. Soon he began to tell her about where he and Vivian had met, and about their three children, one who had died early on and one, a daughter, who lived nearby and visited them every weekend. He told Amelia how he'd probably still be living in his old house if his wife hadn't "gotten sick."

"I need to be as near to her as they allow. To help her remember who she is," Hal said. "Until . . . well, until she can't anymore, I guess."

Amelia wanted to say something, but was at a loss. Hal looked not so much sad, as simply resigned. Resigned to their lot in this last chapter.

"So, Hal," Amelia said, her voice falsely bright. "What did you do for work, all those years?"

"Me? Hmm. I was an engineer. Proud of it too." He rubbed his hands together and shifted in his chair. "I just liked to build things. And imagine building things."

"Oh, that's great—so you were one of those math and engineering geniuses I never could stand in my classes," Amelia offered. "What kind of engineering?"

"Oh, back in my day an engineer was just an engineer, not like these fancy boys today, environmental and all that. I did a little bit of everything all those years. But my favorite? My favorite was my first, ships."

Amelia caught his eye and drew in a breath. "Really? Like Liberty Ships?"

"No, no my dear. But the next generation of them."

"Oh." Amelia stopped to think for a moment, late to recognize her error in matching his age with war years. "My two grandfathers met working in the shipyard, you know, during the war."

"Really?" Hal asked, as he leaned toward her.

"They were electricians, both of them. Actually, so was my daddy. He always wondered what happened to me, going into the business world, although I can in fact understand basic wiring, just so you know," Amelia boasted.

"Tell me about them. Amelia Bedelia," Hal said.

"My mama's daddy, his name was Jackson. Jackson liked fixing things." Amelia stopped and looked at Hal. His solid stare encouraged her onward.

"The story goes that by the time he was thirteen, neighbors were knocking on the door, asking if Jackson could just this once please help them with something. A light switch or an oven or who knows what all. He seemed to take it as a challenge to fix it, even if he didn't know what he was doing. His mama wasn't so sure he wasn't going to outright kill himself." Amelia took a breath and hesitated.

Hal gave a chuckle.

"Once he did burn his fingers pretty badly," she said. "Luckily he didn't shock his whole body. When my grandma, Janet, learned about that episode she liked to talk about how he fried a bit of his brain. My grandma was lucky, by growing up in the same neighborhood she knew all these stories." Amelia smiled at Hal. "No way was she not going to use to her benefit what she could always hold over his head. Anytime she wanted to get a rise out of him, later, after they were married, she'd say, "Careful, Jackson. Remember your shock treatment?""

Amelia stopped and Hal smiled, emitting a quiet, polite snicker.

"As they got older and he tired of this line, he'd tell my grandma, "You know, Janet? That's not funny anymore. Never was.""

"Can you tell me more?" Hal asked.

Amelia continued on with the story—how, as Jackson got older he began making a few dollars fixing things people needed repaired. Later his mama told him she suspected these neighbors had begun to feel they were taking advantage of him, expecting he'd just do it out of the goodness of his heart as he fit it around his job bagging groceries nearby. It was then, Amelia remembered her dad telling her later, he started thinking he'd earn a living fixing things, rather than toting people's heavy bags of groceries out of the store, or cleaning up the muck spilled when someone dropped a carton of eggs. "And that's just what he did, except it was pretty limited work, and it would never have been enough money or stable enough to support a family. He knew that."

Amelia stopped abruptly as she realized she had been talking this poor old guy's ear off. "My dad used to talk so much about his in-laws. Of course, so did my mama. They'd laugh so much over those old stories."

Hal smiled at her. "Better in-laws than outlaws is what I say!" He chortled.

Amelia laughed back and silently recognized how she had never thought about that.

"Vivian, my wife, liked to tell me when we were younger how I was an engineer, not a comedian. But now she'll laugh at me once in a while." Hal looked toward the window. "I'll do just about anything to get my girl to keep smiling, these days."

Amelia could hear the clatter of plates and silverware amidst voices coming from downstairs. "Are you sure you don't need to eat lunch?" she asked, self-conscious of how much she was talking.

"Oh no. I already ate something. How often do I get to hear a story about men of my old world?" He lessened the grip of his hand on his cane, and it fell against his chair. "Please. Please do carry on. If you would."

Amelia gathered her thoughts as to where she left off. "Well, he got a little business here and there, but times were tough I think, so when the call went out for workers in the shipyards, he realized it was a golden opportunity. And because of just how many were needed, those war years, he didn't feel so alone in his skin amongst the others flooding to work." Amelia hesitated. "He was placed on night shift, which worked okay, for a while."

Amelia looked Hal in the eyes, she had been looking off to the distance for much of her storytelling. "He later told me he realized early on that he was a night guy. But with Janet, his wife, my grandmother, trying to gather hours as a maid, it made it hard for them. They tried though. Unlike most of the other guys on his shift, who'd come home and sleep half the day. He and Janet tried to adopt the opposite schedule. Coming home to their 'evening' as the real day launched into mid-morning. Pulling the blinds, Jackson would sleep through the afternoon, while Janet headed off by bus to her cleaning jobs, leaving a breakfast awaiting Jackson on the table. It seemed to mostly work until Andrew, well, my uncle, came along. But by this time, they saved a bit of money, Jackson's talents had been recognized and the union had stepped up to make him feel he had some security. Once Janet started to get rounder with baby, Jackson suggested she lay off the cleaning. One house she begged to keep, having created a friendship with the woman of the house. And Jackson agreed, though he worried for the safety of his, what he hoped, to be a boy."

Amelia took a deep breath. All the storytelling was exhausting. This was the way her mama would have told this story, with her dad a passenger, coming along for the ride, but smiling throughout. She needed to finish, she realized, to complete the story for Hal's sake. "And my Uncle Andrew came out just fine. If not a bit of a live wire. Janet knew at that point, that she wanted nothing else but to be home and be his mother. And then, a couple of years later, my mama was born. And she pretty much spent her childhood trying not to be overshadowed by Andrew." She looked up at Hal. "And that's pretty much their story. In a rather drawn out nutshell, I guess you'd say."

As if planned, at that moment a young man, one Amelia hadn't seen before, got off the elevator and headed toward them when he spotted Hal.

"Harold, you can visit Vivian now if you'd like," he offered. He smiled at him and then quickened his pace back to the front desk.

"That's my cue. Time to see my wife. I'll tell her your stories." He looked off and said something else softly, to himself, that she couldn't make out. "I'll see you again Amelia Bedelia?"

"For sure," Amelia answered, catching her breath, feeling better than she had in a long time.

Chapter 21

Full circle
March 2017

SARAH TRIED NOT to react when Gloria told her she couldn't believe she had never taken Amtrak to Seattle; she was trying to be less reactive these days. In fact, their relationship was beginning to astonish her. Although her mother's forgetfulness was disconcerting, a new softness was forming between them, as though the roughest edges of their life together had been filed smooth.

Amelia had startled Sarah with her newly discovered friendship with Gloria, although Amelia didn't divulge many details. In the end, it added to the relief Sarah felt as Gloria adjusted, even if just a bit, to life in the Institution, as she called it: Gloria named it "GHI" for Gray Haired Institution. It was only now that Sarah allowed herself to observe, and often enjoy, what a comic Gloria could be. Many days now, Sarah looked forward to taking her mother out. They'd go to lunch or walk near Gloria's old house by the river, and, only recently, Sarah had begun to ask her about things from long ago. As much as Gloria got mixed up about what she did today or had for dinner last night, the past lay firmly in her memories. At least for now, Sarah reminded herself.

On this morning, Sarah awaited the train at Portland's Union Station, surrounded by people of all ages—the Coast Starlight Amtrak train heading north. On the rare trips she had made previously, she had always driven herself or traveled with Tony—or even longer ago, Alison's dad, when they had headed north on I-5. But now, she was excited, not just for what awaited her in the Emerald City, but for the four hours she would have to herself to look out the window and not worry about traffic. To simply be.

Amelia had helped her prepare for her interview, offering to accompany her on the trip when she learned how nervous Sarah was. As much as Sarah wanted to bring Amelia along, deep down she knew it was her time: her moment to try to trust herself. Amelia's help—sitting opposite her and posing a long list of difficult questions—had been a beginning. It had been over fifteen years since she had sat through the job interview for her current job. And she knew this job she was vying for would be much more competitive than anything she had set her sights on earlier.

Only recently did Sarah have energy to look beyond the walls of where she worked. Once she began imagining the possibility of a change, though, she couldn't let go of the idea. She hadn't wanted to use anybody to get a job offer, yet she knew how simply being considered for jobs these days often got down to who you knew, with hundreds of people applying for positions. *And it wasn't as though Phillip pled her case.* He did let her know about an opening that sounded perfect for her and helped her learn how to use the internet to find clues about the company—their "market share." These things she had never thought much about before. Above all, she could not believe how kind he was to her. She had never known a man like him, and she was forced to acknowledge what traits had attracted her to the men she had chosen so far in her life.

Sarah shook her head, rested her bag on the shiny tiled station floor, and pulled at her strands of hair as she did when she was trying to push thoughts aside. An older gray-haired couple, the man with a cane, were standing in line. Sarah wondered how many years they had been together. She watched a young couple with a toddler in front of her, anticipating the train's arrival from Eugene. The little boy's eyes were huge as he looked at the crowd around him, crying out, "Thomas is coming?" His tired parents lugged two overstuffed daypacks and a paper takeout bag of food. But they smiled at him—Sarah watched them catch each other's eye: excited for their son's train trip, she bet. Like her. Other days it might have made her wistful to see a happy couple, but on this day, she was content to be a solo traveler.

Sarah followed the people in the line ahead of her to Car 11, one of the cars seating Seattle-bound passengers. She carried her lightly packed garment bag and large handbag: she was staying only one night, with her interview scheduled first thing the next morning. Although she had never traveled much, she felt comfort in knowing she had short walks both from the train station to the hotel, and then to the company's corporate office. If she got the job, it would be in Portland, but it made her feel she had a fighting chance by being asked to meet those she assumed were the regional store bigwigs.

A short time later, Sarah looked up from her phone to see the train crossing the Willamette River, past unfamiliar territory. She didn't recognize this part of Portland, and yet they had pulled out of the station only minutes ago. She looked out the window to see its industrial northwest followed by the greenness of Portland's Sauvie Island. Soon after, they crossed the Columbia River too—not far from the bottle's final landing spot. That bottle, the start of so many good things for Sarah, had once flowed under this trestle, although she would never know which channel carried it.

As the train chugged northward, Sarah knew she should focus on the interview, but it was hard for her to stop thinking about her last visit with her mom. Gloria had issued a formal invitation—even written on a card in heavy block letters—to a lunch date set a few days after Sarah's return from Seattle. Sarah had told her about the interview, noticing the relief on her mother's face when she learned, if she got the job, it would be in Portland. Gloria cleared her throat, and told Sarah—in what sounded almost like an official proclamation—how she had to tell her something very important. She wanted it to be over a glass of champagne.

Sarah had hesitated, wondering how much more her mother didn't know about her. Sarah had successfully withheld many details, secrets, through the years. Protecting herself from Gloria's attempts to handle her life. It shocked Sarah at this moment, though, to imagine that perhaps even her mother didn't have a clue about her drinking. Or maybe, she had only forgotten.

Gloria continued to explain to her how she had called her favorite restaurant and set a reservation, or at least that's what she told Sarah. She tended to believe her because Gloria had added, "They thought it was odd to have a reservation for over two weeks out for two, as if they were some fancy place in New York." But Sarah thought the oddest part of the conversation was when Gloria told her to remind her before they left for the date to grab a note—spelling out to Sarah how the note was already written, awaiting their date in her top dresser drawer, the one with her underwear.

"I knew then what I needed to say," Gloria had simply stated, in anticipation of Sarah's questioning look. "Who knows what I might be thinking about next week?" She hesitated. "And, Sarah, I'm sorry. I wish I had told you way back then."

Finally, Sarah closed her eyes to her curiosity, the motion of the train comforting the joints of her body and questions within her heart. When she next realized it, she was jerked awake as the train neared a station.

Shit. So much for being awake.

Her chin was wet against the side of the chair, and she quickly wiped the drool from her mouth with a tissue she had in her pocket. Instinctively she looked around: embarrassed if anyone had seen her. She was in a four-seater, alone, a quiet day for traveling by rail. She looked out the window to spot a sign near the station advising her they were nearing Burien, a town she knew to be not far from Seattle. She realized she had missed the one scenic highlight she had been told to be sure to notice as the train rounded Puget Sound's Point Defiance: Amelia had made a point of telling her to look for it. She made a mental note to pay attention on the way home.

No passengers appeared to get off on this stop, but a man and woman with two small children entered, looking bewildered. Clothing stuck out of a bag the man was carrying, with some of it almost dragging on the floor, and the woman tripped on a piece of luggage she tried to step over. A little boy of three or four was crying, holding the corner of a blanket in his hand. Sarah didn't miss days like that. The foursome stood in the aisle unable to find an available block of seats, and chose a pair of seats in tandem when Sarah stood up and moved toward them.

"You can have these," she offered.

"Oh, no, we'll be okay," the man said.

"No really," Sarah said. "I'm traveling alone, and it'll make it easier for you."

The woman smiled at her in relief and pulled the little boy toward the offered seats, while the older girl followed close behind.

"Thanks," the man said. As if needing to explain the crying boy, he added, "He fell asleep on the way to the station and is crabby."

Sarah gathered her two bags in the overhead bin, double-checked that her phone was in her pocket, and moved down the aisle of the car, searching for a single. She sat herself next to a young girl immersed in a book. The girl looked up, nodded, and then returned to her page. Sarah, sitting now in an aisle seat, looked across the girl to watch billboards popping up in the skyline and concrete filling up the landscape. Just ahead the sparkling waters of Elliot Bay were becoming visible.

She looked at her phone—they'd be arriving in less than thirty minutes. Maybe it was good she had slept, as she did feel more rested and less anxious. She hadn't ever spent much time in Seattle, and suddenly wished she was able to take more time for this trip, but she needed to get back to her job, as it had turned out she'd lost more than a week recovering when Tony beat her four months prior. And, she needed to be back for Gloria. But she did promise Amelia she'd take time to visit Pike Street Market: Amelia had been surprised to learn Sarah had never been there before. Sarah suddenly wished Amelia was with her, and hated it when she noticed—like now—what an anxious, scared woman she was. *This wasn't how she wanted to be.* She let out a long sigh and then inhaled deeply.

Her call yesterday with Alison came to mind. It was more of the same: with Alison admitting that drugs were fucking up her life, but also making it clear to Sarah how she had no intention of changing, at least not yet.

"I will if I really need to," Alison had added.

No matter what Sarah had said over the past year or two, Alison pushed back, denying she had a problem. Even though she had lost two jobs last year, and only now pieced together odd jobs bouncing between waitressing in a dive, and occasionally working in a friend's coffee shop. But for now, Sarah's recent introduction to Al-Anon, thanks to its initiation by a friend of Amelia and Phillip, was helping her chart new territory for herself.

Sarah hadn't been able to forgive Gloria, all those years ago when her mother had stepped in and issued the infamous intervention. She was so angry that her own mother had stepped above her to do what Gloria had thought best. To Sarah, it felt that Gloria was continuing to control her, even though she was no longer a child. And when the rehab clinic didn't work, Sarah could never bring herself to thank Gloria for trying: knowing she had spent her own savings, money earmarked for retirement, on her granddaughter. And then, for so long after, what hurt Sarah the most was finally believing Gloria had been right. And yet the pain of that experience had cost them ten years of uneasy communications and a continued withdrawal of her relationship from Gloria.

But, the past is past. She looked out the train window and took a deep breath from her diaphragm: She and Amelia had agreed they were both going to try to be better to themselves. And even though, on a fleeting moment she might still occasionally wonder what it might be like to have a relationship that was beyond platonic, she accepted that a deep friendship was what mattered most.

Sarah fidgeted in her chair, as she tried to slow her rambling thoughts. *This was not what she wanted to think about.* She felt movement in the chair next to her, and looked over to see the girl rustling through papers, all within a folder embossed with lettering spelling out "Seattle University." She looked more closely at the girl's face: she would have guessed her to be no older than fourteen, certainly not college age. Though she reminded herself how many of the shoppers in her department looked younger than they were.

The girl saw her looking at her and shyly smiled.

"Visiting Seattle, I take it?" Sarah asked.

"Well, yes, for now," the girl said. She smiled nervously, "I'm hoping next fall to be living there."

"Oh, wow," Sarah said. Trying not to sound surprised. "Are you a student?"

"Well. Finishing high school." She was quiet and looked away for a moment, as if considering what to say. "You see, I have an interview. I'm actually really nervous. It's for a lot of money and, well, it'll decide if I can go or not." The girl looked up at Sarah, her eyes sparkled as if with a glorious secret. She looked down at the papers and maps on her lap, and then back at Sarah. "I'm trying to make sure I know where to go."

Sarah smiled at her. She wondered what it might have been like to have been motivated at that age.

"Actually," the girl said, with a very shy smile, "it makes me feel so happy to be heading back to the campus, even if I'm nervous." And turned to look back out the window. "That's where the Seahawks play. Though I'm not really into sports. Don't ask me what they actually do in there."

Sarah laughed, thinking, I'm with you, girl. She looked out, straining to see the urban expanse extending toward Puget Sound. It felt so much larger than Portland.

The girl looked back at her. "That was stupid of me to say. You've probably been in there. Are you from Seattle?"

"No," Sarah said. "I'm just coming up for a job interview."

The girl gave her a nervous look. "Ooh. That's exciting. And probably kind of scary, I bet. I know it's not the same, but I remember how even more nervous I was earlier this year for my first interview at college." A triumphant look flooded the girl's face. "But I got through it. It's what I keep telling myself now."

"Yes, I understand the feeling," Sarah said, nodding. And then she felt compelled to add, "You will do great. I can just tell." She didn't really know, but she hoped for this girl, that everything went her way.

They were quiet as they listened to an announcement through the public-address system: they would be arriving in just a few minutes—pick up things around them. Then the voice went on to announce the departure gates for trains leaving for Bellingham and Vancouver BC.

The girl gathered her over-stuffed daypack, and stood. "I'm sorry, do you mind if I sneak out ahead? I can catch a bus up to campus if I hurry. I'd rather not hang around too long down near the station."

"Of course," Sarah said, as she moved her feet closer to her seat and out of the aisle. "Good luck to you."

"You too," the girl said. "I hope you get the job."

"Thank you. And nice to talk to you. My name is Sarah," she said, as the girl started to move into the aisle.

"Thanks," the girl said. "I'm Annie." And she disappeared down the aisle into the next car.

Sarah stared after her. She felt the train halt to a stop, its brakes screeching. The jolt nudged her to look out the window, beyond. She imagined a bottle made out of green glass and smiled in wonder. She reached up above her and grabbed her bag from the rack, pulled her handbag around her shoulder, and pushed out from the staleness of the train into the welcoming freshness of Seattle's marine air.

Afterward

The Notes

Annie's Note—May 6, 2012

To whoever finds this bottle. I know this river goes on for many, many miles and finally to the ocean. I hope that someone finds it sometime. That would be so exciting! If you are reading this note, then you must have found it! Maybe you wonder about me. I am 12. I hope someday to be a teacher. I think it would be good to be a teacher because they are so important for kids. Especially kids like me. Because especially one of my teachers really understands me and talks to me when things are hard. Hard at home. Because they are hard at home a lot. I don't know if people know about that. But some of our secrets can't be shared. So, I don't do that, but somehow Mrs. Marquam understands me. She seems to understand me without asking any questions. It's so hard sometimes I just want her to know what a big exciting but scary secret I have. Some of our secrets are bad. But there is one that Dad says is so big and exciting, but that I can't share it because maybe someday it will be our ticket to not be poor anymore. And for it to be him and me against the world—away on our own—kind of like in a book I read once when I was little. I don't know whether to believe him because he lies a lot too. And I don't think Mom believes him anymore because she gets tired of his lies too. Anyway, that's why I want to be a teacher so someday I can meet a kid like me and help them make bad days better. Sometimes I worry that this big secret won't ever really save us, and then I'll just have a bad life like mom says we all will because dad never does what he is supposed to do. And I also think I worry that maybe the secret won't save me but will make things worse. But I guess if I knew this bottle got all the way to Japan or someplace far like that maybe it'll be found by another kid like me who might want to be a pen pal and share stories.

And maybe this kid might have some kind of sad stories like me but we can help each other feel better. Because right now I know that in June I will be done with the school and I won't see Ms. Marquam any longer. And what if my next teacher doesn't listen like her? Or maybe she'll make me tell her what is wrong and think I'm lying if I say I can't tell. So also I have one sister and one brother and one dog and one cat. My sister and I share a bedroom and she is older and tries to be nice to me but gets really cranky. Our cat doesn't pay very much attention to me, but our dog is named Charlie and he's pretty fun. We can't let him sleep in the house but we still love him, at least us kids do. I also like to write. Maybe you can tell because this letter is getting kind of long. Writing makes me feel better sometimes. So I hope if you find this that you are a happy person. Because everyone deserves to be happy. At church they say you deserve to be happy if you believe in Christ but I think everyone deserves to be happy no matter what they believe in. It only seems right. I mean as long as they are a good person. Then they should be happy. So I will give you my address because if you find this it would be really fun if you wrote back. And then maybe if you are a kid like me we could be pen pals. Or maybe even if you aren't a kid you would want to be a pen pal. And maybe even if you live in Japan you can send me a letter except I think it might be really expensive. I told my brother Danny I was going to send this letter in a bottle and he laughed at me. He told me it wouldn't even make it down the river but would fill up with water and sink. He told me I was stupid to even try to do this. But I don't think he's right. So I will list my address and my phone number. Okay. I better stop writing so I can get this in the bottle. I worked really hard to get a bottle. I even had to clean a really gross bathroom to find it. So goodbye. I hope I get a letter soon.

Your friend. Annie

My address: 2399 River View Road, Newberg, Oregon
My phone number: 503-601-2929

June 8, 2013

Dear Annie,

I was so happy to see your green bottle in the river! I have to admit, I had spotted it quite a while ago, but was kind of lazy. I kept thinking that the current would knock it out of the snag it was caught in. But finally, I did finally get my energy together and brought it in. Imagine how surprised I was to find your note! I wanted you to know that you did a really bang up job of protecting it from getting wet. Seeing that you live way up the Willamette River, you can be pleased that your bottle did almost make it to the Pacific Ocean—and maybe might have made it to Japan. In fact, did you know that your bottle made it over the Willamette Falls? The Willamette Falls are bigger than almost all of the falls in the United States. And it also made it all the way through the Willamette River and into the larger Columbia River. It did get spit out into the Columbia River, and in fact got caught up in a bit of a cottonwood snag. Again, had I known how much you hoped for it to make it to Japan, I would have left it in the water. Sorry about that. But I think you should be pleased that it did make it as far as it did. The way I figure it, your bottle traveled dozens of river miles during its year of travel. Of course, it might have gotten held up somewhere else, too, for a while.

Your bottle got me thinking about its path. Kind of like the path of life: like all those things you talked about in your letter, your dad and your brother and your mom and your sister. Your dad sounds like a dreamer. You know, Annie, some dreamers do make things happen and some don't. All dreamers need to have someone they love who help them figure out if their dreams really might happen or if they are an endless sea of pipedreams. Sometimes we can try to help those people and sometimes we can't. You can always love them though, you just have to use your own heart and brain to make sure you keep yourself safe and healthy. Make sure you also sometimes listen to what your mom thinks about all this, because I bet she knows a lot about your dad too. You know, life is full of these things that happen that seem bad and hard. But sometimes I think when these things happen you have to remind yourself there are also these other little things that move you forward, and sometimes you don't even know they are happening. Special things, sometimes. Just like your bottle: how that little bottle moved through two huge rivers to me. And just how excited I was to find it, and to learn about you! I am mailing back to you your note, your bottle and stopper, foil and red string just in case you want to try again to find a pen pal your age. I would be happy if you wanted to send me a letter back. But, Annie, I am an old man, and someday soon I won't be here. But you should know that you are a special girl. I know you will be missing your special teacher, but she will go on to be special to other girls and boys who may need her. And you will move on and find other special teachers, I am sure. Thank you for letting me find your bottle and giving me the chance to write this letter. It reminds me of the letters I used to write to my daughter. Like you, I too find that writing helps. And sometimes it's easier than talking. I am sorry that I don't get to meet you, but I just can't drive that far anymore.

Your Friend. Ernest
108 Ferry Road, Westport, Oregon

Epilogue

"Hints from Beyond" by Anne McDonald, September 2018

When I was a little girl, I put a note in a bottle, carefully placed it in our local river and prayed that a girl, my age, in Japan would find it. My bottle with its accompanying note traveled miles through the gentle currents of our Willamette River, stayed intact over the wild Willamette Falls, and gently dumped into the Columbia River as it journeyed toward the Pacific Ocean—and to a new friend.

It got stuck in the snag of a tree mid-journey, sitting patiently for the person who might notice its presence. The person who just might be the right one. The one who had a message to deliver to me. I didn't know it then, but when I did in fact receive the phone call from my new friend Ernest—a man as old as my grandfather might have been, if he were still alive—it offered me a message. A message about hope, and trust, and willingness to believe. And most of all, an invitation to look for those signs that await and connect us.

I don't know where my friend Ernest might be these days, where he came from or really anything about his life. I know that he and I connected in those few moments in a way that taught me a most important life lesson. And so, it is Ernest I thank for being the one to pull my bottle out of that snag: To lead me on my path to accept life; the happiness and the sadness, the goodness and the evil. And all the other degrees along the way. I look toward the clouds—at one moment in time—and I am reminded of, for whatever reason, a poem I thought about writing one day long ago. Another day, I see an old woman on the bus: I catch her eye and she smiles. I smile back and I know that the smile we share, for only a few seconds, will carry her to her next stop. And it is now I know, in being open to these moments and being willing to believe in the power of beauty and human life, that I too will help others as I continue my journey in life.

Acknowledgements

Thanks to my editor and publisher, Casey and Claudia, of Bedazzled Ink Publishing for so quickly appreciating and supporting this book.

Nearly five decades ago, a West Linn man, whose letter I no longer have nor name I remember, fed my imagination and sense of adventure by finding a bottle I placed in the Willamette River. I thank him for taking that moment to retrieve the bottle and scribe a detailed response, leaving me with an idea to begin this story.

Although we write in solitude, I have learned how a writer may never finish a book without a circle of friends and supporters. I thank Patty Montgomery for being the first to hear this story, and encourage me to pursue it. I appreciate my readers who took the time to read *Beyond the Ripples*, in various stages, and give me the early support and critique it deserved: Karen Bonoff, Karen Lennon, Diane Harju, Sara Elgee, Karen Griffith, and Kris Beam, and Gordon Gregory and Maura Doherty, who pushed me to go deeper into plot and character development. I thank my fellow author friends, colleagues, and workplace associates for support beyond what I ever imagined.

Finally, I thank my grown daughters, Erin and Emily Axelrod, and my husband, Russell Axelrod, for their continued support of me and my passion to write.

Dede Montgomery is a sixth generation Oregonian whose family ties have instilled in her a deep connection to the land. Dede was a 2019 Oregon State Capitol Foundation Speaker Series presenter, sharing her 2017 memoir *My Music Man* on Oregon's February 14 Birthday. During the day (except when she escapes to scribble new writing ideas), Dede works at Oregon Health & Science University in worker safety, health and well-being research and education. Dede lives with her husband in West Linn, Oregon where she never tires of exploring the banks and ripples of the Willamette River. Learn more at https://dedemontgomery.com